BORDER ANGELS

Anthony J. Quinn was born
in Northern Ireland's County
Tyrone and majored in English at
Queen's University, Belfast. After
graduating, he had a number of
odd jobs – social worker, organic
gardener, yoga teacher – before
finding work as a journalist
and author. His first novel,
Disappeared, was published by
Head of Zeus in 2014.

BORDER ANGELS

ANTHONY J. QUINN

A Mysterious Press Book
for Head of Zeus

First published in the United States in 2013
by MysteriousPress.com/Open Road Integrated Media

First published in the UK in 2015 by Head of Zeus Ltd
This paperback edition published by Head of Zeus Ltd in 2015

9 7 5 3 1 2 4 6 8

A catalogue record for this book is available from the British Library

ISBN (PB): 9781781858639
ISBN (E): 9781784088132

Printed in the UK by Clays Ltd, St Ives Plc

Head of Zeus Ltd
Clerkenwell House
45-47 Clerkenwell Green

London EC1R 0HT

WWW.HEADOFZEUS.COM

For Clare.

BORDER
ANGELS

1

She knew about border country. There were wolves, bears, and buried land mines in the one she had left behind, those snow-covered oak and pine forests that divided her homeland from the outside world.

During her enforced stay in the decomposing cottage, she dreamed of her homeland until the shadows of its trees stretched as far as this new border country. She could almost picture, in a dark corner of her mind, the forgotten light of her grandmother's farmhouse at the edge of the alpine forest. But when she opened her eyes, all she saw was a cracked windowpane glittering in the moonlight, and the figure of yet another man hitching up his trousers, tucking in his shirt, and stumbling out the door.

As a teenager, she had been hungry for journeys, to be on the road to interesting, colorful places. She wanted to escape the forests that bounded her village, to travel where war had not, where politics bored people and music played all night long. She passed her time waiting for true love, or an adventure, one that would transform her life and help carry her to new destinations. Little did she realize that one man's cruelty would do the job much more efficiently.

After two months in the farmhouse brothel, she was no longer interested in what happened to her for its own sake. A part inside her could not be touched or changed. She just watched. It was November. The sloe berries in the thorn hedges dripped with heavy drops of rain. From her window, late at night, she could hear the roar of a deep river devouring the darkness along the Irish border.

2

A sinuous flow of headlights made its way to and from the border brothel on weekend nights. Jeeps and expensive German cars snaked along the overgrown lanes, shifting down the gears, the barely controllable nature of the motorists' urges resulting in haphazard parking; tires sinking into mud and gurgling ditches; handbrakes pulled abruptly; bonnets lurching one final time under the sodden thorn trees.

Jack Fowler was in no mood to be discreet. He drove up to the farmhouse in his flashy Mercedes, knocking the wing-mirrors of a Land Rover and a BMW along the way. He looked the part of a shrewd businessman in expensive clothing come to spend some of his hard-earned money.

Horseflies spun round him as he trudged into the farm-house. In spite of his unsteady gait and the drops of sweat forming on his forehead, he had the air of a man who was in perfect control of the world, and his own life. In truth, however, his mouth was filled with the bitter taste of defeat. Deep down, his soul grieved over his avarice and the string of mistakes he had made in the property market. It was too late now to retrace his steps and correct the pivotal error of his greed. The value of his investments plummeted as each day rolled in with more news of job losses and business failures, one black wave after another, sweeping him closer to ruin.

He had knocked back several whiskies before seeking out this border hideaway, and already he could feel the approaching drum of pain behind his forehead. The cottage swam toward him, the door flapping open as if pushed by a gust of wind. A guilty feeling of transgression drafted through him. He closed the door behind and waited for his eyes to grow accustomed to the dim light.

At first, he was just anxious to talk to someone. The women whispering behind the red velvet curtain turned out to be Eastern European. Not many of them knew English well enough to carry on a conversation. He introduced himself to a girl called Lena, noticing that her eyes were clear, free of hate or disgust, or the signs of drugs.

She responded to his attempts at conversation not to please him but out of loneliness. Sometimes she went through the entire day without speaking to another soul. When they ran out of small talk, he paid the money and left. It had been the most expensive conversation he'd had about the weather in his forty-two years.

When he came back the next week, he asked specifically for her. This time they had sex, and afterward he fell asleep on the bed.

When his time was up, she poked him awake.

He roused himself quickly and searched for his clothes, but something made him stop. He leaned toward her, startled.

"Did I hurt you?" He sounded horrified with himself.

She hesitated for a moment. "No."

"Those marks on your body." He reached out to touch a line of bruises, dark blue smears against the pale marble of her rib cage. She had tried to hide them but there were too many.

She dragged the blanket over her shoulders.

"The man who guards this house came up last night. His name is Sergei. My presence makes him feel like a coward. So every now and again he takes his anger out on me." She reached for a cigarette.

"How can you stay in this place?"

She did not reply.

"I came here seeking pleasure but…" He opened his mouth, closed it, and tried again. Nothing came out. His eyes were bright with confusion. He was like a man under-water trying to avoid suffocation.

She finished the sentence for him. "But all you've found is pain." She lit her cigarette. "Pain of the ugliest type. The pain inflicted by men who hate women." Her voice sounded different, savoring the words like the cigarette smoke she was inhaling.

"Is there another type? Can pain be anything but ugly?"

He reached out to touch her but she flinched.

Yes, of course there was. The pain caused by nature was never ugly, like when you ran barefoot in the snow, but she did not tell him that.

"You're right. There is nothing but pain here."

She closed her ears to his soul-searching.

"How do you keep going?"

She took a deep drag of the cigarette without taking her eyes off the opposite wall. "You know how the cliché goes. The one about separating the personal from the professional."

"I've never understood that one."

"The truth is I'm no longer afraid of anything."

He stood up, made to leave, stopped at the door.

"How long have you been here?"

She flicked the cigarette ash. "I wish I could say. I don't know. A couple of months. It feels like a year."

His silence was more uncomfortable than the silence that usually came over her clients. She tried to dismiss him with her eyes.

"If you want to be left alone, just say so."

"Yes. I mean no. I don't want to be alone. Why have you stayed? What else do you want?"

He dropped into a chair in the opposite corner of the room.

"I want to help you."

"Then save me from this hell."

The minutes passed and neither spoke. The word *save* seemed to echo in the air between them. She was his prisoner, trading this intimacy for the promise of freedom.

"There's nothing I can do right now," he said eventually. In the half-light he appeared as solemn as a priest. He sat down on the bed next to her. Her face looked empty. He pulled her toward him, his fingers fumbling, light and then

6

rough. He tried to wrap his arms around her. He almost overpowered her. Several times, she felt she might lose herself in his embrace, but then she crept away to the bottom of the bed. She felt relieved to know she had not yet crossed that territory where a man might care for her. She began to think there might be a way back to her old life after all.

A fierce gust made the cracked windowpane shift in its frame.

"This is a dangerous place," she said. "The people who run this house are violent and evil."

He stared out the window and nodded. The closer one came to the border, the deeper one fell into the nightmare domain of terrorists and criminals. He felt uneasy. He listened to the buffeting of the wind and an owl hooting in the darkness. He knew that out there lay a wild terrain of disappearing lanes and blown-up bridges, uninhabited farms and thick forests, a smuggler's paradise and the ultimate refuge for people traffickers. He picked up his jacket and stood at the door, wishing he could just walk out with her, but he knew that was too dangerous. He would have to organize something more cunning. His solution lay somewhere outside in the darkness of the border and in the shadowy corners of his past.

"Can you help me?" she asked.

"It will mean digging up some old comrades," he replied, half to himself. "It will cost me. And I'm not just talking about money."

He stared at her face. Was it his imagination or had her skin grown paler? For the first time, he noticed the

7

dark rings under her eyes. He wondered who she was, this woman who made him want to risk all he had left behind in his life. She had a lovely body and a pretty face, but these attributes were common in the places he frequented. Although she held his gaze, he had the uncomfortable feeling he might be little more than a shadow to her, one of countless others that passed through the room. He began to suspect that she had deliberately revealed the bruises on her body, as a way to seek his protection. If he had any sense, he would leave now and never come back to this house, which offered nothing but pain and despair.

"I'll return in three days," he told her. "I should have a plan in place by then."

Before he left, he wrote down a mobile phone number on the back of a cigarette box.

"If anything happens before then, ring this number. It belongs to an old friend of mine. One with the right sort of connections. He should be able to help."

Afterward, she could not sleep. The promise of escape penetrated even her subconscious. She lay on her mattress waiting for his return, and in the darkness her mind turned to the plight of the other trafficked women. She drew up a list of the girls working in the brothel, along with the contact details of relatives back in Croatia. She asked them questions about Jozef Mikolajek, the man who had hoodwinked her into traveling from Croatia to Ireland. The name was familiar to all of them. He had promised each of them something; if not love, then work, or simply the opportunity to escape poverty. In return, he had taken each girl's whole world away. She felt the hairs stiffen on the back of her neck. Mikolajek was a predator, and they had been his prey. She had seen him on several occasions, walking through the farmhouse late at night, his face plunging by a crack in the doorway, his eyes shining like a wolf's as he weighed up the girls he had brought to ruin. The pent-up anger rose within her and threatened to fly off in all directions, harming anyone who was near—herself, the other women, the pimps and their clients, even her rescuer. However, her anger had only one real target, and that was Jozef Mikolajek.

At her bedroom window, she contemplated the blackness outside. This was a dark country, peopled by ghosts and dangerous men, she thought. She would not let herself become part of its painful history. The impulse to act burned within her. It struck her that she could not leave the farmhouse and all its terrible memories for good without taking revenge on the men who had robbed her and so many others of everything. She would concentrate and pounce at the right moment, she decided. Only then would her nightmare be over. She stared at her reflection, tethered in the blackness of the window like bait to the men who roamed border country. After a while, it started to snow. She watched the wind swathe her shadowy face with flakes. The thought of revenge thrilled her. It was easier to kill when a part of you was already dead.

The evening that Jack was due to return, Lena crept into the next-door room and sat down at the edge of the bed. When the girl lying there woke up, she held her hand.

"Have you decided?"

"Yes. I want to help you kill them. Now. Tonight."

"We have to wait our time. We have to be like hunters and lure our prey toward us."

She stroked the girl's cheek and handed her a small rag doll. Inside it was a piece of paper with the telephone number Fowler had given her, as well as the personal details of the women Mikolajek had trafficked. The girl hid the doll under her pillow.

"It's a horrible thing to do," she said to Lena.

"But we've been made to do horrible things."

"It has to be done, then."

Lena repeated those words to herself as she waited for Jack to return. The hours passed slowly, but there was no sign of him. After midnight, she got up and sat at the window. She waited for the headlights of his car to light up the snow-filled lane. She had almost nodded off to sleep when the reflection of a hunched figure appeared in the glass and startled her. She turned round. It was her pimp, Sergei. He smiled at her look of surprise.

"Get up. We're going on a little trip."

"A trip? Where to?" She had a horrible premonition that somehow her plans had been rumbled.

Without saying another word, he took her out to his car. He opened the front passenger door for her, but she climbed into the back. He flashed a look of annoyance and lit up a cigarette. In the flaring light, his eyes looked unsteady, hovering on the pivot of violence.

"Take off your shoes," he growled.

She did as she was told.

"I don't want you making a run for it."

He sat at the wheel and examined her for a long time in the rearview mirror. With her bare feet and legs folded beneath her, she resembled a child. She had grown used to captivity like the others, he concluded. No matter how much they wished to escape, they could never break through the bonds of fear. He flicked on the headlights and the forest came into view, rising out of the depths of the night.

As he drove, she leaned back into the cold leather of the seat and struggled to think clearly. It was best not to take any rash chances, not to rush anything, she thought. However, she knew that if she did not escape soon, all would be lost. Her heart pounded. She tried to swim through her anxiety and stay focused.

Suddenly the car braked. The road winding out of snow-filled darkness halted like a frozen film. The headlights picked out the shape of a lorry jackknifed across the narrow road, and beside it, rammed into the ditch, was a new-looking Mercedes. Recognition hit her like a punch in the stomach. It was Jack's car, but there was no sign of the businessman. Only a police officer waving a red torch in the middle of the road.

Sergei turned to her with a grim face.

"I knew I should never have left the house with you," he said with a snarl. "You're bad luck."

He stuck the car in reverse and steered it at speed back up the road.

She pulled at the door, but the handle clicked lifelessly. The car dipped and skidded as he floored the accelerator.

An urgent sense of desperation took hold of her. She began to strike him but he hit back with his free hand, the car clinging to the curves of the road as though it knew them by heart.

"We have to stay clear of police," he tried to explain, batting off her fists.

Now even the car seemed to be whining and snarling at her as it struggled to stay on the road. She heard a churning noise as the wheels bit into the snow-covered verge and then the rasp of branches scratching its bodywork. She crouched down behind the leather seats just as the driver lost control. The rear of the vehicle slewed deep into the hedge, spun round, and hit a tree trunk.

When she came to, snow and the cold night air were gushing hungrily through the smashed rear window. Sergei lay slumped against the steering wheel, semiconscious, his head a dark bulk against the oncoming lights of a car. A torrent of thorns and branches had ripped through the canvas roof of the coupe. She crawled out the back and stumbled onto the road. Deep in the hedge, the car had filled its barbed cage with the glitter of smashed glass and the eye-smarting reek of leaking fuel.

Above the sound of the approaching vehicle she heard the wind swishing through snow-laden trees. She wondered if that was the sound death made as it drew close to the living.

The front door of the crashed car swung open, and Sergei leaned out, spitting a mouthful of blood. He sought to compose himself, reached for a cigarette, and flicked the lighter. A look of derision passed across his face as he caught sight of her backing away. The cigarette flared. With the speed of a chemical reaction taking hold, the car erupted into a fireball, the blaze running through the vehicle like a quick-moving liquid, flowing over his hunched back and shoulders, drowning his face in flames.

Lena felt the heat and pitched into the darkness, her arms stretched out to break her fall. The night air was resonant with fragments of noise—the sound of a car skidding to a halt, followed by the urgent shouts of the police officer broken into echoes by the roar of the fuel tank igniting.

Her ears must be deceiving her, she thought. The policeman's garbled voice sounded familiar. She even thought he was calling her name.

She took one last glance at the burning car, the leather seats spitting out tongues of flame, the arms of her pimp melting to amputated stumps, his face disappearing behind a mask of flames and charred flesh, the mouth wide open but silent now.

Then she ran in her bare feet. The snow felt soft at first, but soon the freezing cold bit into her feet like a steel trap. She was still only a short distance from the farmhouse, but instead she ran into the trees, sending clumps of snow bouncing from branches. Her flight set the quiet forest astir, her numb legs toiling through snowdrifts, twigs whipping her face. She was used to running barefoot in forests. The only thing that could keep pace with her was the wintry eye of the moon, blinking through the shaking trees. She kept running, listening for the sound of footsteps behind her.

She knew by intuition the hiding places in border country, and its traps—the blown-up bridges, the crumbling sheds and outbuildings occupied by gunmen, the lorries and cars driven by smugglers at breakneck speeds, as well as the obstacles posed by mountains, forests, and rivers. She dashed headlong into the deepest shadows, searching for a secret place to hide. She also understood that human life was expendable in border country. It was easy for people to disappear when they had no passports or documents to prove their identity.

With her breath lurching in her chest, she came to a void in the darkness. A deeper darkness pushed by her with dizzying speed. It was the river that marked the border. Despite its fast swells and impenetrable depths, swimming it was not out of the question. An excess of water splashed her feet. She took a deep breath, but the cold made her gasp. Her entire body quivered. Death was the final hiding place in border country. The last escape route. She had nothing to lose now. A light flashed in the distance and the policeman's shouting grew louder. Her heart shook, caught between her past and her future. Before she could come to a decision, pain burst from her frozen feet and she felt the ground give way beneath her.

3

Inspector Celcius Daly opened the front door of his cottage on the southern flanks of Lough Neagh to find a basket of open-mouthed trout sitting on the doorstep. He guessed that his neighbor Owen Nugent, a fisherman of forty years, had left them after a night of poaching on the river Blackwater. Daly sniffed the fish. They had been caught only a few hours previously, he surmised. He had a keen sense of smell when it came to the decay caused by death. Several times it had warned him to be on his guard on entering dangerous situations. Violent death, in particular, had a dank slickness that stained the air even after the corpse had long vanished.

Unfortunately, his nose had been less successful in guiding him through the pitfalls posed by the living, in particular, the women in his life, who had writhed before his senses in alternating gestures of seduction and dismissal. His ten-year marriage to Anna had broken down the previous year, and his heart still felt stranded in the jaws of their unpleasant separation.

Anna had phoned him the night before, to discuss what to do with his boxes, the remnants of his past life that were still taking up valuable space in her attic. *Out with the old and in with the new,* he thought afterward. However, on the phone he had reacted with a baffled blankness, unable to decide what to do with all those memories heaped up in cardboard boxes. She explained that she was not being hard-hearted, only brave and decisive. *Our past will smother us to death,* she warned him. She even offered to take the boxes to the local dump, but a form of cowardice made him ask her not to. Although he still wished to cling to the past, he was unwilling to expose himself to its sorrows. It was the same inertia that prevented him from deciding what to do with his father's run-down cottage. His ex-wife had scarcely been able to hide the mockery in her voice when she heard he had still not sold it and was planning to spend another spring within its damp confines. When he replaced the receiver, he felt a crushing sense of discontentment with his life and a yearning for the human heat and scents of the living.

In the meantime, the thought of fried fish for breakfast was enticing. Daly carried the trout into his kitchen, smacking his lips in anticipation. He felt a twinge of domestic pride that would have either amused his ex-wife or irritated her. He lit the gas cooker. It was February, and the fish would be fat and succulent. He collected some overwintering cress from the windowsill. Then he filleted the trout and slapped them onto the hot griddle, skin side down with a little melted butter. Even though it was late morning, he had to switch on a light to see what he was doing. The weather had changed since dawn, transforming a hopeful, sunny morning into something darker, more brutal. Heavy clouds filled the sky. A flurry of fresh snow spattered against the windowpane. Daly fried some bread in olive oil and was about to dress the fish with the cress leaves when the phone rang.

It was Detective Derek Irwin.

"Remember the complaints we received about a brothel near Dunmore?"

Daly had to think for a moment before his memory swung into action. Complaints about suspected brothels had grown more commonplace in the past year, especially along the border between Northern Ireland and the Republic.

"We're going to have to check this one out."

"Why?"

"There's been a violent death there. A man in a burned-out car."

"What's this got to do with the suspected brothel?"

"We believe he was the pimp."

"Is he local?"

"No. Croatian, we think."

"Okay."

After the phone call, Daly placed the half-cooked fish on a platter and covered them, hoping to revisit the culinary high point of his week later that day.

Since Irwin suspected the body was that of a foreign national, Daly stopped at the police station and contacted the newly appointed antiracism officer. Twenty minutes later, Constable Susie Brooke was climbing into Daly's car with an almost schoolgirl excitement. She had accompanied detectives to the scenes of numerous race-hate crimes in the city—vandalism, arson, and assaults—but this was going to be her first assignment in border country, as well as her first violent death. She snuggled in under the seat belt and smiled at him warmly. The car filled with her perfume and a sense of intimacy that felt oddly perilous.

"This is a serious crime investigation, but you might as well come along," he said. "Let's just hope it's not the start of something."

"The start of what?"

"I don't know," he mumbled. "The border's a brutal place. Especially for people who don't fit in." Then he warned her: "This won't be a pretty sight."

She did not look worried, just pleased to have been invited on the investigation. Her blue eyes sparkled.

"If this turns out to be racist killing, then I'm going to have to deal with the crime scene at some point," she said. "Foreign nationals in this country are four times more likely to die a violent death. Even those living in remote areas."

Daly did not respond. She might have sounded like a statistician, but she certainly did not look like one. Glancing away, he eased the car into first gear. He wondered if his behavior had come across as awkward or, worse still, standoffish. He racked his brain for something lighter to talk about as his eyes prowled the windshield, absorbing sideways the details of her profile, the long aquiline nose, the dark swirling hair, the bright eyes. Her lips moved slightly, but she did not speak. Perhaps she was waiting for him to continue the conversation, but somehow, his tongue had been banished to the long-lost muteness of his adolescence.

He turned right at a junction. Again, his attention was snagged by the delicate length of her nose. On another woman, such a feature would have been ugly, but on Constable Brooke, it was like a snaring device, luring in the eye. He rammed the gear stick between second and fourth, the tires slithered on the fresh snow, and then finally they were off, heading into the hills of South Armagh.

The road climbed and grew bleaker as they drew near to the border. The ragged patches of snow deepened, swallowing up the grass verges and dry-stone walls until only a few lone thorn trees could be seen rising out of the white depths. Nothing moved across the mountain fields but the wind trailing swirls of snowflakes.

Ten minutes later, they dipped into a valley and a haggard farmhouse swung into view. They pulled up behind an ambulance and a police car parked at the warped mouth of an iron gate. Daly could not see Detective Irwin anywhere.

As he clambered out of the car, a gust of wind dislodged a lump of icy snow from the trees onto his shoulders. He shouted with the cold shock.

A paramedic stepped out of the ambulance with a puzzled look. Daly introduced himself and was directed to the bottom of the lane, where the burned shell of a car lay like a spent cartridge case. A damp acrid smell reminiscent of a firing range stung Daly's nostrils.

The blaze had been furious but contained, leaving the car a study in violent black against the whiteness of the snow, the driver burned beyond recognition. His body rested against the skeletal rim of the steering wheel like a man-sized cockroach. Daly briefly examined the face that resembled a black mask slipping off the skull, the eye sockets darker than any blindness.

"Get stuck behind a flock of lost sheep?" asked a voice from the hedge.

Detective Derek Irwin stepped out of a gap in the gorse bushes where he had been sheltering. The question was his unsubtle way of trying to make Daly feel like a schoolboy late for class.

Daly felt a familiar flicker of annoyance as he stared at the younger detective's smug face. The Special Branch detective knew how to put people on the defensive right from the start. It was a professional technique he had borrowed from the interrogation room.

"Not at all," Daly replied. He waved in the direction of Constable Brooke who was gingerly making her way down the lane. "I decided to bring along our new antiracism officer."

Irwin, however, did not appear to be listening. His face had grown attentive, a look of soft awe widening his eyes as Brooke's tall figure approached.

"Who's the girl in self-important boots?" he asked a little too loudly.

Daly looked away in embarrassment. Being a chauvinistic pig seemed to be Irwin's natural talent.

Brooke grimaced at the sight of the burned car. "I'm not used to dead bodies," she said, almost in embarrassment. "It looks barely human."

"It's a shocking sight for anyone to see," agreed Daly.

Even though it was more than six months since he had last smoked, Daly felt a sudden urge for a cigarette. The sight of the dead body threatened to shake him loose from the usual moorings of his self-control. Murder was the ultimate act of rule-breaking. Someone had crossed the line, so why shouldn't he? In comparison, lighting up a cigarette was only a minor transgression, a futile act of defiance.

He was about to return to his car and search for a half-empty packet when he saw something that made him stop in his tracks. He stared at the ground. Etched in the snow was the bare footprint of a child or a young woman. *The cold must have stripped the person's skin,* he thought. He came across several more prints. The person had been running, possibly in the dark. A wild, heedless flight like that of a frightened animal. On a thorn tree he found a torn strip of a dress and a thick strand of black hair, low down. *A girl or a woman,* he thought. He tried to picture her, the clothes she had worn, a blue dress, entangled in the twigs with her long hair. He looked up, scanning the dark horizon of the hills. He sighed. The cigarette would have to wait for the next emergency of the soul.

From the tree, he followed the footprints along the edge of a field and into a forest where the snow lay in drifts. He felt a clear sense of mysterious invitation, urging him deeper into the trees. Concern for the girl, whoever she was, had short-circuited his awareness of the police team, the forensic investigators, the photographers, and all the protocols for dealing with important evidence. He plunged into the trees, head bowed to the ground, arm fending branches off his face. He lost the tracks at the bank of a fast-flowing river. On the other side, the snow was clean and unmarked. The roar of the river rushed in his ears. He spent half an hour scouring the briars and undergrowth for scuff marks, hoping the footprints would reappear and take off again, but had disappeared.

When he returned to the burned car, Irwin strode toward him and took him aside. His face wore an incredulous expression.

"How are we going to investigate a murder case with Miss PC looking over our shoulders?" He jabbed his thumb at Constable Brooke.

"Be nice to her. We're trying to prove the police take racism seriously," replied Daly.

"You shouldn't have brought her along. This is a critical murder investigation. It has nothing to do with racism. Tell her we don't need her help."

"Don't overreact", snapped Daly. "She might provide us with some valuable information. An insight into these people's lives."

"I'm not overreacting", Irwin grumbled. "I just don't want her to get in the way."

They walked back to the car.

"Tell us what we know about the deceased," asked Daly.

Irwin kicked the back of the vehicle, knocking a shower of metal fragments to the ground.

"There's not much until we identify the body. But I can tell you he drove an Audi coupe. Nice car. Once. It's always the same. The lower the life form, the more expensive the taste."

"Who's the registered owner?"

"Sergei Kriich. He has a conviction for threats-to-kill and ABH. According to our files, he works at the local poultry factory."

"Ever known a chicken catcher to drive a coupe?"

"He must have caught a lot of birds," replied Irwin. "We asked the factory if Mr. Kriich turned up for work today, but they said they'd no one working under that name. We have a photo of him in our records but, unfortunately, we can't match anything to a burnt cinder."

Irwin turned and stared at Brooke with the stance of a shortsighted man. She ignored him, as if refusing to acknowledge a predator might make it go away. Daly cleared his throat.

Irwin snapped his attention back to the crime scene. "We've been trying to put this brothel out of business for the last month or so," he said. "Then the criminal fraternity comes in and sorts the problem out in one night."

"You think a rival gang did this?"

"The evidence seems pretty clear."

"I've learned that evidence rarely tells the whole story."

"Then listen to this. The fire service has already examined the seat of the blaze. They found something unexpected."

"What was that?"

"There were two types of accelerant. Petrol and diesel. They believe the diesel leaked from the car's tank, but it appears that someone also threw a petrol bomb onto the fire. They found broken glass and a burned rag a short distance from the car."

"Why would someone do that?"

"Obviously, someone wanted to do more than kill him. They wanted to destroy all evidence of his identity, or anything else that might have been in the car."

Daly drew Irwin's attention to the footprints in the snow.

"There was a girl with him," he said.

"A girl with no shoes," replied Irwin. "Whoever she was, she belongs to the bottom of the food chain. A prostitute, probably. Or the victim's girlfriend. Maybe even a relative." He smirked. "Or all three rolled into one. You never know with these people. My guess is we'll have to go a little higher up the chain to find who did this."

The smile grew across Irwin's face as he glanced at Brooke. She walked past them, back up to the ambulance, her body leaning to one side as though battling a shift in gravity. The grim look on her face said it all. The world had shed its skin and revealed its cruelty.

"Did something I say offend her?" asked Irwin.

Daly stared at the tracks again trying to link them to the burned-out car and the deceased. Each footprint was planted cleanly and deliberately in front of the other—*a strong runner,* he thought. Right here, on the spot that he stood, someone's journey in life had ended suddenly, and another's had begun. Something happened here that altered two people's lives forever. A big death and a small death. He sat down on his haunches and touched the prints.

"I want to know what happened next," he said.

"Why does something have to happen next?" asked Irwin.

Daly regarded the younger detective. Was it his imagination or had they been arguing since they had met at the burned car? Irwin's tone was even, unwavering, but behind it, he detected a subtle form of tension. An undercurrent. Irwin's opposition to Daly's working style had been honed to a fine edge ever since headquarters had transferred him to Special Branch a year previously.

"This is where a young woman's journey started," said Daly. "Her lack of footwear suggests she was in a very vulnerable position. We should find out where she came from."

They walked back up the lane to the abandoned farmhouse. The doors and broken windows were wide open, but inside a stale odor hung in the air. Daly sniffed. It was the smell of imprisonment. In the front room, a velvet curtain wafted in the breeze. Behind it, a row of threadbare dressing gowns hung from hooks on the wall. Irwin's eyes flitted about in his head. A faint glow of excitement colored his cheeks. He appeared to be taking a secret glee in the investigation.

"So this is the brothel?" asked Daly.

"We believe so. Welcome to a forensic technician's worst nightmare. Just think of all the deposited bodily fluids."

"Tainted evidence, indeed," said Daly, stamping his feet to keep warm.

They walked through a side door into a tiny bedroom where there was just enough space for some unimaginative sex on a narrow mattress.

"We found a stash of condoms and sex aids," said Irwin, proud of being thorough. "Also, quite a lot of cash and jewelry. Gifts, I suppose, from gentlemen callers. You should see the amount of tire tracks in the front yard. The place must have been heaving on weekend nights."

"What do you make of it?" asked Daly.

"Well," replied Irwin, "there's half a dozen dressing gowns on the wall. Six girls at £50 a session. I'd say this place was a crock of gold."

"What happened to the women?"

Irwin shrugged. "One of the officers thought he saw a shadow move in one of the outbuildings."

They looked out through the window. The sky darkened behind a row of sheds and a lorry container. Some of the buildings were half demolished, others filled with rusting machinery. *A place like this should be teeming with shadows,* thought Daly.

"Let's have a look," he said.

On the way out, a mobile phone on the coffee table began to ring. Daly picked it up.

The caller's voice was dry and uncertain.

"Is that Club Paradise?" he asked.

"No."

"Club Tropical?"

"No."

"What about Heavenly Delights?"

The caller rattled through several more names as if they were keys to unlock the gates of paradise, but the farmhouse brothel failed miserably to live up to any of the exotic titles. It was more like Daly's worst nightmare of hell. He supposed that was the whole point: prostitution advertised under fancy names in the backs of Sunday newspapers to give punters the necessary emotional distance.

"This is a brothel," Daly told the caller. "Run by criminals."

"Who's this? Where's the guy in charge?"

"He isn't able to speak anymore. He's dead."

The caller hung up quickly. Daly placed the phone in an evidence bag. Forensics would go through the numbers later.

He led the way outside. At the gate to the yard he fumbled to release the frozen latch, then heaved himself over. As he approached the sheds, the snow suddenly turned a sickly green and he felt himself sink. He clambered sideways to solid ground.

"Slurry tank!" he shouted at Irwin. "Watch you don't drown in cow shit."

Twigs and mud, dislodged by a crow from its nest, slid sharply down a tin roof. The noise startled the detectives into an exchange of glances.

Daly swung his body carefully into the first outbuilding. The effect in the darkness was like immersing oneself into a pool of dung and animal sweat. He heard a wet snort of breath and tensed, as his eyes grew accustomed to the poor light. Before him were the manure-caked buttocks of a cow, huddling against a pile of hay bales for warmth. He lifted his boots out of the deep muck and stepped back into the farmyard. Irwin stood at the gate and grinned. Daly continued the search. The other sheds were filled with

27

the detritus of many decades of failed farming enterprises, chicken coops, hay balers, feeding troughs, potato sacks, and a dusty pile of turf, but no signs of life.

Daly walked up to the back of the lopsided lorry container and pulled down the shutter. This time he found himself staring at the baffled faces of a group of young women. Daly inhaled a suffocating breath of stale food, cosmetics, and alcohol and felt a sense of relief. His mute suspicion of something shadowy and sinister hanging over the farmhouse had been confirmed. He had found the source of that uneasiness. For a moment, no one spoke. The eyes of one of the women swam fiercely with tears or the cold. *They're like goods ready to be sold from the back of a lorry,* thought Daly.

"Where are you from?" asked Irwin, joining him from behind.

The women huddled together with the forlorn air of schoolgirls on an excursion that had gone disastrously wrong. They did not appear to understand Irwin's question. Their faces had a closed-down look.

Then one of the women stepped forward. "We are from Croatia. Albania. Serbia."

"What are your names?" Irwin turned to Daly. "Some of them don't look old enough to have a driving license."

"Their pimps take away their IDs, if they ever had any in the first place," said a voice behind the detectives. Brooke had returned. "It deprives trafficked women of their ability to travel and strips them of any legal status."

There was enough mess in the lorry container for a dozen

people. Magazines and clothes lay strewn with makeup containers and empty vodka bottles. A gas stove flared dimly in the corner. Brooke appeared calmer in this female territory, even though it lay in disarray. She walked over to the women and offered them chewing gum. She spoke to them in halting German.

"These women are hungry," she announced. "They've been hiding here since the accident."

Irwin studied Brooke for a moment and then forced his eyes away, not wanting to recognize the young woman as a legitimate part of the team.

"They did everything their pimp said," said Brooke. "He could have twisted them around barbed wire if he wanted to."

The women walked out of the container, their puffy eyes blinking, clutching each other as they made their way through the wet snow.

"Men!" said Brooke.

"Men," repeated Daly. *Letting the side down again*, he thought, but he had enough personal faults to brood over without taking on a few more for the team. He pulled the collar of his coat up around his neck, feeling the cold wind of female anger.

"How could anyone come out here and take advantage of these poor girls?" she asked. "Look at how miserable they are."

Daly stared at them. Although they were barely out of their teens, their faces had given up any softness, turned sharp around the chin and cheekbones. Their eyes shone with an unstable light. One or two of them wore short skirts, their legs smooth but discolored with bruising and the cold. Daly's eyes flicked away. There was such a gulf between him and these frightened women.

"I'm wondering the same thing," said Daly. He shrugged his shoulders. "But that's the sex industry for you."

Constable Brooke could not help spilling her disgust. "I don't understand why a man would drive all the way to this godforsaken place to give money to violent criminals. It's not an industry. It's a horrible experiment in human cruelty."

She glared at Daly.

"Don't ask me to explain why men come to places like this," he said. Even though his voice was quiet, he felt his words punch the cold air. He looked away. Branches of sloe berries hung their frozen heads along the hedgerows. The call of a pigeon wobbled from somewhere deep within the frozen thorns.

Brooke was right, thought Daly; the farmhouse was a sinister place, but then this was border country. For prostitution to flourish, it had to be a furtive business operated by dangerous criminals, like smuggling or terrorism. So different from the cities, where sex was at the other end of the continuum, advertised in glossy magazines and neon strips, a highly visible industry, sold as part of the nighttime economy. In border country, sex came clothed in shadows and stank of drunkenness and farmyard smells.

"Ask them about the girl who was with the pimp," suggested Daly.

One of the women came forward. She had understood

his request. "Her name is Lena Novak. She told us she would come back and rescue us after she found her..." She struggled to find the right phrase. "Her knight with shining armor."

Irwin snorted. "She was a prostitute with no shoes, not a fairy-tale Cinderella."

Daly spoke slowly to the women, emphasizing his words. "You are rescued. You'll never have to come back here, we can promise you that. No one can harm you now."

"Yes, they can," replied the woman. "It doesn't matter where we go. They know our families back home. We still owe them money."

The women huddled closer together with worried expressions that suggested their troubles were multiplying by the moment. Daly surveyed them, the run-down house, the lane with the burned car and the mysterious footprints, and tried to discern if anything resembling a pattern or story was beginning to emerge. Not much. At least not yet, anyway. Only a single, wispy strand. A runaway prostitute in search of her knight in shining armor.

4

One theme constantly cropped up in the investigation team's first meeting, and that was the lack of a tangible trail of evidence. It was as if the clues the scene of crime officers had gathered at the burned car and abandoned farmhouse spoke a different language, one the detectives had yet to decipher. Normally in such a local setting, the path left by the killers would practically glow before their eyes.

Daly tried several times to bring a sense of firmness and clarity to the investigation, to define its shape and direction, but he struggled on each occasion.

"The women we found in the lorry container, did anyone else get the feeling they were holding something back?" he asked.

"I think they were suspicious of us," suggested Brooke.

"No. There was something else."

"What?" asked Irwin.

"I don't know. It's just an instinct. Something in their collective spirit. It was there. I just couldn't pick up on it at the time."

"They're still under police protection. We can question them anytime we wish," said Irwin.

Daly grunted. "Perhaps I'm adding to it after the event, and what I felt was really nothing."

He went on to argue that in the absence of any positive leads, the footprints in the snow offered the only promising direction for the investigation to follow.

"After all," he said, "this is a missing person case as well as a murder. Lena Novak might not have family or friends searching for her, she may even be an illegal immigrant, but that doesn't mean we should ignore her plight."

However, a cursory search of the river and forests had revealed no trace of her.

"We don't have the manpower to launch a full-scale search," complained Irwin.

"The river marks the border with the Republic," said Daly. "As such, the Garda should be involved." He asked Ciara O'Neill to take responsibility for liaising with Monaghan Garda station. "We have to work without making any assumptions, but it's clear to me that this woman is the key to finding out how the pimp Kriich died," he added.

"The problem is where to start looking," said Irwin.

O'Neill spoke up. "One of the women told me they believed Lena was dead. That night the women raided her drawers and a suitcase. They fought over whatever clothes she had left behind."

"Perhaps this is more your territory, Susie," said Daly. "Where do you think Ms. Novak might have gone?"

"If we assume she is still alive, then she's a stranger lost in one of the most dangerous parts of the country," she replied. "The only people she can turn to are her captors. Her only other contacts are the trafficked women and their clients. We don't even know if she can speak English."

The room was silent. The investigation was only a day old but already a mood of pessimism had descended upon the team of detectives. Most of them anticipated further trouble. This was not going to be a routine investigation into the sordid little death of a pimp. The barefooted girl had run away from a dangerous world of international criminals, one governed by the powerful forces of sex and money. Perhaps she had been captured or, worse still, killed, if she had not already succumbed to the freezing cold.

"We've searched the neighboring farms and outbuildings and drawn a blank," said Irwin. "No one heard or saw anything, apart from a report of an accident between a car and a jackknifed lorry not far from the brothel."

Daly nodded. The law-abiding residents of South Armagh did not like talking about brothels and trafficked women. They did not want to think that sort of thing happened on their doorsteps.

"We should give special attention to this accident and the drivers involved," he said.

"There was no official report given to the police," replied Irwin.

"Perhaps the drivers just exchanged insurance details and agreed to sort it out between themselves," suggested O'Neill.

"Lorries speed on that road to make the early morning ferry from Newry," said Daly. He asked O'Neill to check with the local haulage companies to see whether any of their drivers had reported an accident.

The discussion turned to finding a motive for Kriich's murder.

"Maybe there was a feud, or fighting over a woman. Perhaps the pimp had bad-mouthed someone," suggested O'Neill.

"No doubt he would have had enemies, but would they have had reason to murder him, and in this way?" asked Daly.

"Our only sources of information are the women in the farmhouse and the men who visited them," said Irwin.

Brooke read the notes she had accumulated from her interviews with the women. There was little on Lena Novak. None of them could give an explanation as to why her bare footprints were beside Kriich's car. Their stories followed the same pattern. They all mentioned a man called Jozef Mikolajek and described how he had persuaded or lured them from the villages and farms of Croatia and Albania.

"What information do we have on Mikolajek?"

"There have been some inquiries over his involvement in credit card fraud and the manufacture of false passports," said Brooke, "but we haven't got close to arresting him. He's registered legally as the manager of an agency that supplies cleaning staff and care assistants. They bring over Croatian women and employ them to clean houses and offices, and work in nursing homes."

"I want you to find this man and give his business dealings a thorough examination," Daly told Detectives Brian

Harland and Declan Robertson. "Run one of his vacuum cleaners over him and his paperwork, an industrial one if necessary."

The effort to trace the men who had used the brothel on the night of the murder had also yielded no results. Daly assigned two additional officers to concentrate on this.

"We need to find the clients, especially the regular visitors," said Daly. "Get a list of all the numbers that rang the farmhouse. These men will want to disappear off the face of the earth but we must locate them. And get them to talk. Threaten them with criminal charges, if necessary."

"We'll be met by a wall of silence."

"Then we'll have to break through it."

"There's one question we haven't asked," said O'Neill. "How did Lena Novak escape this trap that had been set for Kriich? She must have been there when the blaze started. How did she survive?"

The officers stared at each other, blank-faced. No one had any theories. The meeting broke up and the officers filed away to their separate tasks.

In the following days, the weather got colder, and Daly employed as many officers as he could in the search for the missing woman. Wasn't that the whole point of police work, he said to his chief, when he resisted requests for more personnel—to create a circle of security, a protective chain around the frightened and vulnerable? Daly hoped that his team would reach out to and connect with Lena, and bring her back to safety, but there were too many absent links and missing hands in the chain, and their search proved fruitless. The missing woman's trail simply disappeared like a ghost's into the darkness of a deep river.

It was a month before the first clues about her whereabouts surfaced.

5

During the summer, the swimming pool belonged to the children with their army of inflatable toys and floats, but after the long cold winter, its murky waters had a ransacked feel, the toys long gone, the wind churning a mass of dead leaves on the surface, the rotting dregs slowly sinking to the bottom.

Jack Fowler had allowed himself the luxury of a silk dressing gown and a double gin as he took a final tour of the pool and garden. A knot of nostalgia for happier times tightened in his stomach. He surveyed the mansion and its grounds hacked from the surrounding moorland—a landscape of impoverished-looking gorse and thorn bushes that formed a groping backdrop to his landscaped gardens. Even a week ago, a similar walk to the white-tiled pool edge would have made him feel like a king staring across at a battlefield of vanquished enemies.

He could hear noises from the kitchen where his wife was getting their four children ready for school. Somehow he had to get through the morning routine, survive the first hour of the day, and escape his children's questioning gaze. Then, afterward, he might be able to think through a plan of action.

He raised the shivering meniscus of his drink to his lips and sucked greedily, but not even the numbing effect of alcohol could lighten the dread weight of the financial and legal disaster that burdened him. The previous day, an officer from the Fraud Squad had delivered the news he feared the most. The shock of the words had almost made his body bend in double.

He looked up suddenly, blinked, and raised his arm in self-defense. A ragged flock of crows fell around his head. He tried to brush the swooping wings away, but the birds dove at him with such insistence that he feared God had finally unleashed his anger. Surely, he was being punished now for his greed and his ill-advised affair with the Croatian prostitute. He thought ruefully about Lena Novak. The unattainable Lena with her mysterious eyes. Rescuing her from that brothel a month ago was the one selfless act he had done in his entire life. It was also the most stupid decision he had ever made, he thought bitterly. No wonder it had led to the unraveling of his private and public life.

Greta, his wife, had just finished helping the children put on their school uniforms when she glanced through the French doors. She was surprised to see her husband standing by the pool on such a cold morning, his dressing gown fluttering against his bare body. A flock of crows flapped around his hunched shoulders, the birds gathering and dispersing as though an invisible web had entangled them in his arms.

Seeing him like that, when normally he would have been showered and dressed in a smart suit, made her feel uneasy. Carefully, she opened the doors, and was surprised once again—this time by the sound of his voice praying. She had assumed he had forgotten how to do so. To her knowledge, he had not uttered a single holy word since they'd moved into their new house. The fervent tone of his voice heightened her uneasiness. She would have stepped back into the house had he not chosen that moment to turn round. He stopped praying and beckoned at her.

"What is it with these bloody crows?" he complained when she drew close. "Look at them, they won't rest. Their beaks have picked the thorn hedges clean but still they're not happy. What drives them on and on?"

A swell of mountain air lifted the birds high above the pool and then dropped them back toward her husband. Their caws were like gashes in the restless wind. Greta clapped her hands sharply and the flock disintegrated, the crows flying off at low angles.

"That's enough!" she shouted at him. "Stop talking about the bloody birds. Have you gone mad?"

He turned toward her, and for a second she saw the desperation in his face. He ran his hands though his heavy black hair as though he wanted to uproot it. His feet were blue with the cold, and the belt of his dressing gown trailed in the pool. She feared he might follow it in at any moment.

"I can't live with you if you're going to behave like this," she said.

It was then that he revealed the disaster that had found a shortcut into their lives, the contagion that traveled through their bank accounts and their portfolio of properties and investments as quickly as disease or death itself. The alcohol and her soothing presence loosened his tongue and softened the frozen grimace of his face. He told her his fear of ending up bankrupt had turned him into an empty shell. His heart was broken and he was unable to stop himself going mad. If only they could go back to their old life, to all that was familiar and dear to them.

"There'll be a police investigation," he said finally, the breath squeezing from his chest. "They might charge me with fraud and embezzlement."

She saw a look of terror in his eyes and wanted to comfort him, but the children were waiting in the car. The youngest would start wailing soon.

"We'll survive this," she told him. "Let's get away from here. We'll book a hotel for the weekend, leave the children with my brother."

He lowered himself into a deck chair and poured another glass of gin.

"Just treat all that money as if it didn't exist in the first place," she urged. "We've been through so much together. They can't take everything from us."

He emptied the glass, dropped it beside the chair. "How are the children?"

"They're fine. They're so busy with homework they don't notice what's going on."

"And Luke, too?"

He was their youngest, the only boy.

"Luke, too."

"I can't bear the thought of him visiting me in prison."

"Don't tell me anything more. I've already seen the letters and answered the telephone calls. I know too much already."

She walked off without glancing behind even though she knew he was waiting for her to do so. She knew that if she looked back, his misery and fear would cling to her, too, and drag her down with him.

Where had all the money gone? she wondered. Not so long ago, her husband had been one of the richest men in the country, vaulting from business deal to business deal so successfully he had moved in the most powerful political circles in the land.

Greta managed to rally herself by the time she returned from the school run. These days everyone in the country was anxious about money, she reasoned. They were not the only family facing financial annihilation because of the depressed property market.

She rushed into the garden feeling a surge of the love she had for him in spite of his recent transgressions. Those faithful feelings were unchanged in the face of his infidelity and the deplorable state of their finances. *We'll be all right,* she wanted to reassure him. However, by the time she reached the swimming pool, it was too late. A more brutal tragedy had swept into their lives. She was forty-two years old, had given birth to four children, suffered two miscarriages, and seen the deaths of both her parents, but nothing could prepare her for the sight of her drowned husband's body floating in the wind-ruffled waters of their swimming pool.

6

"These people don't just live in the asshole of nowhere, they have their faces shoved right up it," said Irwin as Daly pulled the car up to the brand-new electronic gates. He was right. The bog had been the drowned man's nearest neighbor. Jack Fowler had been a millionaire several times over when he built his three-story mansion at the end of a turf-cutter's road, on a clearing in the wilderness, an expanse of mountain moorland that was as desolate as a rough sea. The harshness of the setting added to the precarious solidity of the house, its wide, triple-glazed windows reflecting an unstable panorama of storm clouds rushing in from the west. Only a thin hedge of laurel separated the manicured lawns from a hundred square miles of mountain and bog.

A house sign welcomed them to Tara na Naomh, hill of the saints. Daly recognized it as a reference to the Mass rock in a nearby wild glen and the anonymous hordes of pilgrims that congregated there during times of religious persecution. He studied Fowler's house as they approached, imagining the expensive things inside, the furniture, the paintings, the statues, the latest playthings for adults and children all piled amid the ruined emotional lives of a family who had just lost their father.

Daly could not help but feel a twinge of distaste at such ostentatious signs of wealth. The mountain's reputation for sanctity had been diluted by the early twenty-first-century race toward prosperity by men like Fowler. Three hundred years ago, in a nearby glen, persecuted Catholics prayed in secret amid the holy thorns—nowadays their descendants built mansions with swimming pools on the tops of hills and holidayed in second homes from Portugal to Dubai.

They parked the car and walked up a set of garden steps to the back of the house, where a group of paramedics had gathered at the edge of the pool. Opera music reverberated through a set of French doors, adding a manic edge to the mountain breezes and the muted flight of several curious crows.

They took in the scene. The landscaped grounds, the patio tiles, the brick barbecue, and the children's play area with its wooden swings and climbing frames. A deck chair was positioned next to the pool, an empty glass and a half-smoked cigar sitting on the tiles. A folded parasol hung over the nearby table like the remnant of a summer dream. Something was missing from the scene, however, something else had been wiped from the poolside with a dreadful finality.

The two detectives stepped to the side of the pool and stared at the floating body with its bloated silk dressing gown. No one spoke. Even in death, Jack Fowler looked like a man who knew what he wanted. He had put on the perfect dressing gown, selected the perfect cigar, put on his perfect piece of music, at just the right volume so that it would emanate through the windows, which held the perfect view of the swimming pool and the backdrop of mountain and moor. The only thing out of place was the ugly bruise on the front of his head, the wound enveloping the hair in a halo of flowing blood. *The scene has been orchestrated like a play,* thought Daly. One that was over barely before it had begun.

He looked back at the cold shell of the house, its windows streaked with rain, and then to the pool as the paramedics dragged the body out of the water, the dressing gown entangling the arms like a straitjacket, water and rotting leaves seeping from the sleeves. He wondered if the drowning had simply been a case of Fowler slipping on a wet tile. How else could he have so casually left behind his glass and cigar, the mansion and family of young children, a life overflowing with abundance?

"Looks like his garden parties are over for good now," said Irwin.

A doctor stepped up to examine the body. His stethoscope fluttered across the pearlescent chest, then rested on the sternum. The ripple of urgency dissipated from his hands. He removed the earpieces and felt along the side of the neck. The dead man did not resist. The doctor took his face by the chin and using a pen torch examined first his mouth, then his unblinking eyes. Finally he looked at the head wound, gingerly pulling the skin and hair back. He glanced back at the assembled team of paramedics and detectives.

"I'm on shaky ground here," he said.

"What do you mean?" asked Irwin.

"Medically speaking. I'm a GP, not a pathologist, but I believe the deceased was struck on the head before he drowned. However, that's for other professionals to decide. All I can certify is that Mr. Fowler is dead."

At this point, the laurel hedge began to rustle and a man burst through to the garden. He stopped, collected himself, and gave the detectives an uncertain salute.

Daly introduced himself. "This is the scene of a police investigation," he said sharply. "What are you doing here?"

The man's face was a blank. Not a tremor or a blink or a tightening anywhere.

"I'm his brother-in-law," he replied, staring at the drowned body.

"That may be the case, but I want to know your name and what you were doing in the hedge."

The man nodded. "My name is Frank Cassidy. Greta asked me to come down and look for their pet dog. He's been missing since this morning."

Daly raised an eyebrow.

"Tell me about your brother-in-law."

"He is—was—a businessman," said Cassidy.

"What sort?"

He grinned, revealing a gap in his teeth. "One of those who threw money at houses like there was no Gomorrah."

"A property developer?"

"Yes. But he had other strings to his bow, too. He was the director of Gortin Regeneration Partnership, a

47

community group." He spat on the tiles. "God knows what skeletons you're going to unearth if you pick over Jack's life. You know, a long time ago, he was a crew member on *Samra Africa*?"

Daly had no idea what he was talking about. Cassidy explained that the *Samra Africa* was a boat that had set off from Malta in 1991 with a ten-ton cargo of AK-47 assault rifles and Semtex, courtesy of Colonel Gadaffi's Libyan government, bound for the IRA. However, the Spanish customs seized the boat close to Gibraltar. It was one of the biggest arms seizures in the history of the Troubles.

"The six-man crew, including Jack, spent four years in a Malaga jail," said Cassidy. "The Spanish thought they were so dangerous they kept them in solitary confinement in a concrete bunker."

Daly looked around him, finding it difficult to resolve Fowler's past with the opulence of his family home.

"How well did you know his private life?"

"Well enough to know he was having an affair with a Croatian girl." Cassidy produced a photograph of a woman from his jacket. "Greta found this on the deck chair by the pool. She asked me to remove it. It's a photograph of his mistress."

Daly took the photo, catching a scent of perfume. He examined it with interest. What he saw was a picture of an attractive young woman, dressed in a man's jacket, lying sprawled across a sofa. *She has the kind of body that would look good in anything,* thought Daly. No matter how shapeless the clothing, everything found its fit. He looked again at her pretty face. Although she was smiling, he thought he detected a hungry loss in her eyes, as though she had just fled a war or massacre, her body forcibly resettled to that sofa, seeking refuge in the shapeless jacket that sagged so fetchingly for the camera.

"My sister phoned at the weekend," said Cassidy. "She wanted me to take her to the priest for advice. She'd just discovered what Jack was up to."

"Wouldn't a decent solicitor have been more useful?"

"My sister wanted to save her marriage, not end it. Besides, Jack was not the sort of man to have his personal life dragged through the courts."

"What do you mean by that?"

"He didn't have much time for the law of the land. Everything had to be done his way."

Daly nodded. His interest in Fowler's personal life had been piqued, but it was too early in the investigation to pry into the dead man's past. There were set routines that had to be adhered to, procedures that had to be completed before the investigation went any deeper.

"That's all for now, Mr. Cassidy," he said, putting the photo of the mistress in his wallet. "In the meantime, keep an eye on your sister. We want to talk to her later this afternoon."

"What do you mean? Is her life in danger, too?"

"Just don't leave her alone with her sleeping pills."

"Thanks for the concern."

"I just want her fit for questioning, that's all."

"Come on. You're not suggesting she did this to Jack?"

"A scorned wife is just about the worst thing for an errant husband to run into."

49

Cassidy turned and stared at Irwin, who introduced himself as a Special Branch detective.

"Why is Special Branch interested in Jack's death?" asked Cassidy cautiously.

"A few days ago, the Fraud Squad was due to question Mr. Fowler over his financial dealings," explained Irwin. "Unfortunately, he didn't show up at the arranged time. Technically, when he walked out here this morning in his silk dressing gown, he was a fugitive from the law. That's why we have a professional interest in finding out how he died."

Cassidy shook his head. "So he cheated on more than his wife?"

"That's what we're here to find out," replied Irwin.

The wind leaked out a whimper, the sound of a dog yelping in distress. Cassidy remembered the task he had been assigned by his sister and made off briskly. A front of cold rain pushed Daly and Irwin away from the comfortless poolside toward the shelter of the house.

"The possibility that someone murdered Fowler doesn't make sense to me," said Irwin. "He finds out that his financial affairs are under police scrutiny and his wife discovers his affair. Then he walks out to the pool in his dressing gown on a cold morning, leaving behind a photograph of his mistress. That suggests suicide to me. Not murder."

Daly did not answer. It was certainly the plot, the set, and the location for a suicide, and the photograph suggested the events leading up to Fowler's death had been high on emotional drama.

"We need to find out if there's anything else that might

suggest he took his own life," said Daly. "A suicide note, a history of depression, previous attempts, but for now, we'll keep an open mind."

"If he was murdered, what was the photograph doing at the scene?"

Daly pondered the question. "Maybe his killer wanted to announce Fowler's infidelity to the world. Or throw us off the scent."

They retraced their steps around the house and then back down the steps to the car. Irwin surveyed the bleak landscape. "Pity there's no neighbors to call upon."

"We'll have to rely on the autopsy report and his wife's statement," said Daly.

"You're forgetting the woman in the photograph. A man will tell his mistress things he would never tell his wife."

They ran into an officer who had been searching Fowler's house.

"It looks like Mr. Fowler was planning a romantic break," the officer said, holding up a large brown envelope.

Inside it were Fowler's passport and two plane tickets for a flight the following Saturday to Malaga. One of the tickets was made out to Fowler; the other bore the name of Lena Novak.

Daly heard the name echo inside his head. He was surprised. The prostitute had found her knight in shining armor, he realized. Unfortunately, Jack Fowler had failed to sweep the missing woman off her feet. Instead, he had left her with one foot in a fairy tale, the other at the center of a crime scene.

7

Even though Easter was early, the sky was blue and the sunshine warm in the hilltop Andalucian village. Ashe relaxed in the grounds of the shrine to La Virgen de Nieve. He watched the Semana Santa parade wind up the dusty track, the heavy crucifixion scenes carried on floats by barefoot pallbearers, the doleful music punctuated with hysterical cries from a straggle of wizened women dressed entirely in black.

He leaned against a holy statue and joined in with the prayerful crowds, their voices echoing across the hillsides, which were dotted with the dark green foliage of orange and lemon trees. The spectacle was more like a mass mourning event than the drunken, noisy fiestas that usually filled the streets of the Spanish village.

Ashe was taller than the other spectators, who were mostly old and infirm. The dangerous muscularity that ran under his dark shirt seemed out of place amid the religious fervor of the procession. In addition, his praying voice was tenacious, practiced and hard. It jarred with the theatrical wailing of his coworshippers.

It was Ashe's habit to join in the procession every year as part of his journey away from violence. However, sometimes he feared his attendance was simply a means to alleviate the deep disquiet of his soul, which was the totality of all the demons he had invoked during his youth, when he had been a gunman for the IRA. He feared that this disquiet was untreatable, no matter how stubborn his prayers.

When the procession had passed, an elderly Englishwoman in a lavender hat turned round and smiled up at him.

"Good evening," she said, clutching a palm frond.

There was a frailty about her face that momentarily entranced him.

"Oh. Hello. How are you?"

"Just wonderful. Absolutely." She appeared pleased to be asked the question.

A man, who Ashe presumed to be her husband, walked up and joined them.

"What are you smiling at?" Ashe asked her.

"The procession," she replied. "It was breathtaking. At times like this, don't you think the world is a wonderful place? That we are so close to God?"

Ashe glanced at the remnants of the procession. One of the hooded pallbearers had stopped to steady himself against a stone wall. He wore Nike trainers and was carrying a can of Amstel and a half-smoked Ducados in one hand.

"Your vision is very limited," he said.

However, the woman did not appear to be listening. Her eyes were fixed on the sweep of his shirt beneath his left arm, where a gun was neatly holstered. Her brow furrowed.

Her husband delicately gestured her away, and Ashe went back to saying his rosary. He had been reciting it all evening with weary efficiency. Moments of transcendence were elusive and had to be earned by effort. He knew that. He also knew that the woman was wrong. Try as he might, he did not feel closer to God. Nor was the world a wonderful place. In fact, it was a nest of boundless evil and calamity that made the very notion of goodness seem as out of place as the drunken pallbearer in running shoes.

He put away his rosary beads and walked back down to the village where the familiar evening aromas of coffee and garlic were wafting onto the streets. He had a limping gait and his progress was slow. He shunned the bars and restaurants that were beginning to fill with the crowds released from the holy vigil. He bought a lemon ice cream at a *heladería*. The taste of it was refreshingly real and cold. On his way back to his hostel, a man standing in one of the throngs gave a sudden start and slipped quietly out of view.

Instead of going straight up to his room, Ashe sat on a sofa in the foyer and buried his head in a newspaper. Patches of his journey back from the shrine began to take shape in his mind like a print emerging from a solution. He got an impression that someone had paused behind him earlier in the town.

A waiter walked by, and Ashe ordered some coffee. He finished it quickly. The feeling that there was someone out on the street, very close, grew stronger. Someone was following him, he realized. Several times a year he stayed in this hostel, and almost everything was familiar.

The excitement of this new sensation helped fill a little of the emptiness he felt within. He guessed that the person watching him, whoever it was, had a connection with his past, but he was unsure as to what extent the person wished him harm. How should he act? Was he meant to make a run for it and imitate fear? Or would that prolong the suspense unnecessarily? Through the hotel window, he watched a pair of cats scavenge through a heap of discarded tapas wrappers. He leaned forward and stared at the hostel doors. Whatever violence the evening held for him, he was glad that at least he had spent the day in prayerful meditation.

He walked to the doors and looked up and down the street. He was like an animal that needed a den with many exits. He made his way out to the olive and fruit groves that bordered the village, the tension in his body making his knee hurt more than usual. The dogs that lay slumped in the shade of the trees roused themselves to bark at his passage. Along the hillside, water gushed through the irrigation channels, weaving through trees hung with ripening citrus fruit.

He climbed through the terraces and stopped under the branches of a leafless almond tree. A dry spiced scent filled the air. There was little cover beyond the tree. The mountainside turned into a flinty wilderness stretching several hundred feet toward the snow-capped peak. He surveyed the fertile terrain below and caught sight of a familiar figure from his past clambering through an olive grove. Screwing up his eyes, he tried to fix on the details. The man had a severe haircut—or perhaps he'd grown bald—he was too far away to make out. Unfortunately, he had spotted Ashe and was now waving to get his attention. It was too late to evade him.

"What are you doing here?" asked the man as Ashe slithered back down the hillside.

"I came to pray." Ashe clapped the dust from his hands. "I haven't finished yet."

"No amount of praying will undo the past."

"There's no mistaking that," said Ashe, hobbling by him. "If I'd known it was you following me, I'd have made sure you never caught up. I would have slipped town and you'd never have seen me again."

"You've always wandered where you wanted," replied the man. In spite of Ashe's limp, he had to run to stay up with him.

"I'm on a journey."

"Isn't life a journey? Good or bad?"

"What do you want from me? Why have you followed me here?" Ashe stared at the man's face, absorbing the detail he had been avoiding, the ugly scarring that pockmarked his cheeks and nose. What he saw resembled a botched plaster-cast mask of the face he had known all those years ago.

"I've been sent to offer you a job. We have a problem back home. One that the party bosses are very concerned about."

"I've already done my service. I've paid. Many times over. Fifteen years in jail. The best years of my life."

"Haven't we all?"

"But I've quit the organization, cut my ties. It's been ten years since I even set foot on Irish soil."

"Don't you think I deserve at least a little of your time? After all we've been through in prison?" The man's eyes briefly clouded over. A spasm ran through his facial disfigurement.

Ashe's mind resurrected images of the cell they had shared, and another darker recollection from the time before—the bombed framework of a building, exposed like a doll's house, its ravaged contents spilling out onto the street, a dead body hanging in pieces. He felt his life slip slightly out of its axis.

The man noticed Ashe's reaction. The expression in his eyes changed. "There must be a good restaurant somewhere in town," he said. "All this mountain air is giving me an appetite."

"There's a taverna at the edge of the village," replied Ashe. "The serrano ham and huevos rancheros are the next best thing to an Ulster fry."

Ashe hoped that the man smiling up at him would prove a better partner to his conversations than the demons inside his head.

They ate in a small restaurant off a cobbled courtyard hung with geraniums and scented jasmine. In the middle of the courtyard was a fountain surmounted by three rusted iron crosses.

Ashe's companion surveyed the scene as the waiter brought them beers. "Perfect," he said. "Catholic guilt never felt so good."

He shot Ashe a grin. "You're enjoying life here?"

"I suppose you could say so. I didn't used to, but I've changed."

"A better life than in Ireland then?"

"Yes, of course."

"At least the Ireland you remember."

"I know no other."

"You can't imagine how much it has changed, for the better. Have you thought of returning?"

"What's your point? I'm content here. This place brings me as close to a sense of peace as I ever dared imagine. The only problem is money. Or the lack of it."

"Bound to be worse now with the recession."

"Money's tight everywhere. They say spending's gone out of fashion."

The man placed a wallet on the table. "In here is some cash, a credit card made out in the name of Frank O'Neill, and other personal documents."

"What use are they to me?"

"If you agree to this assignment, I can make you Frank O'Neill. A passport in that name will follow. I have a bank account set up in Northern Ireland to cover your expenses."

Against his better judgment, Ashe felt intrigued by the offer. For one who had taken the vow of exile, there was something dangerous and exciting about returning home under a new identity. He had been dead to his homeland, but now he saw an opportunity to rise again like Lazarus.

"Frank O'Neill," said Ashe. "Sounds familiar already." He flicked through the wallet, sorted the documents and cards. "The only thing I don't see is a piece of paper with 'here's the catch' written on it."

His companion allowed himself a brief smile. "That information's too dangerous to be written anywhere."

They were edging closer to the proposition. Their voices lowered.

"OK," said Ashe. "This problem you have. What, or more precisely who, is it?"

"A community organization run by the party has been swindled out of money. Taxpayers' money from the British government."

"How much?"

"About three million in peace funds." The man stared at Ashe, dead-eyed.

"I'm guessing that doesn't look good for the party's socialist credentials."

"We left that ethos behind long ago. We're all capitalists now, and like all good capitalists we're desperately searching for the missing money."

"Who's in the frame?"

"The community organization was run by an old friend of yours. Jack Fowler."

"I remember Jack." Ashe did not know whether to be pleased or saddened at the mention of the name.

"Then you know his style. Jack wheeled and dealed with the best of them—politicians, bankers, developers; he turned them all inside out. No one guessed the financial tricks he was pulling. He diverted some of the peace funds into the account of a consultancy firm he set up. The company was given a wide-ranging mandate, to look at ways to develop the run-down village of Gortin and draw up a set of plans. But, really, its primary interest was property. As it turns out he used the company to buy up every derelict building and inch of development land in the area."

Ashe thought for a moment. "Sounds like a foolproof scam."

"Exactly. Investment money to develop a dilapidated village is siphoned off and used to buy up land and buildings. When the investment plans are announced with their promises of jobs and community facilities, the value of property goes up. The land is quickly sold to developers eager to build homes, and the funds are paid back into the community organization's accounts, minus the fat profits, of course."

"Jack always knew how to look out for himself."

"He did. But then the credit crunch cracked open the property market and revealed it for the rotten egg it really was. Property prices plummeted, and the company was unable to sell the land and buildings. So Jack's scam was exposed."

Ashe studied the man as he spoke. He observed the listlessness in his eyes, the frozen frown of his mouth, and the scarred skin of his cheek and jaws that made it look as though he was communicating from behind a lifeless mask. A long time ago, they had been imprisoned in Long Kesh during the hunger strike, but Ashe suspected that the real world in the intervening years had been harsher to his old cellmate than any regime in Long Kesh. His companion looked like a man who had been forced to eat his colleagues just to survive.

"What has Jack got to say on all this?"

"Not much." The man's frown grew more haggard. "Jack's dead. He drowned in his outdoor swimming pool two days ago. No suicide note. Only a photograph of his recently acquired mistress."

"Is that all we have to go on?"

"It may be enough. The mistress is a Croatian woman called Lena Novak. Before he died, he set her up in a new apartment, showered her with credit cards, even made her the director of a holding company. He emptied what was left of the community organization's entire funds and deposited them in a foreign bank account, which he registered in her name. We found the paperwork in their love nest."

Ashe watched his companion. He was holding a bottle of Stella but apart from wetting his lips at the start of their conversation, he had not drunk a drop. There was something suspect about his manner. Ashe had the feeling his lines had been practiced and carefully honed. He tried to focus on the silence at the end of his replies. The man's sentences seemed to finish too abruptly, as though his flow of thoughts kept pulling him back from a dangerous brink.

"The party bigwigs are extremely upset. Especially the new leader, Owen Higgins. He's taken it the hardest. We're supposed to be the party of the people for Chrissakes."

"We used to be an idealistic bunch of terrorists," replied Ashe. "But look at us now. Property deals, expense accounts, mistresses, and chauffeur-driven cars. How did we become so vulgar?"

"Ambition's not a sin."

61

"But greed is."

"Listen. The bottom line is we need you to help us find the missing money by making contact with this Croatian woman. We've alerted party activists the length and breadth of the country to be on the lookout for her. Discreetly, of course."

"Here's an outrageous thought. Lena Novak took the money and ran. She's on the other side of Europe now."

"That doesn't appear to be the case. According to our inquiries, the money hasn't been touched. We believe Lena has gone to ground somewhere in South Armagh along with a bunch of her compatriots. Our fear is she may withdraw the money at any moment. Time's at a premium."

"For you or this woman?"

"The party bigwigs are anxious to have the money returned to the community organization as soon as possible."

"If they're so annoyed, why aren't they leaving it to the police and the Fraud Squad to sort out?"

"We don't want the British government getting suspicious about where its money has gone. Anyway, the police won't investigate Lena Novak's disappearance properly until they believe she's committed a crime. At the moment, the evidence is not stacking that way."

"If I was the suspicious type, I might suspect the party is trying to link this woman to the missing money so that party members can cover their backs. Or maybe they want to know how to get their cut of it."

"This is too serious for personal greed or reputation. The peace process is in a perilous enough state as it is. If this falls back at the party's door, it could derail everything."

Ashe examined the photo. He felt a dangerous tug drawing him to the mysterious Lena Novak. He took the wallet and documents and placed them inside his jacket.

"I know a temporary solution for the political crisis," he said.

"What's that?"

"Guinness. Fishing on a cold river in Donegal. Fresh salmon for supper. More Guinness."

The man grinned. The scarred skin on his face stretched like a shredded garment, barely concealing his uneasiness.

"Sounds perfect. I'm glad you're coming back. We'll head to Donegal when this problem is sorted." He tried to meet Ashe's gaze. "If we get drunk, we can always call at Owen Higgins' holiday home and ask him to put us up for the night."

"He'd curse us the whole way to hell and back," said Ashe, and they both laughed.

8

Greta Fowler's face was covered in makeup and tears, a mask of bitterness and grief that shook as she laughed harshly to herself. She was sitting on a pale avocado sofa, her bare knees almost touching a mica coffee table in the expansive sitting room of her mansion.

Daly had just asked for a list of people who might have wished to do her husband harm.

"How many hairs does a dog have?" she replied derisively.

"Have any of them threatened him recently?"

She nodded, not having to think too hard.

"I was in the kitchen the evening before he died, making dinner for the children." She took a deep breath. "He'd left his jacket over the chair. The breast pocket began to buzz. It was his phone, switched to vibrate. I answered it."

She grabbed her cigarettes, lit one, inhaled, and emptied her lungs. For a teetering moment, her eyes watered. Then the nicotine took effect, keen as venom, hardening her face and mouth. The words came to her quickly.

"I didn't say anything. The caller didn't wait. 'You're a bastard,' he said. 'Do you hear me, Fowler? A bastard. You will pay for what you did.' Then he hung up."

"Describe the voice," asked Daly.

"It was muffled. Deep. He had a foreign accent. I'm not sure which."

"Any idea who it might have been?"

She drew on the cigarette. "Someone from his past?"

"But who?"

"I can't think."

"You have to think, Mrs. Fowler. You have to make sense of what was going on in your husband's life."

Something came into her eyes, a stab of cold light. As if she knew what he was talking about. Then the smoke and her heavy eyelids closed it off.

"Jack liked to keep his business secret. I suppose he thought his deals too complicated for his little housewife to understand." She looked away bitterly. "In fact, you could say he was good at keeping secrets. It was something he learned during the Troubles. How to compartmentalize his life."

"Your husband was once involved with a terrorist organization," said Daly. "What did he do?"

"What everyone did," she replied. "He did what he was told."

"Some people were told to do terrible things."

"Jack didn't hide his past. Not like that bunch that's running the country."

"What skeletons did he have in his cupboard?"

"He never killed anyone, if that's what you mean. He was involved in the business end of things. Raising cash, buying weapons."

"If it wasn't for men like your husband, there would have been no bombs. No killings." Daly could not prevent an edge of aggression creeping into his voice.

She stared at him provocatively. Her mocking gaze suggested he had no idea what he was talking about.

"Mrs. Fowler, I have to get to know the type of man your husband was, and the type of people he came in contact with."

She shrugged. "I'm not even sure I knew. I could never figure him out. Even that morning when I saw him standing at the poolside, he surprised me."

"How?"

"He was praying. I mean really praying. As though his life depended on it."

How much do we really know about our nearest and dearest? Daly thought to himself. He produced the photograph of Lena Novak.

"We need to get in touch with this woman," he said. "Do you know who she is?"

"Please, I don't want to go down that path."

Daly understood the request and said nothing. His instinct told him he had more to lose by aggravating her at this early stage in the investigation.

"Jack made his mistakes, but he always told me everything," she said. "I helped him confront his demons. That woman tried to get her claws into him, but he broke free."

Pain etched an almost vulnerable human face on her hard features. "We were married for over ten years, but Jack liked to be carefree. Deep down he still thought he was twenty-one. That's all I can say for now."

Afterward, Daly returned to his office and contacted the duty inspector in Monaghan, the nearest Garda headquarters. He suspected that with her lover dead under mysterious circumstances, Lena Novak might have escaped across the border into a different police jurisdiction.

He did not recognize the inspector's name, but he had a friendly voice. Daly introduced himself. He described Fowler's girlfriend and found himself poring over her photograph. He took in the curves of her long body leaning back in Fowler's oversized jacket, the slack features of her bored but pretty face, the tilt of her half-closed eyes, and the glimmer of what might have been vengeance or fear in her dark pupils. What made her so different from the other women Fowler had met in the course of his high-powered life? Daly thought he could detect the fatalistic attraction, the air of detachment in her face coupled with a lonely vulnerability that must have made Fowler's imagination take flight. In an unsubtle way, Lena Novak could be summed up in one word. *Risk*.

Daly was glad he was a policeman and not a gambler like Fowler. His brain had grown sharper and more perceptive to the dangers such adventures posed. He was also glad he had not invested in the property market or sold his father's run-down cottage when even disused sheds commanded six-figure sums. His chances of growing rich had passed him by. Poor men could not afford to take risks, which made them unadventurous lovers but better citizens.

When Daly described Lena, the policeman on the other end of the line paused. "Pretty girl?" he asked.

"Yes. We believe she was trafficked from Croatia."

"A prostitute?"

"She'd been forced to work in a brothel."

"I'll put out an alert for her, but don't count on anything. A girl like that will have disappeared like smoke. She won't need to worry about picking up a lift. Is her English good?"

"I don't know. I haven't spoken to her."

"What has she done?"

"Nothing. Yet. But we believe her boyfriend might have been murdered."

"Lena is a popular name among Croatians. So too is Novak. As common as Murphy or Kelly."

"Are you suggesting she's using an alias?"

"I'm only telling you it's a common name."

Daly put the phone down. He had no way of knowing if Lena was her real name. In fact, her entire identity was as nebulous as a ghost. The only hard evidence of her existence was this photo and a set of footprints in the snow that had melted away. They were like the first clues in an interesting game of hide-and-seek. He stared at the photo, examining her image closely, her slender slouching shape, the body that was hers but somehow not her own. In his mind's eye, he saw her half-sleeping eyes open wide and her face lean forward to mouth the words *Shall I take off the jacket now?*

He put the photo away, feeling tense, as though he had opened a door that could not be closed. The darkness of her eyes had threatened to pull him down into a deep river rushing through the night.

9

When Lena awoke, the first thing she felt was anger at men, and in particular her lover, the businessman who had promised to rescue her from her violent pimp but had succeeded only in opening the door to more dangerous enemies. Then she remembered she did not have a lover anymore. Nor a home, or any place she could regard as a safe refuge.

She slid her arm from under the blanket and checked her watch. 7:15 a.m. She began to organize her thoughts. Each time she had awoken in the past six months, the second feeling that invariably followed her anger was one of overwhelming homesickness. This morning was no different as she stared at the crystal chandelier dangling above, glittering in the early morning sunlight. Despite its closeness, the chandelier belonged to a distant world. The unattainable world of mortgages, well-paid jobs, and nine-to-five respectability.

She had a bunch of keys in her purse and could have chosen any of a dozen houses to spend the night in, all of them still smelling of fresh paint and varnish and furnished with every comfort she needed. Everything, that is, except the security and warmth of a home. This house with its crystal chandeliers was not her home. That place lay somewhere deep in her past.

The keys belonged to her dead lover, Jack Fowler. They represented what was left of his property empire. The doors themselves and everything else about the houses belonged to the banks. She owned the keys now, but in financial terms, they were worthless to her.

A couple more days and I'll be away from all this, she told herself. All she had to do was get to Dublin, purchase a false passport, wait for Jack's money to come through, and then book the first flight home. True, there were obstacles to be surmounted, and events had taken a dangerous turn for the worse. She was a fugitive now, on the run from not only her torturer and pimp, but also the police and all those to whom Fowler owed money.

Carefully, she made the bed and plumped the pillows, ensuring no trace of her presence remained. At 7:25 a.m., she slipped out the back door of number 84. She ran like a guilty party guest past the neat lawn, the clipped foliage, and the For Sale sign. There was no other evidence of human life on the street. Rows of identical houses stared blankly at their mirror reflections, each with its own collection of tired-looking For Sale signs. She had become an invisible woman hiding in an estate of empty homes, a ghost estate.

A taxi waited for her on the main road. She climbed in and gave the driver directions. It was not the first time she had directed a taxi to take her by Fowler's mansion, but it was most likely the last. Previously, her secretive excursions left her feeling foolish and excited as she succumbed to the recurring daydream of a settled life with her lover. In her mind she kept looping over the same fairy tale—that she was his Cinderella and he was her Prince Charming. She had hoped that some day she could just enter his life, right at the happy-ever-after ending.

However, this time she had returned to make sure the fairy tale was over. She scanned the tree-lined drive, the side gardens, the front of the house, the double doors that she always suspected would never open for her, in spite of Fowler's promises. Everything looked as she expected. However, she still wanted to make sure. She counted two police cars, what she took to be a forensics van, and four private cars. She knew the swimming pool lay at the rear of the house. She asked the driver to switch off the engine and wait for a moment. She said good-bye to the mansion where her lover had led his normal family life, tucked in his children most nights, drank a glass or two of wine before climbing into bed beside his faithful wife, while, unbeknownst to her, his libido was pulling his life in an entirely different direction.

She rolled the window down a chink and leaned back, lowering her body slightly. The wind smelled of the first wild blossoms of spring fed from the hedgerows. Men and women in white forensic suits bustled around the house, carrying bags and different types of equipment. Everything was silent. Not the usual silence that hung over the house and its grounds. This time the silence was different. Deeper. No matter how expert the forensics people were, she doubted if they would ever be able to fathom the depths of that silence.

A window opened on the second floor. It was as if the house had suddenly woken up and blinked at her. A young girl stared out. She appeared to be looking straight at the taxi. Lena slid down farther and asked the driver to move off.

She had found out about Jack's death by accident. He had not rung or answered her calls, and then in a supermarket she saw his face staring from the front page of a newspaper. She did not understand all the words, but worked out he had drowned in his swimming pool and that either suicide or foul play was suspected.

In shock, she bought a bottle of vodka and stepped onto the street. Cars raced by and she trembled. Behind her, she could hear the patter of quick feet. She sensed the press of pursuit and wheeled around, but all she saw was a group of schoolgirls giggling together. Her dress fluttered in the wind of a lorry hurtling past. She was alone again. She resisted an urge to ring Jack's home number and fire questions at whoever answered. Her deepest fear was that Mikolajek had found Jack and murdered him in revenge. Unfortunately, it would be difficult to make inquiries about his death without drawing attention to herself, and doing that was the last thing she wanted.

Someone tapped her on the shoulder and she turned around.

"Is this yours?" One of the schoolgirls stood with a purse in her hands.

"Oh. Yes. Thank you." The purse lay open, displaying a picture of Jack.

"Is something wrong?" The girl waited, hesitant.

"Not me. Him. Yes."

Concern and curiosity showed in the girl's face. "Do you need someone to help you home?"

"I don't know where home is."

"What do you mean?"

Lena tried to smile. "I have no home."

"How can you not have a home?"

Lena walked away quickly. *At least Jack had made it home,* she thought with sudden bitterness. Even at the moment of his death, as he toppled toward the water, he would have been able to raise his eyes and take one final look at the house he had built for his wife and children.

She went back to the flat he had rented for her and packed what she needed. Over the sink, she cut her hair. Soon the bowl was brimming with loose black strands. She did not wait to get it right. She just wanted it as short as possible. Her hair fell like a set of curtains over the final moments of the old Lena and all the disappearing dreams of her future.

After the taxi pulled away from the mansion, she directed the driver to the town's ATM machine. However, a mound of rubble surrounded by police tape and an abandoned JCB digger greeted them. The driver informed her that a gang of thieves had been ripping out the machines in towns all along the border. "Someone must have trouble remembering their PIN," he quipped.

Determined to get her hands on as much cash as possible, Lena asked him to drive to a garage on the road south. She remembered the assistant at the till, a sleepy-looking, overweight young man. Each time she went in to buy cigarettes he had hitched his jeans up, smoothed back his hair, and followed her movements around the shelves.

This time, his eyes locked on her as soon as she entered. She did not feel nervous. She convinced herself the life she was moving through was someone else's. She forced herself to return his lustful stare and watched the tremor of foreboding that briefly clouded his features as she drew closer. She placed the credit card bearing Jack Fowler's name on the counter, and he glanced down at it with a strained look.

Without a trace of emotion, she asked for one hundred boxes of cigarettes. King-size.

He scratched his neck and glanced briefly at the manager's office. Then he looked at the card, shrugged, and put it in the chip reader. When the machine verified the PIN, he began packing the cartons in several large bags. She was relieved to see that the card still worked. When he had finished, he looked at her and frowned. He appeared reluctant to hand over the bags.

"Is there a problem?" she asked.

His frown deepened. "Don't you know smoking is bad for your health?"

She relaxed. "Everyone needs a vice."

He breathed out a sigh. "Now, that's the truth."

Afterward, she took the cigarettes to a house in the town. A woman with an anxious face opened the door.

"Lena!" she said, in surprise. "You can't come here."

"I wasn't expecting an invite."

"If you want to get yourself killed, do it on someone else's doorstep."

"This is business, Martha," she replied. "I need cash."

She pushed the bags of cigarettes at her. The woman looked inside and nodded.

"You've left a big mess behind," she warned. "It doesn't look good for you, but I'll give you the money for these. That's all I can do."

Afterward, Lena walked to the bus station. For the first time in a couple of days, she felt good. Untouchable. In charge of her own destiny. Stuffed into an empty cigarette box in her purse were more than five hundred euros in notes, all flying the flag of the European Union.

A bus was due to leave at 6:00 p.m. for Dublin. She bought a ticket and boarded it. The city would be less oppressive than this lonely border country, she told herself. In a few hours, she would step off the bus and disappear into Dublin's noisy streets, leaving behind her cramped fears forever.

However, as the bus began to pull out of the station, she was seized by a feeling of uneasiness. She stared blankly at her reflection in the window, her shorn head hanging over the darkening countryside like a fading image from an unfinished dream. The bus trundled down the road. It was not the memory of all that had happened to her that preoccupied her, but the thought of all she had left undone. She realized she was not yet ready to leave this border country; it had become part of her. She carried a secret knowledge of the men who had visited her. Their inner lives were etched into her consciousness. Her mind churned through their stories, their fears and complaints, the miserable little crosses they carried on their backs. The sense of revulsion inside her grew strong. The border country had turned her into its prey, and she could not bear the thought that in some way she had been its victim. Her eyes clouded over. Her fantasies of escape dissolved, and in their place, a darker and more desperate plan returned to preoccupy her mind. She had to put things right before she departed.

Grabbing her bag, she ran to the front of the moving bus and told the driver she was feeling sick. He pulled in at the next lay-by and opened the door.

She jumped out before the vehicle had fully stopped. Life was a parachute jump, she told herself; you just had to hold your nerve.

10

On his way to his ex-wife's house in the city, Daly stopped at a florist's and bought two dozen freshly cut daffodils. He hoped they would remind Anna of the spring they had met, when the flowers bloomed in wild profusion along the banks of the river Lagan.

A young man opened the front door with a fixed smile and blank blue eyes.

"Hello," said Daly. "I'm Anna's ex-husband."

"Oh, yes. She's expecting you."

"Brian is it?"

"No, Tom."

"What happened to Brian? You change so often."

"Anna's needs are very complex." There was a slight hint of reproach in his voice.

"I'm well aware of her needs," said Daly coldly.

"You'll find her in the living room."

Anna had just had a massage. She lay on a bed in the middle of the room. The smell of lavender oil hung in the air.

She was asleep. Daly placed the flowers in a vase and peeked at the rest of the house. The walls had been painted white and the blinds removed from the windows. Most of their furniture was gone. He wondered how she could live in such a blank space. The layout of the rooms had also changed. She had installed a bathroom downstairs and lowered the worktops in the kitchen. Anna had reorganized her life completely. He glanced into the study, which had been formerly his refuge, the place where in the evenings after getting back from work he would stretch out on the sofa and play his music. She had converted the room to a laundry. The cozy house in which they had spent ten years of married life and whose walls contained many happy memories was gone forever.

He went through the other rooms of the house, his eyes scanning every horizontal surface and corner as if he was searching for a clue, or a missing household object. All the time his mind raced through his memories. He was about to climb into the attic and start loading up his boxes when he heard her stir. By the time he came back down the stairs, Tom had brought in a wheelchair and was positioning her for a lift. He slung her arm around his neck and swiveled her to the edge of the bed. Daly tried to help but next to Tom's expert movements, his efforts were blundering, inexperienced. His hands grasped at her lower back, but she brushed him away.

"Tom's the nurse, not you. I can manage without your help."

"Of course you can," he replied. He noticed that her hair had been cut short, spiky at the top. Her clothes were different, too. More casual and tight-fitting, the high sleeves of her blouse revealing her toned muscular arms. She noticed his gaze and touched her hair self-consciously as if trying to smooth it down. He suspected her new image was a way of making a fresh start, as if she had to adopt a disguise to escape the pain of the past.

She wheeled herself into the kitchen and began putting away the dishes and pots from the dishwasher. She swung the wheelchair about the room with a determined vitality as though making a show of how well she could cope. She had convinced herself that apart from the assistance of the nurses, she was competent and independent. And he had done the same. It was a game they had played, to delude themselves into believing that nothing had changed after the car crash. But, of course, everything had changed. When she learned she would never walk again, she built a barrier of privacy around herself, one that was breached only by medical professionals. He thought her disability would make her more vulnerable, but the loss of her legs had hardened her heart. Six months after coming home from the hospital, she became the executioner of their troubled marriage.

"We need to be apart more than we need to be together," she had told him. "I can't stop blaming you for the accident."

"I blame myself."

He had tried to save their marriage, making all sorts of promises. He told her he would apply for a part-time position in the police force, but she rejected his offers. He feared the accident had changed her personality or induced some sort of emotional amnesia. Their marriage may not have been perfect, but it wasn't a disaster zone either.

"Having you at my side makes me think of the time I could walk, and that's my past, not my future," she said. "Every time you touch me I feel like a foreigner in my own body."

The pain of their physical separation burned within him, but deep down he felt grateful. That was the paradox. The more time he spent with her, the more he chewed himself up with guilt.

After the nurse had left, he went into the attic and began bringing down the boxes. He lifted out a silver leaf plaque, an award for dedication that he had received at the start of his police career. It was still in pristine condition, unlike most things from that period of his life. Downstairs he handed it to her.

"What's this?"

"A gift." He felt like a man alone on the deck of a sinking ship handing over all the last of his precious cargo.

Reluctantly, she took it and placed it on the worktop.

"I'm glad you're doing this. The house feels lighter already."

He stared at his feet, reasoning that he should not feel so bad.

"Do you need anything? Some shopping? Any odd jobs about the house?"

"I have everything under control." She took a tray from the fridge. On it were two freshly poured glasses of champagne. She handed him one, sipped the other. He downed the contents of the glass as quickly as he could.

"Is this it?" he said, his voice flat. "Is this good-bye?"

"No," she replied. "Good-bye you should only have to say once. I just wanted to mark the occasion, that's all."

"Shall I leave now?"

"Yes."

11

The low winter fog shrouded the motorway as Daly drove home, hunched over the steering wheel. The boxes touched the roof of his car, blocking his vision through the rearview mirror. He found the effect disconcerting. Police officers in Northern Ireland took an unwritten oath to keep a wary eye fixed on the road behind when traveling through border country. However, on this occasion, it was not dissident terrorists but the ghosts of the past that made him anxious.

He was half an hour from his cottage when he pulled off the motorway and delved deeper into the labyrinth of byroads crisscrossing the border. Armagh's crooked, introverted little lanes were as familiar to him as the processes of his own mind. Thorn trees leaned out of the fog, their branches sweeping over the road, twigs scraping the car as he took flight from the city and his troubled past.

A dark valley swallowed up the road. He drove as though hell-bent, descending into an underworld to escape the convoluted feelings of guilt and loss that were crippling his libido. Soon the car wheels bit into the loose stones of a lane. He stopped and switched on the headlights. The bulk of a dilapidated farmhouse appeared in the mist like an unsteady reflection on water. He killed the lights and waited for a while, his breath forming a cloud against the windshield. He was back at the border brothel. He had returned because he felt a need to reacquaint himself with its shadows, to find out more about the women imprisoned there, where they came from, and why they had been unable to escape even when they knew their pimp was dead. Sometimes, the bonds of cruelty were just as hard to untangle as those of love.

He got out and stretched his legs. The house and outbuildings were a collection of gray fragments in the mist, the air still enough for a frost. At the bottom of the garden a pile of tree trunks, knotted with brambles, caught his attention. Their branches loomed out of the fog, smooth and sleek, like a gleaming jumble of female bodies, limbs floundering as if turning over in sleep. Then he noticed the smell, a faint scent wafting slowly through the darkening air from the shadows around the farmhouse. Daly recognized it instantly. The perfume on the photograph. The smell of roses and soap, female flesh and promised sex. He stood still and studied the silent house. He had not noticed the scent when he first got out of the car. He shifted his weight slowly and moved off the gravel path onto grass. It took less than a few seconds to scoot along the garden to the rear of the house. He peered through the windows, but the broken panes were sheets of blackness. The back door hung slightly

84

ajar. He eased through it, half expecting a hand to grab him out of the darkness. He listened carefully and heard the sound of a foot slowly pressing onto broken glass.

Something brushed the side of his head with a clacking noise. His heart leaped in his chest, as he instinctively dove for cover. A dark bird, like a crow, gave an angry caw and flapped into the mist.

When he looked up, the pale face of Lena Novak hovered above him.

"Don't you know?" she said. "Birds hate being trapped. They like to take off in any direction they choose."

For a moment, Daly thought she was going to disappear, too, but instead she stood and watched while he dragged himself back to his feet.

"My name is Inspector Celcius Daly," he said. "I'm a police officer."

"Welcome to Club Paradise, Inspector Daly," she replied, melting back into the darkness of the house.

12

Lena's voice floated through the dark interior. "Watch you don't trip, Inspector. This place is a mess."

Daly switched on his torch and followed her into the cramped rooms. His light swung over her for an instant. She was wearing a short fur coat, jeans, and black boots. Her long hair had been cut roughly. Although she was too young and fresh faced to have worry lines, he saw the tension beneath her skin, the instinctive distrust that pulled at her facial muscles, and the practiced gaze of her eyes, the intensifying of the pupils, which suggested she had seen a lot, and not all of it pleasant.

"I'm investigating the death of Sergei Kriich," said Daly.

"I'm glad to hear he's dead," she replied. "He was a piece of shit."

"I didn't think the news would leave you choked."

"No one should give a damn for people like him."

"Someone has to, though, Ms. Novak. Law and order have to be upheld."

She sat down at the edge of a sofa. Daly placed the torch on a low table so that it lit up the wall opposite. A flurry of shadows rolled over a set of hooks and dressing gowns. Lena looked at Daly. Her gaze was challenging, bleak.

"I've met policemen in this country. They're not so different from the policemen back home."

"People are the same wherever you go."

"In my experience they do the same things."

"What sort of things?"

"Who are we talking about?"

"The policemen here."

She pulled a face. "What all men do who visit places like this. They're crazy. Sex crazy."

She had raised the question of sex. Exploited sex. The thought of it left him feeling tired.

"You were with Sergei in the car. What happened that night?"

"I don't want to talk about it." She gripped her arms against the chill in the air. "Are you going to arrest me now?"

It was not really a question. More a challenge.

"I want to help you."

"That's a line I heard before." She reached down and slipped off her boots. She rubbed her stockinged toes, flexed them on the carpet.

"Chilblains," she said. "What you get for running barefoot in the snow."

"Why have you come back to this place?"

"I had to collect personal things." She held up a small rag doll. "My grandmother gave me this. She said I should keep it with me always."

"Is it meant to bring you good luck?"

"If I take care of it. Yes."

"What about taking care of yourself?"

"I patch myself up best I can."

Daly thought he understood why she had returned for the doll. It was a type of blessing. A reminder of happier times to pit against the darkness of her current predicament. Her life was in danger and she needed whatever sense of comfort the past provided.

"If I can stay as quiet as her, I shall be safe," said Lena.

"I want you to know you have nothing to fear. We have everything ready for you."

"What do you have ready?"

"A safe place. A refuge run by women. We don't want anything to happen to you until we find out who murdered Kriich and what happened to Jack Fowler. You can stay there until the investigation is over."

"That sounds cozy. What happens afterward?"

"If you committed no crime, then a visit to immigration and a short flight home. Back to your country."

He saw the guard drop from her face, and a range of vulnerable emotions spread themselves out on hopeful display. He saw anticipation and homesickness, fear and relief, and what might have been tears in her eyes. Somehow, her beauty exaggerated her need for reassurance. Daly felt as though he were about to be cajoled into granting a favor.

"And what if there was a crime? What will happen to me then?"

"I'm a policeman. I would have to arrest you."

"I have no passport, no visa. That makes me an illegal immigrant. Why don't you arrest me right now?"

"That's a matter for another department. I'm a detective. I want to know what happened the night of Kriich's murder."

She did not answer.

"Perhaps you acted in self-defense?" suggested Daly. "Did he threaten you? Was your life in danger?"

"I didn't like the cologne he was wearing."

She stood up and made toward the door as if to flee. Daly did not move. She stopped and gave him a backward glance.

"Let me ask you a question," she said from the doorway. "Have you ever feared for your life? Not in a split second, but on a daily basis? With a person whose violent threats are as common as talk about the weather?" She paused and stared at his silent face. "I didn't think you had. Look around you at this place. This is not a part of the country or the life you know. This farmhouse belongs to a different world. You're the foreigner here, not me. Let that shed some light on your investigation."

She looked fatigued. Dark rings marked her eyes. The shadows of the house had worn away at her.

"What about Jack Fowler?"

She shrugged. "He saved me from this hell."

"He was found drowned at his home."

"I know nothing about that."

"You must have some idea why he died. Your photograph was left at the scene."

"Jack told me he was going to leave his wife. He wanted me to run away with him, but I couldn't."

"Run away where?"

"Malaga, first. Then Croatia. I don't know where after that. He didn't know himself. But I couldn't leave immediately. I had things to get."

"What things?"

"A passport. And some souvenirs."

"Souvenirs?"

"Yes. Presents for my younger sister and brother at home. I wanted them to think my trip to Ireland was happy and fruitful."

Daly felt drawn to the cold glitter of her eyes. Her pain was something dangerous and formidable, a weapon he could never disarm. Instinctively, he felt he had come to a threshold, a point of no return, over which men like Fowler had crossed. Travelers drawn to a fire that would never warm them.

"Poor Jack," she continued. "He was deluded. I did not love him in that way. Not enough to run away with him."

"I find your story interesting."

"What are you saying? That you would like to be in my shoes?"

"I didn't say that."

She sat down on the sofa beside him. Daly shifted uncomfortably. He began to fear their conversation had drawn them closer not only in understanding but also in complicity. Much closer than he wanted to be. She sat turned slightly away from him. Her fur coat slipped, revealing a long slender neck where her dark hair had been brutally shorn. She was a strange creature, he thought, wary and suspicious one moment, trusting and intimate the next. He stared at her pale neck. The memory of his wife's new hairstyle swam into his consciousness. For several moments, his thoughts ran awry, and the image of Anna's face rose before him, so radiant with sadness he wanted to reach out and hold her.

Lena turned to him and gave a start, as though something in his face had frightened her. He placed his hand on her shoulder to reassure her, but the tendons of her elongated neck tightened. She sat up quickly, pulling her fur coat around her shoulders. He spoke, called her Anna by mistake, and cursed under his breath. She hurried out of the house.

"Lena!" he shouted, running after her into the night. His voice hung in the cold air, but she was gone, her running figure scooped up by the mist. He shouted her name again, this time with hoarse vehemence. From deep in the forest, he heard a brief shriek. He ran into the fog, the blurred branches of trees ghosting by his face. In a dense thicket, he found the rag doll dangling from a bramble, like a crumpled miniature version of Lena, its costume torn by thorns.

He called her name again, this time less aggressively. He wondered if she hiding somewhere close by. The fog lifted, drifting off through the trees. After a moment's hesitation, he floundered deeper into the forest, stumbling over ditches, sudden hollows, and fallen branches, but there was no sign of her. She had dissolved like a fragment of mist.

The sodden undergrowth penetrated his clothes, and he felt a chill come over him. What a miserable shelter the forest would make against the coldness of the night, he thought. He worried that if she did not get help, she might succumb to hypothermia.

"I only want you to be safe!" he shouted, cupping his hands so that his voice would travel farther. He listened carefully, thinking he could hear the rustle of her departing footsteps fade into the depths of the night.

He returned to his car, half hoping she would be standing there, waiting, ready to be taken to the warmth of the police station, ready to sit opposite him and communicate, if only with those mysterious blue eyes.

There was no sign of her when he returned. He slammed the car door shut, annoyed. He had spent too much of their conversation trying to foster a sense of trust. He should have cut to the chase and demanded information. The names of the gang that had trafficked her and the other women, for a start, as well as Jack Fowler's movements in the days before his death.

He drove the car slowly down the lane, still hoping to pick out her figure in the headlights. He resolved not to tell his colleagues about their encounter. He could hardly report the conversation they had without raising doubts over his effectiveness as a detective. After all, how many suspects in a murder case managed to escape after challenging a police officer to arrest them?

13

Daly sat with Irwin in the interview suite. Little of what the woman said was easy for him to follow. He leaned forward, straining to hear, to understand. He poured some water from the jug and swallowed a scant measure. The tang of cleaning chemicals soured his mouth. He tried to weave her narrative into the events of the night before, his conversation with Lena in the grim farmhouse, her abrupt departure and flight through the trees, and then her scream and the doll caught on the briar.

"Go slowly," he said. "Give us a chance to get this straight."

"I was driving along the Mullybracken Road," the woman began again.

"What time?"

"About eight p.m. I almost ran over her. She came rushing out of the forest into the path of my headlights. I rolled down the window, but I couldn't understand what she was saying. She was foreign. I tried to calm her down, coax her into the car, but she was too frightened. Her blouse was torn as if someone had tried to rip it off her. There were scratch marks on her arms. Then I heard a man shouting her name. I think it was Lena."

Daly flinched. He swallowed and breathed deeply.

"Are you sure about the name?"

"I could hear his voice clearly. It wasn't foreign. The woman looked very frightened."

"What happened next?"

"She ran off."

"What did you do then?"

"I waited for a while, hoping she would reappear. Then I got scared. I thought whoever was chasing her might attack me if they found me there."

When Irwin showed her the photo of Lena Novak, she nodded in recognition. "That's her. Except her hair was shorter."

The two detectives left the interview room.

"It sounds like it was Lena Novak," said Irwin. He stared at Daly. "Shall we organize a full-scale search around the farmhouse?"

"I don't know. This doesn't add up." He found it difficult to merge the woman's account with his own recollection of what had happened.

Irwin did not reply. He looked strangely at Daly. "What do you think this woman saw then? A lovers' tiff? A game of hide-and-seek?"

"It's very vague. She couldn't even understand what the woman was saying. I don't think she's a reliable witness, but we'll send out some officers to search the area anyway."

Irwin frowned at him. "You look like a man who's seen a ghost. How much sleep did you get last night?" Daly saw his eyes glide over the scratch marks on the back of his hands. Irwin was quiet.

"Am I free to go now?" asked the woman when they went back into the interview room.

"You can leave anytime you like," said Daly, before taking down her details.

As Daly drifted off to sleep that night, the crow of a rooster jolted him awake. His father's hens, he remembered. He had been so distracted he had forgotten to feed them that evening, and now they were hungry and cross. The flock was part of his inherited smallholding, a brood of leghorns that his father had kept for company and the odd egg.

The rooster's protests stopped when he threw in a bucket of meal. He swung his flashlight at them and was annoyed to see the rooster bully the hens away from the food. It scratched and strutted through the grain with its feet as the rest of the trampled flock recoiled into the coop. Daly watched it gobble up the food and preen its glossy black feathers. A quiver of anger ran through his chest. He thought suddenly about killing the bird or at least releasing it into the night where a fox might snatch it. *You're little more than a bully,* he thought, *and a noisy one at that.* He was sick of its cranky abuse in the hour before dawn, hauling him too early from sleep when he still felt dazed by his dreams. He reached in through the wire enclosure, but his scrabbling attempts at capture sent the rooster into a frenzy of aggression, its wings beating in violent rhythms. Only exhaustion and the imagined rebuke of his father prevented Daly from trying again. He threw the rooster a glance as if to say its number was up. The bird gave him a sideways glance and flapped its wings. Daly walked back to the cottage, wondering who was really in charge of the smallholding, himself or the rooster? He got into bed just as a rainstorm broke.

14

During the night, rain fell so heavily it flooded the makeshift smoking shelters erected behind Armagh's sprawling pubs and discos, and it filled the streets with so much running water it threatened to join them with the river Callan. By the time the downpour eased, the crowds of drunken revelers had disappeared, leaving a watery silence wedged in the town's gullet. Empty food cartons floated in a ragged wake down side streets as narrow as canals. A few police patrol cars swished by on wings of water. The pubs were as dead as their reflections in the puddles, and even the taxi companies had their shutters pulled by midnight.

It was a relaxed morning for the police officers in Armagh station. When Daly walked into the control room, all the desks were empty. The officers on duty had few alcohol-related crimes to investigate, and it was payday. Irwin had gathered a group in the canteen, and they were discussing where to go out drinking that weekend. Daly avoided them and made for his office. He had stayed up late the night before placing basins around the house to collect the water dripping from holes in the roof.

He checked his messages. One interesting fact had emerged from the search of Fowler's house. The painstaking examination uncovered only one set of fingerprints that could not be accounted for. They were on the cover of the opera CD that was playing when Fowler's body was hauled from the pool. Daly stared at a photograph of the album cover. It was Verdi's *La Traviata*. He wondered who had selected the opera, and what did it reveal about his or her state of mind?

There was also a message from the pathologist, Ruari Butler. Daly leaned back in his chair and called him.

"We have some preliminary results through on Jack Fowler," said Butler. "Unfortunately, we're having trouble determining the thing you most want to know."

"Whether or not he committed suicide?"

"Correct. To sum up, Fowler had enough alcohol in his system to put him twice over the legal drink-drive limit. His head injury may have been due to a fall against the side of a table or the edge of the tiles, or even a blow from a blunt object, but the immediate cause of his death was drowning."

"So no murder yet."

"I'll fax you the details so far."

Daly had just sat down to study the report when a voice interrupted him.

"Can I speak to you, Inspector?"

Susie Brooke's tread had been light on the carpet. He looked up in surprise. She was standing at arm's length, the smell of her perfume wafting under his nose.

"Can't you talk to someone else?" he said, a little off-handedly. "I have two important investigations to deal with."

"This is important, too." She smiled at him. She was good at that—just holding back on being pushy, confident that her charm would draw people to her instead.

"You're the only person in the station who can answer my questions," she added.

"Okay, then. Fire away."

He offered her a seat, but she remained standing. Something about the sudden intensity of her gaze made Daly feel uneasy. She looked like a girl about to take a walk down a dangerous street. He didn't know whether to reassure her or warn her off.

"Have you read the court pages recently?" She placed a pile of local newspapers before him.

Daly glanced at them and looked back at her. She had come prepared.

"No," he said.

"Nearly every drink-drive story is about an Eastern European motorist. I'm worried that this kind of distorted coverage will stir up racist feelings."

"Editors will always print whatever they think sells newspapers. We can't be held accountable for that."

"But I've been studying the latest drink-drive figures. Two hundred fifty motorists were convicted in the past year in the local district, one hundred sixty-two of them from Eastern Europe, and thirty-four from the Republic of Ireland. The newspaper editors aren't biased in their coverage. Your officers seem to have an obsessive interest in catching drunken foreign nationals."

"What do you mean?"

"The figures suggest they are targeting foreign drivers more than locals. The drink-driving laws shouldn't be used as a tool to punish one section of the community."

"Let's stick to the facts," said Daly, grimacing as he fought to keep his temper under control. "Police officers don't just pull over a motorist because he looks like an Eastern European. Read the drink-drive reports. You'll find they usually begin with an officer noticing a vehicle being driven dangerously or the suspect staggering out of a pub before he gets behind the wheel. Breathalyzers don't tell lies. Nor are they racist."

"That's what gets reported. Things happen that are never written down."

Daly noticed that she did not flinch under his heavy stare. He leaned forward and flicked through the newspapers.

"I think you should be treating this as an education issue," he said, keeping his tone even. "We need to reach out to these communities and make them aware of the law, and not just their rights. Many of these people come from countries with more relaxed drink-driving laws, or at least from a culture with a more relaxed attitude to drink-driving."

"These people?"

"Yes. These people."

"Put it this way. If seventy percent of convicted drink-drivers were Catholic, wouldn't you suspect your officers of being sectarian?"

He blinked. "I don't understand why you're bringing this issue up. Policing is about catching criminals, not worrying about what the newspapers report. If an Eastern European is caught breaking the law, it's his own drunken fault, and not because my officers are racist."

"It's not just your officers who might be racist."

He stared at her.

"What do you mean? Are you calling me a racist, too?"

"It's widely acknowledged that racism is a general problem within the police force that needs to be tackled."

"So all police officers are racist then?"

"Some more than others."

"This might surprise you, but I think I know my staff a little more than you do. When I leave this station tonight, I'll do so confident in the knowledge that in my absence a bunch of racist police officers won't be spilling across town, sirens flashing on the hunt for Eastern Europeans."

"Fine. I'll be around. Call me when one of your officers plans to arrest another drink-driver."

The police radio beside him crackled. "You'll be the first to know," he said, his mouth sour.

The racist accusation had troubled Daly deeply. He left the police station and drove into Armagh. He drove with apparent purpose, but in reality, he was aimlessly patrolling the disorganized streets around the local meat factories. The redbrick terraces narrowed in—cramped houses rented out to Eastern European families. The anger had settled into his chest, to be replaced by something else, doubt, and the grim knowledge that police officers were human after all, liable to expect the worst in strangers and prone to fear, the fear of the unknown.

Daly surveyed the bleak streets. Ten years ago, this place was a Republican stronghold, with its own brand of political unrest, riots and carjackings, defiant murals, and standoffs with the police. Now families from different lands had taken their place to weave new tales of discrimination and alienation.

Two thousand immigrants arrived in one year. Three thousand the next. Life was different here. You could see it in the cars, cheap-looking imports from Eastern Europe with blackened windows. The same vehicles driving up and down the street all evening. *Motorized loitering,* he thought to himself.

But mostly you saw the difference in the people walking the streets. A siren sounded a change of shift in the nearby chicken-processing factory, and the pace and number of pedestrians changed—ranks of men and women, hardworking and tenacious, all of them under forty, many of them dressed in army-style jackets, a forceful wave of labor, walking as though in convoy toward the open gates of the factory.

Daly knew that immigrants took the jobs that no one else wanted. They worked the longest shifts, in the most grinding of conditions, were docked pay even for toilet breaks, and then went home to sleep in overcrowded houses, climbing into beds that had just been vacated by workers on different shift patterns. They spent their nights and weekends anesthetized by physical exhaustion and alcohol. It was a new model of democratic calm for this part of Northern Ireland, he thought, civil stability of a sort.

He pulled up at an off-license and waited behind the wheel. After about fifteen minutes, a man stumbled out of the shop. He leaned against a black Lada and raised a bottle of spirits to his lips, knocking back a slug with the practiced disregard of a circus performer swallowing a sword. Climbing into the driver's seat, he tilted the bottle again, this time taking a deeper swallow. The sound of children playing football in a nearby street arced through the air. Daly felt anger balloon inside. He waited until the man started the engine.

The driver looked up when Daly tapped the window. An angular face with gray stubble. For a second, he looked at Daly, his eyes brightening as though they might share a past, were second cousins or neighbors from a different town, a different country.

Daly banged on the glass and flashed his ID.

"I'm a police officer. Open the door."

The look of recognition rapidly faded. The driver replaced the lid on the bottle and slid it between his knees. He was like a man woken abruptly from a dream.

Daly informed him of his rights and that he was arresting him on the suspicion of drink-driving.

"Do you understand what I'm saying?"

"Yes." The man fished out a creased Croatian driving license. He balled his fists and looked Daly in the eye. The look of sadness in his face was deep and total.

"I have money in my house. Money for you. I am sorry for the trouble." His voice was clotted with alcohol and guilt, and thickly accented. Daly guessed that he had not been in the country for very long.

"You take my money. Yes? No? For the trouble."

"It's no trouble to me," said Daly. "Get out of the car. I'm taking you down to the station for a breathalyzer test. Do you understand what I'm saying?"

"I not drink anymore," he protested. "I give you my word." He shook his head profoundly.

Daly walked him to his car and helped him into the back.

"I make a stupid mistake," he told Daly. "I live a mile away. Needed cigarettes and vodka."

"Why didn't you just walk to the off-license?"

"No reason."

His stubbled face flushed. "I lose my job now."

"Not my problem. You should have considered that before drinking." Daly started up the engine.

"No, I lose my job. Today. Boss say no work anymore." He sighed heavily and flashed Daly a look so grim, the detective feared he was going to open up his heart and reveal his deepest worries, the dashing of his hopes and dreams.

Instead, the Croatian rubbed his dry lips and stared down. He grunted suddenly. Daly watched him in the rearview mirror. The Croatian rubbed his eyes as though he had seen a ghost. Daly turned round. The man was holding Lena's doll. Daly had forgotten it was there.

"Who owns this?" asked the Croatian.

"A woman. Someone I'm trying to find."

"Her name is Lena Novak?"

Daly stopped the vehicle, looked him in the eye.

"How do you know that name?" he asked the Croatian.

Ten minutes later, Daly had gathered from their halting conversation that Josef Mikolajek had placed a price on Lena's head. He had sent a picture of her around the Croatian community, and a description of the rag doll she had in her possession, one dressed in the national costume of their country.

"This doll, I think he is afraid of it," said the man. "Maybe he's superstitious. He wanted Lena caught or killed, it didn't matter. But what he really wanted was this doll." The Croatian laughed. "When Mikolajek feels threatened by anyone, he has them shot or stabbed. But a doll? You can't kill a doll."

Daly handed the man over at the police station and drove home. He was going to have to work out why the doll was so important to Lena Novak and Mikolajek. It was the key to a dangerous secret, and he needed to know what it was.

Back in the bedroom of his cottage the ceiling was still dripping rain. He emptied the pots and basins that had been collecting the water. During the night he awoke with a start to a loud splashing noise. For a second he thought the Lough had flooded and burst through the cottage walls. Bits of plaster lay on his blanket. In the moonlight, he saw that a part of the ceiling had fallen into one of the basins.

15

Three days after Jack Fowler's drowning, the offices of the Gortin Regeneration Partnership were so washed in blue siren lights that it was difficult for the staff that turned up that day to focus on their jobs. Although how much work was done with the Fraud Squad examining the organization's entire financial history was anyone's guess. A team of police officers as well as agents from Her Majesty's Revenue and Customs entered the building shortly before 9:00 a.m. Contrary to appearances, it was not a kick-the-door-down style of investigation. The previous evening, they had been granted search warrants allowing them to examine computer hard drives, files, and records of e-mail that might reveal crimes committed against the 2006 Fraud Act. A police van waited outside an emergency exit door, ready to transport the evidence.

"Have you found the missing money yet?" A receptionist asked a senior officer as she clocked off for lunch.

"Not yet." The expression on his face showed less than wholehearted enthusiasm for the task that lay ahead.

"If you do find it, let me know. I'm owed a month's pay."

"This place is going to be swamped by people owed money. Like flies to horseshit."

She sighed. "That reminds me of a saying of his."

"Who?"

"Jack Fowler. He used to say that anyone who couldn't make money after the cease-fire couldn't find flies in horseshit."

He winked at her suddenly. "I'll make a promise with you. If I find the missing money, I'll split it with you and we can run away together."

She gave him a look, as though he were small change, and walked off.

In all, the police and HM staff spent eighteen hours over two days sifting through files for evidence. They loaded the police van with hard drives and account ledgers, to which they added bank statements from Fowler's personal accounts and details of his credit card loans and property investments. They soon discovered that Fowler had not been living the dream so much as playing out a grand fantasy, and all with money that didn't belong to him.

"'Take as much prosperity as you can swallow' was the message that boomed from London and Brussels," Robert Bennett, a senior investigator with the Fraud Squad, said to Daly. He had brought the detective to the outskirts of Gortin village, which, in the evening light, looked empty of life, rubble spilling from dilapidated houses, the winding main street empty for as far as the eye could see.

It reminded Daly of a village undergoing a security alert. He half expected to see a bomb disposal squad taking cover behind a crumbling wall. Bennett had brought him here to tell the tale of Gortin's demise and how several fortunes had disappeared down the pockets of Jack Fowler.

"And that's what Northern Ireland did," continued Bennett. "Run-down villages like this and inner-city areas were meant to be the beneficiaries of the flood of capital. Unfortunately, no one rigorously checked what happened to the money one or two years down the line. We've investigated a whole range of behaviors from the careless to the downright criminal. Fowler's business exploits come in firmly at the criminal end of the scale."

All around them were shadows and gaping holes, chunks of crumbling concrete and flooded foundations sinking into the void left by greed and an overheated property market.

Bennett frowned. "It shouldn't come as a surprise to anyone that ex-paramilitaries like Fowler were tempted by the flow of peace money passing through their fingers."

Daly regarded the investigator. Bennett was middle-aged and religious, a member of the Orange Order. It was clear that in his view God's judgment had been passed on the predominantly Republican hill village. It was a morality tale straight out of the King James Bible.

"Of course," replied Daly, "no reason why there shouldn't be as many thieves in the former ranks of the IRA as in any other walk of life."

They reached the once busy main street, which was now a sagging row of worn-out shop fronts enlivened by the odd terrorist mural. Daly remembered how his father had brought him here as a boy on Market Days. For one morning each month, the street became a depository of rusting farming implements and machinery, overrun with panicky livestock and fowl. However, even then, it had been plain to see that the village had fallen upon hard times; the market day the one remaining source of profitable activity for its inhabitants.

"I was sent by the government to track down peace funds that went missing after the collapse of the property market," said Bennett. "The day before he died, Jack Fowler told the authorities he no longer knew the whereabouts of almost £3 million in funding from the European Peace Fund. According to him, the money had dissolved after it was transferred into the coffers of the regeneration group."

"What do you think happened to it?"

"There is only one explanation possible. The money really did dissolve, as Fowler said."

Daly stopped midstride to study Bennett's face, trying to determine whether he had missed something.

There was a measured richness to Bennett's voice as he held Daly's attention.

"Speaking more precisely, the funds were stolen."

"How? We're not talking about a gang of armed robbers."

Bennett squinted in the low sunlight. "I've already examined the accounts and collected a stream of anecdotes from the people who worked for Mr. Fowler. In the hours after the money arrived in the regeneration group's bank account, there was a flurry of international transactions. The funds were first sent to an account in a Maltese bank, and then debited to Vestbank in Frankfurt. There the sum was converted back into Sterling and sent to the Marlborough bank in London. A day later, it was transferred to Maguire Holdings, a cover name for a property investment group with a large portfolio in Tyrone and Armagh."

They had reached a terrace of ruined houses. Behind them, Daly could make out the thin green of broken fields patterned with thorn trees. Brambles trailed everywhere, ready to snare the heel of an unsuspecting property investor.

"You could say the money rolled like a set of dice flung by a desperate gambler until it came to rest here."

They stared at the buildings. Some of the roofs were grassed over and full of holes. The gleam of the low sun caught shards of glass and spiderwebs haunting the darkness within.

"With the money, Maguire Holdings bought this row of buildings and most of the land lying behind the village."

"For £3 million?"

Bennett grimaced. "The money really did dissolve. However, it was the sudden drop in house prices that brought about its dissolution."

The picture became clearer in Daly's head.

Bennett continued: "Fowler's plan was to announce a major redevelopment of the village, promising jobs, business start-up funding, new shop fronts, a sports hall, and a health center. House prices would then shoot up, enabling him to sell this run-down terrace for a handsome profit."

"Surely that's breaking the law."

"The plain fact is that no one in the governing bodies had any way of knowing whether or not the funds had been improperly used. When the homes were sold to new investors, Fowler intended to return the money to the regeneration company's coffers."

"I take it that when the economy went bust, the hammer of reality struck, and Fowler was left with a collection of ruins he couldn't sell."

"That's correct. We suspect this type of fraud was perpetrated on a large scale ever since peace funds began flooding the country."

"A system works according to the people running it," said Daly.

"That's the problem when you pour money into the pockets of former paramilitaries."

"From what I read in the newspapers, a lot of people got greedy. Not all of them were former freedom fighters."

"True. It wasn't just the Jack Fowlers of this world who were up to no good. The banks were at it, too. And politicians. Even the financial watchdogs turned a blind eye."

"Did Fowler confess to you?"

"I spoke to him before he died. He was adamant he had done nothing wrong. He'd used the funds to bolster the local economy, he claimed. It was not so much a crime as an error of timing. If the property crash had been delayed by a month or two, the houses would have been sold and no one would have been any wiser."

They walked on to an abandoned building site. Metal fencing and fluorescent tape surrounded a set of flooded foundations. The place resembled a crime scene. Empty of life. It was hard to believe that the unraveling of one man's greed was responsible for such dereliction.

"Fowler believed in property," said Bennett.

"He owned more than most."

"How relevant is all this to your investigation?"

"A soured business relationship may have led to his death."

"I can provide you with a list of his known business associates."

"Which of them would you recommend I talk to?"

"Michael Mooney, for a start. The two of them go right back to Long Kesh. Mooney was another former terrorist turned community developer. He's still the treasurer of the regeneration group. And a member of the local policing partnership."

Daly took down Mooney's details.

"I have to warn you—this investigation is going to become more political than you can imagine," said Bennett. "Fowler's associates will already have made moves to protect themselves and their reputations. His death triggered minor tremors in the most powerful circles in the land. If it was murder, you're going to have to uncover layer after layer of lies in your hunt for a killer."

"Lies are what interest me. Especially the hidden ones."

The two men looked back down the village. In the distance, they could hear a roaring and bellowing sound, like a set of flailing bagpipes about to burst. A herd of cows rushed abruptly round the corner, whacked by a grim-faced farmer and three young men. Daly guessed they were his sons. They all had the same dogged hunch, their blackthorn sticks lashing the animals' rears. For a few moments, the street teemed with life and the ripe tang of dung. Urine sluiced down the side of the road. The men seemed in an anxious hurry to keep the cattle moving. They passed the pair of detectives as though they were ghostly inhabitants of a village that had lain in ruins for hundreds of years.

"What did you find out about Lena Novak?" asked Daly.

"His mistress?"

"Yes."

"Fowler made her the director of his holding company. He took a big financial gamble on her, setting up accounts in her name and transferring funds to them."

"Why do you think he did that?"

"My guess is that Fowler liked crossing borders. Metaphorical as well as physical. Miss Novak was a classic example of the risks he took in his personal and business life. Most men squirrel away cash and assets in their wives' names; Fowler opted for a prostitute."

"An unconventional choice."

"It seems that he got his thrills crossing into the unknown, following his instincts rather than his head. Unfortunately, his relationship with Miss Novak turned out to be a delusion, like the countless others in his life."

"He had others?"

"Look around," said Bennett, waving a hand at the street's dank frontage. "Imagine what one man's fantasy, fueled by greed, could do to a place like this. Gortin was a Cinderella village, and Fowler was its Prince Charming. Instead of providing a fairy-tale ending, all he did was scatter broken dreams everywhere."

They stood for a while. The sun had gone down, and the air was bleak and cold. The wind blew harder, making a hundred strange noises in the broken windows and collapsed roofs. To their ears, it was the sound of a fortune frittering away.

16

Daly awoke early on Saturday morning and decided his interview with Michael Mooney could not wait until Monday. While his coffee brewed, he rang the police station and checked on Mooney's current address. He was still at an early stage in the investigation, and he felt the particular kind of apprehension that comes with the first forays into a dead person's private life, like that of a balloonist adrift in a new landscape, not knowing where the winds might take you.

The officer working in the information section gave him a brief summary of Mooney's past record, most notably his involvement with terrorist paramilitaries. Daly resisted the urge to make any hasty conclusions. Since his release from Long Kesh prison in 1983, Mooney appeared to have adjusted to civilian life with a measure of success. Republican paramilitaries had cast a wide and ragged net that entangled many young men and women during the Troubles, but since the cease-fire many of them had managed to slip through its holes back to a normal life within their own communities. Nevertheless, as he drove into the mountains of South Armagh, Daly felt a sense of foreboding, as though the investigation were about to enter a squall.

Michael Mooney lived at number 60 Foxborough Mews, a new-build development of mock-Georgian houses situated about a mile beyond the village of Keady. To the west, a pine forest threw out a sheltering arm from the prevailing winds, but in every other direction the estate lay exposed to the elements. There were no streetlights, only a forest of For Sale signs posted along the road. An advertising billboard at the unpaved entrance promised life in a luxury develop-ment for prices more expensive than real estate in Miami or LA. The steamy ad featured a leggy model draped over a kitchen counter with the tagline "Gorgeous Living Comes to Armagh." Foxborough's location at the edge of a moun-tain bog was not referred to anywhere on the billboard.

Daly was surprised to find that the house numbers began at 60. There was no number 58, or 50, or even 1. He parked beside a container full of rubble. It was Saturday morn-ing, and Mooney looked to be the only one at home in the estate. Few of the other houses were occupied. Chances were they never would be. When the tide of cheap borrow-ing withdrew during the credit crunch, it had left behind estates like Foxborough Mews as a monument to the prop-erty madness that had engulfed the entire country. Now it was a so-called ghost estate. But there was nothing ghostly about the houses. Foxborough Mews belonged to one of the most extravagant realities of bricks and mortar the Irish countryside had ever witnessed.

The door of number 60 opened, and Daly got a whiff of foul air. When he introduced himself, the man in the dark hall said nothing. He moved a step closer to Daly, the daylight illuminating his face and exposing in detail his deformity. The skin of his face was scarred and deeply pitted as though someone had thrown a bucket of acid over him. Daly reached out to shake his hand and encountered a palm so smooth and fine it felt like a kind of compensation for the grotesque condition of his face.

Even though the man had not identified himself, Daly knew it was Mooney. He had heard about the former terrorist's facial disfigurement, a legacy of his imprisonment in Long Kesh during the early 1980s. At the time, IRA inmates fought for recognition as political prisoners by smearing their cell walls with feces and refusing to wash. It was a dark time in the conflict, when the paramilitary leaders shifted the battle away from city streets and country lanes to the cramped cells of H-block. Instead of using Semtex and guns, the imprisoned paramilitaries launched attacks upon the prison wardens and ultimately upon their own bodies. Feces, urine, and starvation were the weapons of choice. It was a form of self-martyrdom. For more than a year of his jail term, Michael Mooney's body became the IRA's battleground against the British State.

The prison regime may have been harsh, but it was a skin infection, taking hold in the unkempt conditions, that had shown Mooney the least mercy, ravaging his face and nibbling away at his features. Of course, he got off lighter than the hunger strikers, the ten volunteers who starved themselves out of existence while the international media camped outside the prison side by side with family members reciting the rosary.

"I've come to talk to you about Jack Fowler," announced Daly.

"Why do you want to talk about Jack? He's dead." Mooney's voice had an unfriendly tone.

"My visit is part of a criminal investigation."

"What sort of an investigation? I've already told everything I know to Inspector Bennett. I've cooperated fully."

"The questions I need to ask are about Mr. Fowler's social circle, and how he died."

"He committed suicide." There was a slight break in Mooney's voice, a note of hesitation, even doubt. His eyes grew wary.

"You worked closely with Mr. Fowler. You must have thought a lot about his death."

Mooney stared at him for a long while before stepping back and allowing Daly into the house.

An expensively upholstered seat served host to a tray on which sat a half-eaten meal and beside it a collection of remote control devices. A wash of newspapers had gathered around the leather sofa.

"I understand that the day before he died, Mr. Fowler tried repeatedly to get in touch with you," said Daly.

Mooney said nothing. The scarring made his face a blank.

"Mr. Mooney?"

"What you said was a fact. Not a question."

"You're not denying it."

"No."

"Why was he so keen to talk to you?"

Mooney sighed. "Because he wanted me to prop up his pillar of lies."

He got up and began clearing the tray and newspapers.

"You must forgive the mess. I've been in mourning."

"For Mr. Fowler or your career?"

Mooney grunted. "Both." He tried to bring some order to the newspapers piled on the floor but quickly gave up.

"Every time the phone or doorbell rings I think it's going to be him. Trying to keep up the façade, paper over the cracks. Jack was a born charmer."

"I've heard a lot of things said about Mr. Fowler in the past few days," said Daly. "He came a long way from a solitary confinement cell in a Spanish prison."

Mooney stared at Daly without nodding or frowning. His scarred face gave Daly the impression of emotional emptiness.

"I've heard a lot said myself," said Mooney. He tried to change the topic. "You had no trouble finding this place?"

"No," replied Daly. "I can see you don't get much bother from the neighbors."

Mooney gave a sad laugh. "It was Jack Fowler who persuaded me to buy this house. He was the developer behind the entire estate. Little did I know the place would end up worse than a coffin." He eyed Daly with a vacant stare. "Or a prison cell." His features moved in spasms, fragments without any connection to whatever thoughts and emotions worked their way through his brain. He walked to the kitchen window and pointed outside.

"At night it's completely dark, and during the day, you don't see as much as a dog or a car passing through. Look at all the windows. Not even a plant or a curtain up in any of them. Vandals have started smashing them. First, they targeted the houses closest to the road, then the ones next to those. Soon there'll not be a window left in the entire estate."

As he spoke, a large bluebottle toiled through the air and began dive-bombing the glass pane. Mooney opened the window, closing it again quickly to ward off a swarm of flies swooping outside.

"This house is the only light for about five miles," said Mooney. "At night it attracts a plague of flies and moths."

A whiff of something like raw sewage wafted through the air and hit Daly's nostrils. Mooney appeared not to notice it and went on talking.

"I came a long way, too, like many IRA volunteers," Mooney said with a sigh. "But life in its cruel way arranged that I would end up in solitary confinement once again, imprisoned by concrete. Only this time I'm paying a hefty mortgage for the pleasure." He glanced at Daly. "You probably know that I spent two years in a fourteen-foot cell. All I had for company back then was a bible, a mattress, three blankets, and Jack Fowler. We were Republican soldiers, but the screws treated us worse than rapists. We joined in the Dirty Protest, like everyone else in H-block. We used our bodies as protest weapons. After a few months of smearing the walls with feces, the cell started to crawl with parasitic insects. We became living corpses. Can you imagine smelling your own body rot? At first, I thought it was my imagination playing tricks, but then I was relieved to learn that Jack could smell the same odor from his body. It was the smell of the body wasting away. The same smell you get when paying respects to the dead."

Daly tried not to grimace as another foul-smelling wave overcame him. It couldn't be his imagination, he reasoned. The kitchen smelled like an open sewer. This time Mooney noticed the look of protest on the detective's face.

"Sorry. I've grown used to the smell."

He opened the patio doors and showed Daly a gaping hole in the back garden where a set of sewage pipes protruded into the air. Pools of filthy water bubbled in the weak spring sunshine.

A look of torment twisted Mooney's face. "This place really is Long Kesh circa 1981. About a month ago, the toilets and sinks started to overflow. When the plumbers came, they had to pull up all the pipes to find the obstruction. It turned out someone had poured concrete down a manhole. A disgruntled builder, I suspect, someone never paid for his work. They say it will cost thousands to repair. I'm still waiting for the insurance company to get back to me."

"Tell me about Jack Fowler."

Mooney sat down heavily. "In spite of what people are saying, there was a humane and sympathetic side to Jack. He never said no to raising funds or giving to charity. And you could see it was always his own money that he gave away."

"Perhaps he was trying to salve his guilt?"

"Maybe. In the days before his death, I saw a change in him. He looked preoccupied, haunted. That girl, the foreign national, would be waiting for him in the foyer of our offices. Sometimes they left holding hands. It was very much in everyone's face. Except his wife's, of course."

"What did you think about their relationship?"

Mooney shrugged. "I heard she'd been a prostitute. Fowler rescued her from a violent pimp."

"What does that tell you about his state of mind?"

"Like you say. Perhaps he was salving his guilt."

"Parading her in front of colleagues. Does that not strike you as a strange way to ease one's conscience?"

"No, you're right. It was pure stupidity. In terms of his reputation as a community leader, it was a mistake. On a personal level, I was disgusted. I knew his wife well. But his marital infidelity turned out to be only the tip of the iceberg."

"Tell me about your last conversation with him."

"It was the day of the regeneration association's annual general meeting. We were scheduled to go over the financial report. It was a very unpleasant meeting. I could see immediately that he was edgy. He kept fiddling with his mobile phone and checking it for messages. All his charm had left him. My working life had been based upon indulging his excesses and different personas. It was a reckless form of loyalty, but I believed he was a leader of talent and his commitment to the local community was second to none. However, on this occasion I couldn't give in to his demands."

"What were they?"

"He wanted me to tidy up the financial report, make it more convincing. As though it was the script of a play with a dodgy plot."

"What was dodgy about it?"

"I had uncovered a series of transactions he had made using the regeneration association's headed notepaper, but with his own home address."

"He was working from home?"

"In the worst possible sense."

Daly studied Mooney's expression, but the face gave nothing away.

"I accused him of treating the peace funds as if they were his own money, but he defended himself. He denied any wrongdoing. He'd parked the money in property, he told me. Bricks and mortar. An asset you can touch and see. You know the clichés. Even if it did go down in value it would soon go up again."

"How did you react?"

"I couldn't believe my ears. It was like attending a children's pantomime and being urged to look the other way by the villain. When he realized I wasn't going to go along with his deception, he just stared at me, then he rubbed his hands over his face. 'What am I going to do?' he asked me. 'We can't throw everything away. All our years of hard work.' I told him that things weren't happening the way he thought, but they were happening, whether he liked it or not. The whereabouts of all this money would have to be presented to the board, and the funding authorities. His face crumpled at that. 'Is this how it's going to end,

Michael?' he asked me. He talked about how we had fought the Brits for the right to control our destiny and had built up our communities. Secured good jobs and housing. The property market was on our side, he kept promising me. It had brought wealth and employment in abundance. 'We can't let it come back and terrorize us,' he pleaded. 'It will destroy everything we thought we had won.' I realized there was no point continuing the conversation. 'I'm going to start praying now, Michael,' he said as I left. 'I'm going to pray very hard.' Those were his last words."

"And that was the final time you spoke to him?"

"Yes. He sent me numerous texts and left phone messages that evening. But by then, I was speaking to the Fraud Squad."

"Did he know he would face a criminal investigation?"

"Of course. That was why he was so upset. He knew he was trapped."

"Upset enough to take his own life?"

"I believe so."

Some progress, thought Daly. Suicide seemed a likely course of action for a man in Fowler's position. After speaking to Mooney, he must have felt he was walking powerless into an engulfing storm. He had lost money in quantities that were impossible to imagine. Millions that did not belong to him. And all he left to show for it was a collection of derelict houses and a few thorny fields. Barely a brick had been laid, or a sod of earth turned, and all that money gone. That night he must have gone to bed hoping that by morning his life would resume its natural course, and the events of the previous day would be forgotten as an aberration. But the next morning, it was the other way around. The aberration was the unlivable new reality, and he was a condemned man. Words and prayers would have been of little comfort.

Before Daly left Mooney, he asked, "Did it occur to you that Fowler may have been murdered?"

"Why would I think that?"

"Just asking."

"Who would do such a thing?"

"That's what I'm trying to find out."

"You should be careful about even whispering that word."

"Which word?"

"*Murder.* Unless you have firm evidence. A lot of reputations could be damaged or questioned by the media if there's any suggestion of foul play or dirty tricks. Jack came to a sorry end by his own hand, and that's all there is to it."

"That's for this investigation to decide, Mr. Mooney," said Daly.

17

Ashe had forgotten how cold it got this far north in spring. After his first night back in Ireland, he felt stiff and sore. He stamped some life back into his feet and blew on his fingers, then he crept through the trees and watched where he had parked his rented Jeep. The sun was already a ball of orange rising through the forest. He wanted to make sure that no one was following him or keeping an eye on his vehicle.

Earlier, he had carefully packed his tent, scattered the traces of the fire he had lit the previous night, and picked over the ground for any litter he might have dropped. The good thing about sleeping outdoors was he did not have to worry about wiping down the site for fingerprints. Mother Nature didn't do smooth surfaces, and anyway, her dumb detectives would be nosing through his campsite now, the countless wild animals of the forest, picking up his scent, rummaging through his traces, destroying any evidence of his presence.

When he was convinced the coast was clear, he climbed into the Jeep and headed into the town of Armagh. He drove carefully, wanting to draw as little attention as possible. In a way, he was a fugitive like Lena Novak. He understood the gravity of her situation and its demands better than anyone else, the suspicion and constant vigilance that haunts the pursued, the fight against losing control, and, behind it all, the anxiety of waking up some morning surrounded by enemies, the dread that somehow you might have betrayed yourself in a dream while sleeping.

What made it harder was the fact that as a trafficked woman, she was a human being without an identity. All he had was a photograph and the assumption that Lena Novak was her real name. She had no history in this country, no family contacts, no obvious hiding places, and no clear escape routes. It was easy for her to succumb to her own invisibility. In that regard, she had passed beyond the borderlands of being human; she was more like a wild animal.

He knew that he had to get her moving. He wanted to force her from the shadows because a moving person was easier to find than one who had gone to ground. To do that he would have to pull off a stunt that would set the ground beneath her feet quaking. He had already checked the address given to him by Michael Mooney. As expected, the apartment had yielded no clues, only unrelated fragments of the life Lena had been living and her relationship with Fowler. The police had been unsuccessful in tracing her movements, too. If she had been staying in a hotel or B&B, they would have found her by now. They would have also checked the border brothels and meeting places for her compatriots.

He stopped at a glass bottle recycling point on the outskirts of Armagh. He broke the lock on one of the bottle banks and picked out several crates' worth of empty vodka bottles, which he stowed in the back of the Jeep.

His mobile phone rang. A local number—there was only one person it could be.

"Hello, Michael," he said.

"Where are you?" asked Mooney.

"I'm in Armagh."

"I've called to tell you the latest developments. Do you have time to listen?"

"I've all the time in the world," said Ashe.

"We've been chasing up a reported sighting of Lena Novak. Two days ago a taxi driver took her to Fowler's mansion and then into Armagh. She called at a cleaning company called Home Sweet Home, and then boarded an express bus for Dublin. We posted someone at the central bus station in Dublin to wait for the bus to arrive, but she never showed. She must have made the bus driver stop somewhere en route. Since then she's managed to make herself invisible."

"A disappearing act like that is hard to maintain," remarked Ashe. "Sooner or later she'll have to go back to her old haunts."

"There's word going round town that a contract has been placed on her head by Jozef Mikolajek, a smuggler and people trafficker. Time is running out. We need this situation resolved as soon as possible."

"Don't worry. I've got my own plan."

"It had better be good," said Mooney. "A police detective came snooping by this morning."

"What did he want to know?"

"He's digging into Fowler's financial dealings. The very thought of it is giving me a headache."

"Fowler ripped off the community organization. What else is there to find out?"

Mooney's voice was defensive. "I've nothing to hide from the police, but the less they know the better."

"Then you have nothing to worry about."

"True."

"Time to leave you in peace, then."

The early morning lights of Armagh faded behind Ashe. Traffic on the way south thinned out. He drove into the border hills, passing abandoned military observation towers overgrown with vegetation, like shards of shrapnel trapped in old wounds. Rattling with the crates of empty bottles, his Jeep bounced through a bleak countryside crisscrossed with streams and muddy lanes. He saw innumerable opportunities for ambush: culverts where the road dipped, high hedges, and rocky outcrops casting dark shadows.

He tried to concentrate on the road, but in his head he could hear the echoing sound of bombs and shootings. He kept well within the speed limit, but it was difficult to relax when you worried you were constantly within range of enemy fire. His instinct made him stop every now and again and check the road behind from concealed vantage points.

In the hill villages, he passed fortified police stations, decommissioned now as part of the peace process and standing derelict, surrounded by housing developments. In the staunchly Republican town of Crossmaglen he stopped for supplies. Fresh slogans and murals supporting dissident Republicans decorated the gable ends of houses. He sensed bitterness in the air, the bitterness of a disputed peace.

Closer to the border, he found himself driving through a series of looping lanes and dirt roads, through forests and steep valleys dotted with ruined farms. If anyone were on the lookout, they would see him now. The tires of lorries skulking across the border at night had plowed the roadside verges—the telltale tracks left by fuel smugglers, a lawless herd of modern-day highwaymen dodging the main roads and police patrols. Although the lanes had been busy during the night, they were now empty of traffic. He stopped several times and switched off the ignition. All he heard was silence and the restless sound of the wind nosing through the hedgerows.

The smell of diesel filled the car when he pulled up at a lane blackened by thorn trees. He got out of the vehicle. The cold air was laden with the stench of fuel. A set of sprawling outbuildings lay at the end of the lane, the remnants of an abandoned farm. He hung back for a while. Images of men in berets and balaclavas with Armalites came back to him as he surveyed the outbuildings with a pair of binoculars. A fuel lorry sat next to an overgrown hedge, fresh mud obscuring its number plate. In the yard stood a Portakabin surrounded by several vehicles—vans, pickups, and a sports car, positioned for a quick getaway. At the far end, half submerged in the gloom, were the hulks of two forty-foot trailers, gaping like beached whales. Next to them was the dismantled carcass of another fuel lorry, entangled in pipes and tubing.

His tip-off had been correct; he had managed to find the smugglers' lair. Housed somewhere in the farm buildings was a makeshift chemical lab, built to extract the dye from agricultural diesel bought in the Republic, which was then sold at a higher price as commercial fuel in the North. It was the one part of the terrorist apparatus that had escaped decommissioning. At one time during the Troubles, fuel-laundering plants were the staple industry of border country; now they had been taken over by dissident Republicans with links to criminal gangs from Eastern Europe. Ashe was also able to tell from the stacks of empty bottles that the gang was running a counterfeit alcohol-bottling plant as a sideline.

He waited for a while. He scrutinized the farm again. He spotted a dingy caravan in the corner of a field with a washing line. When he was satisfied that the only signs of life came from the Portakabin, he started the Jeep and drove up the lane.

He kept the engine ticking over outside the Portakabin and sounded the horn. A packet of cigarettes and the butt of a rifle sat in the window. The gun slipped from view. A moment later a bleary-eyed youth stood in the doorway, cradling the rifle.

Ashe rolled down the window and grinned. "I've a load of empty vodka bottles."

The youth walked carefully around the Jeep, squeamish of the mud that caked his white trainers.

"We're not taking any deliveries this afternoon."

"What's the problem," snapped Ashe. "Has there been one already?"

The boy looked down at the piece of paper he had pulled from a pocket. He clutched it next to the rifle.

"I don't see any mention of one here."

"They didn't tell you I was coming?"

The boy stared at him. He put the rifle down and took out a mobile phone. "I'll have to call Mr. Mikolajek and check with him."

Ashe leaned across the window. "Are you going to ask him why he forgot to say I was coming? Rather you than me."

The boy hesitated. Ashe noticed the hand holding the phone was shaking slightly.

"You can ask me as many questions as you like, son," said Ashe, "and if you don't have any, just tell me what I'm meant to do with this load of empty bottles."

The boy shuffled his feet, suddenly anxious to get back to the warmth of the Portakabin.

"Do you know where to go?"

"Don't worry, I can take care of things from here. It's good to see you're so vigilant." He winked. "I'll put in a good word with Mr. Mikolajek."

Ashe drove into the yard and took out his gun, a Glock 17. The workers were here, he guessed, somewhere in the outbuildings. He inspected the buildings one by one. All he found in the first two were rusting farm implements stained with bird shit, and fusty bales of hay. Everything was dark and cold.

The next shed was the largest, wide and high roofed. The only lighting came from Perspex panels in the ceiling. The smell of cheap spirits mingling with the stench of diesel almost overwhelmed him as he stepped inside. It took a moment or two for his eyes to adjust to the gloom. The cement floor was scored with plastic piping and wiring that connected a bank of whirring machines. Next to the machinery sat two containers of cat litter, one fresh and clean, and the other stained with red dye. Beyond the laundering paraphernalia he made out the silhouettes of three women sitting in chairs and filling glass bottles with a liquid that, in the shadows, seemed to light the bottles from within.

They sat up abruptly when they became aware of Ashe's presence. A set of bottles fell to the ground and rolled across the cement. Something about the way Ashe stood silhouetted against the door told them he was not meant to be there. The older of the women attempted to move and let out a cry, but Ashe grabbed her by her tracksuit top and pushed her back to the ground. She let out a dull groan.

"Don't worry, you haven't broken anything," said Ashe. They crouched before him.

"There's no one to help you now," he told them. "You should have disappeared like Lena Novak and found yourselves the darkest hiding place in border country."

When he raised the gun to their faces, they did not resist. Instead, a detached look fell across their faces. Moving quickly, he tied them up with rope, placed hoods over their heads, and bundled them into the back of the Jeep. He had many questions to ask them, about their compatriot Lena Novak and their boss, Jozef Mikolajek, but the time for questioning would come later.

18

The electronic alarm counted down the seconds as Daly fumbled in the dark for the control panel. He punched in the numbers, and the hall was silent.

"Shall we go in?" He turned to Irwin, but the Special Branch detective had already pushed open the door to the apartment.

Daly surveyed the solid wood floors and lavish furniture of Jack Fowler's love nest and wondered not for the first time how Lena Novak had managed to fly so swiftly from the farmhouse brothel to such luxury, from one world to another, from the unwanted attentions of men who degraded and abused to those who pampered and indulged.

"How much do we know about this woman?" asked Irwin.

"Only what one photo can tell, and what we see before us," said Daly, trying to collect his first impressions.

A rictus of a smile formed on Irwin's lips. "I can tell you she had a good sex life, and that her livelihood was her sex life. Fowler must have showered her with money and presents. Look at this place."

Boxes of perfume and ornaments and piles of designer clothing spilled from the sofa and coffee table to the two bedrooms. It was an overloaded apartment. Overloaded with luxury and gifts. Slowly and objectively, Daly surveyed the interior and allowed everything to filter through his mind along with what he knew so far about Lena Novak. Somewhere among the jumbled possessions he thought he might find a lead, but all he got was the impression of a woman who suddenly possessed luxury in abundance, and did not quite know how to accommodate it.

Irwin interrupted his train of thought. "Fowler tried to save her from her past, then he dies mysteriously and she goes missing. Along with several million pounds. If I were a betting man, I'd say she murdered him and stole the money."

Daly nodded. Lena's life seemed to be an epic marathon of escapes, betrayals, and conspiracies with sex at the throbbing heart of everything. In contrast, his own life had the tedium of a monk's.

He walked into the master bedroom, which bore a carpet thick enough for a decadent rock star. He examined her bed. There was an indentation on the pillow. It felt cold, the warmth of her body long gone. He stared at where she had slept and then across at the ransacked wardrobe. He breathed in the scent of perfume. He wondered how long her scent had lingered in the air. Perhaps the same length of time it took for a set of footprints to melt in the snow. Long enough to snag the interest of a detective who had been excluded for too long from the small and comforting intimacies of sharing a room with a woman.

When he opened the door of the en suite bathroom, the curtains blew into the bedroom, upsetting an ornament on the windowsill.

"Who's there?" He turned, startled, but it was no one.

Inside the bathroom, which was as big as his own bedroom, he stood stranded in an ocean of marble and ceramic. He checked his appearance in the mirror, ran a hand through his hair, fixed the collar of his shirt. He noticed the look of exhaustion that enshrouded his features. In his eyes, he saw a hungry light, a glaring need for some sort of comfort. He sighed. It was not just stuff and meaningless possessions that messed up people's lives. Sometimes the thoughts and memories in one's head were more than enough to keep one in turmoil.

In the kitchen sink, he found what appeared to be a wig floating in water. He poked it. The hair was real.

"Next time we see Lena, her hair will be cropped," he said.

"Why did she cut it?"

"An attempt to disguise herself. Perhaps she thought she could cut off the past."

"All those lovely locks gone."

"This tells us she's a woman who faces up to things. Discarding what she has to, even parts of her identity."

If Fowler was a man of lust and greed, thought Daly, Lena Novak was a woman of intrigue and invention. Who had seduced whom? he wondered.

Irwin beckoned him. He had switched on the TV. The two detectives watched as gray CCTV images flickered across the screen. They were from outside the apartment block.

"This is live footage," murmured Irwin.

"Constant vigilance," replied Daly. "That's the price you pay when you're in the pocket of men like Jack Fowler."

Irwin ejected a CCTV tape from the recorder, examined it, put it back in, and pressed rewind. The camera had a side view of the building's entrance door, as well as the approach road. They played through the tape, to that morning and then during the night. At first, they didn't notice the figure transfixed in the upper left corner of the screen, a lean shape wholly fused with the darkness. Then a car drove by, its lights sweeping the front of the apartment block. Shadows jumped out from their hiding places and fell back. In a corner of the building, where the grainy light briefly spilled into a pool, Daly spied the silhouette of a man standing very still. They spooled forward. The clock showed that an hour and a half had passed. The light cast by two cars loomed across the building and briefly picked out the shape of the man, standing in the same spot, before returning him to darkness.

"Who do we have here?" asked Irwin. "A member of Insomniacs Anonymous?"

They scrutinized the footage, watched the figure remain motionless each time a set of headlights rippled across the building. Disturbingly motionless. Daly watched with bated breath. It was the stillness that made the figure's presence meaningful and menacing. Nighttime was a moving forest of shadows, but the figure was so still he appeared to be staring constantly at a fixed point.

The pattern of light and dark on the TV screen flickered but remained the same until dawn. The two detectives watched transfixed, as the rising sun gradually revealed the front of the building. However, by then the figure had disappeared. They spooled through the rest of the tapes but found nothing. Irwin placed the tapes in an evidence bag.

They went back to searching the flat for any clue to Lena's current whereabouts. Daly could find no sign of ID, but he had not been expecting any. What he did discover were credit card receipts. He jotted down the details, intending to put out an alert for the cards. Apart from that, they found nothing more suspicious than the ordinary intrigue of a mistress's apartment. No evidence at all of the void that had sucked away the life of Jack Fowler and threatened to do the same to Lena Novak.

The doorbell rang and there was a pregnant moment as Daly and Irwin stopped in their tracks and stared at each other. The bell sounded again, impatient. Daly flicked on the TV monitor. He swallowed when he saw the figure on the doorstep.

19

"Who's there?" asked Daly as he flicked on the intercom button.

"I'm a friend of Lena Novak," said the caller after a pause.

Daly looked at the monitor. Outside it was a brilliant day, clear and sunny, but a man's dark figure crowded the doorway. It was the same figure from the night before. In daylight, he looked amorphous, like a sack of coal. Irwin leaned closely over the monitor as though he was peering into a nest or cave, the lair of a dangerous animal.

"What do you want?"

"I want to see Lena."

"A lot of people want to see Lena right now."

"This is important."

"She's away at the moment."

The intercom was so quiet, Daly thought the man might have gone, but the CCTV showed he was still on the doorstep. He had the equanimity of a statue. He looked up slowly and gave the camera a blank stare. His skin was tanned, his head shaved. He looked like a man who had spent a lot of time in a sunnier climate.

"Where is she?" he asked.

"Can't say," replied Daly. "Leave your number and name. I'll pass them on to her."

"Why won't you answer my question?"

Daly paused. There was a tenacity in the caller's voice that suggested he was a man who liked to be in control.

"Because there was a stranger outside this building last night. He looked like he was stalking Lena Novak. He looked like you."

The figure was unperturbed under the eye of the camera.

"Why do you want Lena?" asked Daly.

"She's my special subject."

"Lena's my special subject, too."

"Why are you interested in her?"

Daly tried to hook his curiosity. "A week ago, a man died suddenly. He was Lena's boyfriend. When something like that happens, people like Lena have to answer questions."

"Who is this?"

"Why don't you come up and see?"

Daly glanced back at the monitor but the man had disappeared. *And we were just getting to know each other,* he thought.

The detective ran out of the apartment and down the stairs. As his feet pounded the concrete steps, he heard the sound of a vehicle accelerating noisily. He burst through the front door in time to see a black Jeep pull away from a nearby car park. He ran toward it. The Jeep stopped, reversed with meticulous care, and drove toward Daly at speed.

For a moment, he stood insolently in its path, then he turned and ran back to the door. He heard the snarl and whine of the engine forced to its outer limit. He did his flesh-and-blood best to outrun the vehicle, but it gained ground, bearing down upon him. The roar of the engine sounded murderous in its ferocity. Light-headed and heavy-footed, he fell to the ground, bracing against the impact, but at the last moment, the vehicle swooped to the left, away from his hunched figure, toward some other target of which Daly knew nothing. He crept toward safety, gulping deep breaths. The noises of evening life surrounded him, the bark of dogs, children playing, a door banging shut, and, amid it all, the fading screech of the Jeep's tires as it disappeared down the road.

Daly looked up at Irwin's annoyed face.

"You should be relieved, not looking so upset," panted Daly. "He nearly ran me over."

"I couldn't make out the registration," explained Irwin. "Why do you think he wanted Lena?"

"Whatever the reason, he must have decided it wasn't worth killing me for."

"But it was a close decision," said Irwin.

"We must make whatever details we have on Ms. Novak public," said Daly, after getting his breath back. "And release a description of her mysterious caller to the press. No hiding place is safe for her now."

Daly slid into his car, clunking the door shut. He gripped the steering wheel. Raindrops twinkling in the streetlights filled the windshield. The weather had changed in the fickle way it does over the gruesome bogs and gurgling ditches of South Armagh. He switched on the engine and flicked the wipers. He wondered why the caller had gifted him with his life at the last moment. The conflicting emotions of anger and relief caused a heaviness in his mind as he drove north toward Lough Neagh and his cottage.

When he got home, he felt restless, unable to settle in the cramped living room. Outside the air was turbulent. The wind raked through the wild garden, fluttering through the dead thistles and nettles. The hens fussed and beat their wings in their wire enclosure, and in the distance, waves surged against the darkening lough shore. The movements and noises of entrapment were everywhere. Even the tall trees at the bottom of the garden tossed as if held back by a long leash. Daly stood at the threshold of his door listening keenly before jumping a stone wall and running off across his father's hummocky fields.

20

Lena needed to think. She needed to use all her time for thinking now, because to stop thinking meant certain death. She was no longer a victim, but to carry out her plan she had to keep up the pretense of being a victim. She knew that in every hunt there were times to shiver and run, and then there was a time to stay calm and rooted to the spot.

She came early to the café and picked a seat by the window. It was afternoon, and the café filled with single men hungry for food and some form of communal ritual. She stirred her coffee and lit a cigarette. A TV in the corner showed news footage of an illegal bottling factory that police had raided after a tip-off. According to the newsreader, three Croatian women had been reported as missing, but no one was paying attention to the report.

Lena wore a black dress so tight it was molded to her body, and her eyes were heavy with makeup. Every time she shifted in her seat, the male diners glanced up automatically, taking in her figure, indulging themselves half consciously between forkfuls as her long legs rearranged themselves.

Her eyes kept roving hungrily to the door, waiting for her client's arrival. When a waitress asked her to put out the cigarette, she speared it into a half-eaten sandwich. The restaurant had been one of her old haunts when she worked for Mikolajek, and she had been relying on the cigarette to hide her agitation.

"It's nothing personal," said the waitress, walking off.

There was a tapping at the window. Looking up, she saw the tall figure of a middle-aged man standing in the rain. His shaved head made him look like a Buddhist monk. She raised her hand in a half greeting.

The man entered the restaurant with a gust of wind and sat opposite her. This was how prostitution worked, she thought. It was as easy as sitting next to a window in a half-empty café. Her looks and behavior advertised that she was still on the game, no matter how hard she tried to switch off her charms.

"Hello," he said.

She didn't look at him. She stirred her coffee in an off-hand manner, but her tension was visible. Her olive skin had turned pale.

"I just want to talk," he said. "Nothing else."

She nodded. Another lonely soul looking for company.

"Do you want to order something?" He leaned closer to her.

"Are you buying?"

"If you want me to."

"It's okay. I'm not hungry." Her eyelashes moved up.

"My Jeep is outside. Do you want to come now?"

Her throat tightened as she gulped down a mouthful of coffee.

"What if we wait here? For a while."

He looked around. "It's a little drab. Anywhere's more cheerful than here." There was an edge of anticipation in his voice.

She got up and insisted on paying for the coffee and sandwich. The man watched as she handed the cashier a credit card. He seemed to find it hard to drag his eyes away from her.

When she turned back to face him, she hesitated for a moment. She stared at his tall frame silhouetted in the door frame and blinked, uncertain of her next move. If this were a fairy tale, she would have reached for her grandmother's doll. She would have given it a squeeze and its little voice would have whispered in her ear, revealing the true identity of the enemy, and how to avoid capture, but she was on her own. All she had left were her instincts to guide her at every turn in the path.

The man stood in the doorway. He might be a phantom from her past, a pimp or a drug dealer, perhaps even a murderer, she thought. She tried to ignore her distrust and followed his limping gait out to his Jeep. She had seen the look of desire in his eyes. It was the sap that gave her life. Without it, she feared she might vanish forever.

21

She was just out of hearing, a secret thing hidden in the wild depths of the blackthorn hedge, but somehow Daly knew she was there. It was almost nightfall when he caught sight of the hen's feathers in the hedge that formed the final boundary between his father's land and the bog. He expected her to take off, but she stayed still, crouching in the darkness like a ghost of herself. She had a surprise in store for him.

Daly had not seen the hen for weeks and assumed a fox had taken her. Since his father's death, the flock of fowl had been flighty and cross, withdrawn at times, unable or unwilling to lay eggs. The oldest hen, an Andalucian blue, kept escaping, finding holes in the wire enclosure, which Daly repeatedly mended. Now he knew the reason for her recurring flights.

Her feathers had changed in tone, darkened, as though she was in mourning. Her beady eyes were alert and suspicious. He nudged her back until a mound of white eggs and broken shells became visible. Several blue-gray chicks, cheeping feebly, emerged from the warmth of her plumage. Daly held his breath and felt the remaining eggs. Unfortunately, they were as cold as stones. He gathered up the hen and her fluffy chicks and placed them in a snug nesting box.

When he had them settled in the hen coop, he returned to the hedge and searched for any chicks he might have missed. He rummaged through the hedge and heard a faint cheeping. He stopped, listening carefully. The sound was strained, muffled. He knew the chick would not survive long on its own. It was like a tiny leaf clinging to a dead branch. Abruptly, it stopped.

He stood without moving. The thorn trees ached in the wind, and the winter grass rustled in the fields. The noise began again. This time it was wincing, urgent, closer. The chick was trapped somewhere. He stared at the unhatched eggs, and, to his surprise, saw one of them shake slightly. The chick was still inside, he realized, struggling to crack open the shell. Lifting the egg in the palm of his hands, he gently pressed the shell with his thumb and watched as the chick's wet head poked free, its eyes veiled with blindness. It scrambled out, beak trembling, wings dangling behind, drinking in its tiny freedom from the cradle of broken shell.

An exhilaration took hold of him. He ran back to the hen coop, clutching the chick close to his chest, as though it were the prize of his life. He offered the frail bundle back to its mother, who was squawking angrily. He was relieved to see she did not reject her newest arrival.

When he returned to the nest in the hedge, he heard more cheeping. This time the cries were weaker. He found another egg, cracked slightly where the chick was trying to break free. He separated the shell, and the chick slithered out, pained and stiff, a greasy, half-digested thing. He blew over it and tried to warm it gently with his hands, as he hurried back to the nest. He tucked the struggling chick under the hen's feathers and went back into the cottage. He salvaged some turf from the dwindling pile his father had gathered in the summer before his death. He lit a fire and waited for its slow heat to warm his sodden feet. In the green and yellow flickering light, he stared at his hands and arms. Blood prickled from where thorns had raked his skin.

When he had dried his feet, he went out and gave the mother hen some food and changed her water. Discreetly, he removed the dead body of the final chick he had rescued from the hedge. The hen had tried to hide it under some straw as though it were a piece of dirt.

Afterward, he surveyed the familiar folds of his father's fields. For the first time since moving in after his death, Daly no longer felt like an alien dropped in from outer space. The grass still brimmed with weeds and the hedges were a tangle of brambles and thorns, but at least he had helped bring new life to the smallholding.

Back in the cottage, he was just about to sit down with a tumbler of whiskey when his mobile phone rang.

"Are you free to speak, Celcius?" It was the duty inspector from the Armagh police station.

"I'm always free to speak."

"We've got a lead on Lena Novak."

"What sort of lead?"

"A report came through a few minutes ago. One of Jack Fowler's missing credit cards was used in a café. A place called Jenny's in Aughnacloy."

22

When Daly drove into Aughnacloy, the border village was slowly sinking into darkness, like a ship falling to the seabed, its twinkling lights fading one by one. A few men gathered in the shadows of doorways, but Daly could see no sign of Lena. The café had already closed. The window shutters were down and there was no answer when he banged the door.

He drove farther up the empty street. If Lena had used the credit card, she could not have gone very far, he reasoned. He scanned both sides of the road. Driving back up the street, he caught a glimpse of a man and a woman entering the darkness of a side street or alley. The effect was like watching a couple sink into deep water, with no one to raise the alarm or help them in any way. He braked and reversed quickly.

When he ran down the alley, he found an abandoned building site. He picked his way across strewn rubble. He came upon the couple standing by a clogged-up cement mixer, with the air of two people negotiating a business deal. For a second, Daly regarded the half-lit tableau, the figures of a young woman dressed in black and a middle-aged man, surrounded by construction equipment and bags of cement stacked high. Behind them a roll of barbed wire covered a tower of cement blocks.

Daly walked up to them, flashing his ID. Lena turned toward him, but the man remained motionless, his head turned slightly away, unwilling to draw attention to himself. Lena was instantly alert. She lit a cigarette and blew smoke in Daly's direction with evident disregard.

"I don't want to talk to you," she said.

"I keep telling you I want to help."

"This is none of your business. I'm trying to scrape out a living."

"There must be less dangerous ways of making ends meet."

"I trust my instinct. I survive. Most of the men I meet are harmless. They like to indulge themselves. Like my friend here."

Daly turned to the man.

"I don't want to waste your time, Inspector," the man said from the shadows, his cadence smooth, soothing almost. He spread out his arms a little, as though opening himself for contrition. "This is the first time I've ever tried to do this, honestly. I saw this woman and stopped on impulse."

Daly did not believe him. His very presence indicated that he had already lost control of himself, was unraveling away from all that was decent and respectable, falling into border country, an exile from the tight-knit comforts of family life.

As Daly advanced toward him, the man withdrew farther into the shadows cast by the construction equipment.

"Have you considered what a criminal conviction might do for your job prospects?"

The man sighed. His face was completely in darkness. "I'm a businessman. My wife and children would never forgive me if they found out."

Daly nodded wearily. Perhaps his judgment was wrong, and the man had made a thoughtless mistake. Daly tried to study his face. The sight of guilt and fear agitating the careworn features of a family man was not his favorite view, but something about the man's hidden face made him feel wary, uncomfortable. It was as though his shadowy eyes were peering into Daly's soul.

"This woman is a victim of people trafficking," said Daly. "You can't see her chains, but that's what she is. A slave."

"Like I said. This is my first time." The man did not say anything more or make the slightest of gestures. Something about his voice sounded familiar. He watched Daly, absolutely still.

Reluctantly, Daly realized he was going to have to arrest the two of them, if only to make sure he could talk to Lena and find out what had happened between her and Fowler. He could see that she needed a sharp dose of reality, and a police interrogation room was as good a place as any to supply it. Somehow, he had to convince her she was not safe touting for clients like this.

Daly read the man his rights and asked for a form of identification. He had expected the man to beg him, to plead for an informal caution, swearing an arrest would destroy his life. Instead, the man allowed a silence to fall over Daly's request. He stepped out of the shadows and examined the detective with particular interest.

"What is it, Inspector," the man said slowly, "that you want from this woman?"

"Come again?"

Too late, Daly recognized his voice, the stillness of his body. He had seen him before. On the CCTV footage from Lena's apartment. It was the man who had almost run him over. Daly felt a quiver of fear freeze his heart.

23

The reflection of a single streetlight fell across black pools in the deserted construction site. The ragged edges of unfinished foundations surrounded the three figures. Nothing but dark holes and obstacles to negotiate if any of them decided to run for it.

"I'm interested in finding out what your plans are for this woman," the man said to Daly. "Do you mean to jail her or repatriate her? Or are your interests of a more personal nature?"

"What business is it of yours?"

"It's very important to my business. My boss has a special interest in her."

"Who do you work for?"

The question produced a cold light in the man's eyes. An unpleasantness surfaced in his features. Daly knew that he had misread the exact nature of the man's intentions. He had strayed into a more sinister encounter than that of a prostitute propositioning a client.

Daly turned toward Lena, who was backing away with a

look of fear widening her eyes. Everything revolved around her, he thought, even as she was trying to invent a distance between herself and her past. He realized he was not going to find out the man's identity or that of his boss when the man's considerable bulk knocked him to the ground. Very quickly, the stranger was on top of Daly, his knee pressed into the detective's neck. Daly craned his head to see his attacker's face. The man was slack jawed as though about to laugh or yawn, his facial muscles relaxing as he focused his energy on the task ahead.

He took a length of rope from the inside of his jacket and, pointing a gun at Lena, made her tie Daly's hands behind his back. The detective felt her hands work intimately at his back.

"What are you going to do with her?" asked Daly.

"I don't know." The stranger leveled his gun at her face. "It's been a long time since I had the company of a beautiful woman. Perhaps I should buy her flowers and take her out for a meal."

The stranger's calm voice and conversational tone made Daly's heart pound with hope that there might be some means of escape for the two of them.

The man leaned down and repositioned his knee against Daly's neck. "You still haven't answered my question?"

"Which is what?" grunted Daly.

"Why are you interested in this woman? Is it about sex?"

"No."

The man grinned. "Have you a physical problem in that department?"

"No. I'm not interested in her that way. Why are we talking about sex?"

"Because this woman is a prostitute. Surely, you've worked out that piece of information for yourself."

He pressed his knee deeper against Daly's windpipe. The detective thought about kicking and roaring at the top of his voice, but he reasoned that might prompt more violence from his assailant. He thought of a number of options, but the time for action was quickly slipping away. The last thing he remembered was the stranger's face fixed at full effort, and the steadiness of his eyes, like two dead knots of wood, weathering out Daly's final struggles as he drifted into unconsciousness.

Out of a blizzard of shadows, Lena appeared above Daly, her eyes the only clear shape in the swirling light and darkness, eyes without shadow, digging into his unconsciousness, dragging him back to the cold building site. Daly tried to raise his hands to his face, but they were bound tightly behind his back.

"You wanted to talk to me," she said.

"Yes. But I had in mind somewhere more comfortable. What happened?"

"I removed your gun while tying you up. When he tried to strangle you, I pressed it to the back of his head. He didn't wait to see if I would fire it."

"That was smart of him."

"I need your car keys, Celcius."

"What do you mean?" The fact that she had used his first

name seemed almost as significant as the request that preceded it. Was she running away or drawing closer to him?

"You can talk to me later. On the phone. But for now, I need your keys."

"I can't let you take my car. You must know that."

Her hands fished through his pockets and found what they were looking for.

"Listen, Lena, you're being very stupid. Stealing a police officer's car is a serious offense. What I will do, if you release me, is drive you to wherever you have to go."

"No."

"What do you mean, no?" He tried to push himself up with his shoulders.

"You have to catch me first," she told him.

"Can't you see what happened here? That man was carrying rope to take you prisoner. He meant to harm you. He'll find you again, before I will."

She was not listening. She ran her hands along his jacket. This time she removed his phone. She tore off the strip of paper cellotaped to the back. It was where he had written his number in case he forgot it.

"If you do get to make a phone call," he told her, "I suggest you ring a solicitor. A good one. Then have him call me. You're going to need all the legal help you can get."

"I can lead you to Mikolajek," she promised him. "When I get my personal life sorted out. Just give me time."

She squeezed his bound fingers quickly. Her touch set off a reflex of desire in his body. She stared into his eyes, again. For once, her face had lost its melancholy look. Daly saw what lay beneath—the gaze of a lost girl searching for a way back home. And then he saw the flash of something shrewder and more poised—the look of a predator who would do what was necessary to kill. His throat went dry, and a shiver of fear rippled through his arms and back. He felt the ligatures of an entanglement more awful and hopeless than the physical one he was enduring. She had perfected the art of intimacy, he realized, the dangerous, close-up exchange, the hurried caress. He felt an equal measure of excitement and discomfort from her close presence.

"You're teasing me," he hissed between closed teeth, but she was already gone, leaving behind a barely discernible trace of her perfume. He listened to the sounds of his car sparking into life and accelerating away, then he lowered his face to the pavement, defeated, his cheeks flushed.

Shortly afterward, he heard footsteps approach. Relieved, he shouted for help. An elderly man appeared out of the darkness. He helped Daly to his feet and untied his hands. He had the lively eyes of a man who had just stepped out of a pub.

"Thanks," said Daly.

"Are you all right?" he asked. "The village can be a dangerous place at night." He flashed Daly a look of grandfatherly concern.

"I was attacked from behind. Some men came out of nowhere."

"You should ring the police."

"I am the police."

The man squinted at him. "You're the police?"

Daly was aware of a chilly space growing between them. The old man regarded him with an angry stare of suspicion.

"What were you doing here? Snooping?"

"I was preventing a crime."

"You're a nosy Protestant bastard."

"No," Daly corrected him. "I'm a nosy Catholic bastard."

"That's even worse."

Daly walked slowly back to the streetlights, feeling the man's eyes prickling his back. After he had walked several hundred yards, he checked if he was being followed. The street was empty. He leaned against a wall and rubbed his neck. Rain started to fall, washing the caked mud from his shoes. He was going to be drenched by the time he got home.

24

Commander Ian Boyd did not shift from his seat when Daly walked into the room the following afternoon. Daly's superior was as stiffly posed as a shop window dummy, one that had been positioned inside its exact plot of office space by the top brass in Belfast. He had a square chest, a smoothly combed head, and a face that stared down at a sheaf of papers with a look of impatient efficiency. Although the commander was only two months into the post, Daly had already decided he was little more than fifteen stone of form-filling muscle, the type of police officer who had been specially created for an atmosphere of stifling paperwork and protocols.

"I'd like a word, sir," requested Daly.

The commander did not look up. A state-of-the-art paper shredder whirred in the corner next to him. He was feeding pages into the shredder as he read them, each page replacing the last with barely a moment in between. Daly watched the chief and the machine. There was a curious uniformity at work. They were like two parts of a contraption that shared the same controlling mechanism.

"One moment, Inspector," replied Boyd. He gathered up another array of papers and began reading and shredding them. *Read and shred,* thought Daly. The new Police Service of Northern Ireland was quick to promote competence in the reading and shredding department.

Donaldson, the former chief, might have been the archetypal RUC commander, but at least he had dash and style, and a way of working that was completely indifferent to any directive from headquarters. When the shit hit the fan, as it invariably did, he would disappear from the station, usually because of a mysterious "something he couldn't get out of," and allow his senior detectives to make whatever decisions they thought best at the time.

Boyd was a different animal altogether. He was more interested in protocols and policies, and managing budgets, and revealed as much about his personal life as an executioner standing next to a guillotine, albeit a paper guillotine that needed to be fed constantly.

"I'm not interrupting something?"

"Not at all," said Boyd, disposing of the final sheet. "It's my rule to keep the door open at all times. Even when a detective comes to tell me the bad news of their botched police work."

Daly flinched.

Boyd fixed him with a stare. "I've read the report on the discovery of your stolen car. An empty bottle of vodka was found in the vehicle, along with cigarette stubs and scuff marks including the imprint of a woman's boot on the dashboard. It seems that this woman took your car and had a party in it, Inspector Daly."

"If you've read the report, then you'll also know she took the vehicle after I foiled an attempt to kidnap her. Her liberty and probably her life were under threat."

"You're a chief inspector. How often do chief inspectors lose their cars to a missing person?"

"I was knocked unconscious." Daly shrugged. Whatever he said was going to sound like a lame excuse.

Boyd looked him up and down. "Perhaps you need a break. You know you're allowed to take some time off and recuperate."

"I'd rather progress the investigation."

"How do you propose to do that?" asked Boyd sharply.

"I want a press release to help us trace this man with a limp, and also one for Mikolajek. Alert all the media channels and liaise with Interpol if necessary to find out their histories and track them down. I also want to organize a search house by house, street by street, in certain parts of the town, until we have rounded up this gang and whoever else they are paying to do their dirty work."

Boyd frowned but said nothing.

"Do I have your support in this?"

The commander stared levelly at Daly. "You have my growing interest, but not my support."

"What do you mean?"

"I mean we're not going to do anything more in the search for your missing woman. At least for the time being." Boyd leaned back in his seat.

"How come?"

"We can't afford another cock-up. Last night you were

lured into a trap, and Lena Novak was able to make off in your car. It suggests poor preparation and judgment on your part. It also suggests this woman's a lot more resourceful than you gave her credit for. I think there's less to this case than you make out."

"What do you mean?"

"I've read the reports so far from your team. There's nothing solid or concrete there. The crime scenes are vague, and the links to Mikolajek tenuous. Nothing to hang a coat on, never mind a media campaign or an organized series of raids. You're leading my officers down a blind alley."

"I know there are gaps but—"

Boyd interrupted him. "Your plans will raise public alarm. People will wonder what sort of crazy foreigners we have living under our noses if you send out press releases and go in heavy-handed and raid all these houses. It's not in the public interest to create anger and fear."

"What are you suggesting? That arresting Mikolajek could stir up racism?"

"No. I'm saying that bumbling and clumsy police work will. You know this town better than I do. Parts of it are on the verge of a racial war. There are thugs walking the street right now looking for any excuse to petrol bomb their neighbors' houses because of their nationalities."

"The life of a vulnerable young woman is at risk here."

"As I said, I think you're exaggerating the danger she's in."

"Why would I do that?"

"Because your curiosity has been aroused by Ms. Novak. However, this has no business with the realities of detective work. If you had some hard evidence linking her with one of these crimes or proof her life is in imminent danger, then that would be a different matter. Then you could follow the laws of evidence and police procedure, but this has nothing to do with the technicalities of an investigation. This web of intrigue that you have created around this woman"—Boyd summoned his vitriol—"and her mysterious rag doll is a fantasy. One to keep you away from the frustrations and paperwork of ordinary police duties. Let me be clear on this, I want you to drop your search for her. We know she's not injured or sick. We know that she has means and some sort of refuge. Our officers, the Garda, and the public have been given a description of her. We should wait and see what leads develop there."

"You're right. My curiosity has been aroused, but that curiosity comes from training and experience."

Boyd stared hard at Daly. "I think I'm getting to know you now, Celcius Daly. What I see is a police officer with a photo of a missing woman and a hunch. A pretty woman, by all accounts. And the more you search for her, the more personal your motivation becomes."

Daly blinked. The criticism was also getting personal.

"We can't allocate resources to a photo and a hunch," declared Boyd.

"Is this because she's a foreign national?"

"Don't play the racist card with me, Daly." Boyd was being tough now. Gone was the practiced look of efficiency. It had been shredded with the rest of his prepared script.

"You know what the press are like," said Daly. "Any

suggestion we're ignoring the plight of this woman because of her race and they'll be baying like hounds. They'll turn on us and accuse us of racism."

"Her race is not an issue here. We simply don't have the resources to indulge your curiosity. That's the problem with this force, too much inefficiency and time-wasting. I have to account for and budget every action taken by my officers. I want a written report on this investigation so far, and a proposal as to why it should have more resources."

Daly frowned. It was not he who needed a dose of reality, but the commander. In his opinion, Boyd had succumbed to the idiocy of obsessive form filling and bean counting. It was a comfortable refuge for the mind, one where criminals were made of paper and the only transgressions were committed by numbers that did not add or boxes that could not be ticked.

Boyd handed Daly several sheets of paper. They were the agenda for a meeting of the policing partnership. Due to attend were community leaders and local politicians.

"This meeting's tonight. Seven o'clock sharp," said Boyd. "I want you there. Some concerns have been raised by Republican politicians about the nature of the investigation into Jack Fowler's death."

Daly scanned down the list, picking off the names of former terrorists, who five years ago would have committed political suicide by attending such a meeting.

"Good. I'll see you there."

"A word of advice, Daly," said Boyd as the detective turned to leave. "This woman may be in trouble, but it seems to me the trouble stems from the men who try to rescue her from her chosen line of business. The next time one of my officers encounters her and suspects she's on the game, I want her arrested and charged for prostitution."

25

Irwin sprang from his seat when Daly entered his office. He had a lukewarm cup of tea in his hand and deposited it beside Daly's paperwork. He looked pleased with himself.

"I thought you'd be back earlier," said Irwin. "You might still get the good out of that cuppa."

Irwin was not a natural tea boy, and Daly suspected he was there purely out of professional curiosity. Glancing at his untidy desk, he wondered if Irwin had been going through his paperwork.

"What did the commander have to say?"

Daly paused. "A few suggestions about the direction of the investigation. That's all. I think it's time we reviewed Fowler's drowning. Go through the evidence again to see if we missed anything."

"We've already examined everything."

Nevertheless, they spent an hour sorting through the case so far. They dug through Fowler's life and business dealings, but found little to point to a murderer. Daly picked up the bag containing the opera CD. They had yet to identify the owner of the fingerprints left on the cover.

"This was the music playing when he drowned," said Daly. "It must have some sort of significance, sentimental or otherwise."

"For whom? If there was a killer there that morning, perhaps the fingerprints are his," suggested Irwin.

Daly studied the CD, thinking it was time to visit Mrs. Fowler again.

"I almost forgot," said Irwin as Daly was about to leave. "A call came through from Customs officers. They raided a farmhouse this morning close to Keady, after a tip-off about an illegal fuel-laundering plant."

"Did they find anything?"

"The message was unclear. The tip-off claimed a man with a gun had abducted three Croatian women. The place was completely deserted by the time Customs got there. Not as much as a squeak from a rat, but they uncovered an operational fuel-laundering plant with several tankers, also set up for illegal alcohol bottling. They suspect the people working there did a runner across the border."

"Why didn't they call us out to assist with the raid?"

"They have to act immediately on this sort of intelligence and swoop; otherwise the evidence will be destroyed."

"Any more details about the women?"

"Nothing as yet. All they have is the tip-off, and that's secondhand. It'll be impossible to get any witnesses. No one will want to incriminate himself."

"Get back to them and speak to the officers who carried out the raid," said Daly. "Find out as much information as possible about what happened to those women."

"OK," replied Irwin. "The officer in charge of the raid was someone called Dukes, at least that's what I think the duty sergeant said." But Daly had already left.

Driving up to Fowler's mansion, Daly noticed that little had changed since his last visit. There were no portents of the heartbreak that had occurred within its high walls. The solid mahogany doors and triple-glazed windows remained unperturbed by the destruction Fowler's death had visited upon his family. The wind poured down the slopes of nearby Slieve Gullion as fresh as ever, and the cherry trees blossomed reassuringly, shedding fresh petals across the mown lawns.

It was only in the silence and shadows of the rooms within that Daly detected evidence of the tragedy, and in the emaciated figure of Greta Fowler, who was waiting for him in the sitting room. The floor was pale marble, the walls covered in embossed paper. She sat on the same pale avocado sofa, her bare knees almost touching the mica top of the coffee table. The same wind whistled against the windowpane, and the same cut flowers stood in a tall porcelain vase, past their best now, looking as though the slightest of breezes might send them and the vase smashing to the floor. Greta Fowler looked just as fragile, and close to catastrophe, as though she had not moved from the sofa all week. Daly wondered if the questions he had to ask would sink in.

She seemed to compose herself when he explained the reason behind his visit.

"Is there anything unusual you can recall about the day

before your husband died?" he asked. "Perhaps something that didn't spring to mind during our last interview."

"Lots of things," she replied with a sigh. "I did the shopping that day in Marks and Sparks. Then I read a magazine while waiting in the hairdresser's. I had blond highlights put in that day. Little did I know the woman staring back at me in the mirror was going to disappear forever that evening. But enough about my banal little life. I thought you came here to discuss the investigation into my husband's death."

"What do you mean, disappear forever?"

"When I went home that evening, Inspector Daly, I believed my dignity was intact and my marriage sound. I had no idea of the new existence awaiting me." She paused. Tears welled in her eyes, but not a drop fell. "I found a message on the phone from that woman you're searching for. When I replaced the receiver, I was replaced too. By a new version of myself. One freed from the normal day-to-day frustrations. I waited until Jack came home and then I replayed the message to him. He was stupefied. When I looked into his eyes, I saw they were burning with fear. Like a small boy surrounded by bullies."

"What did the message say?"

"She said their relationship was over, and she wanted £10,000. It was blackmail. Very business-like and matter-of-fact. All along she'd been working for her Mafia boss, a man called Mikolajek. She said she'd some important financial documents of Jack's, which she would return when she got the money."

"What did your husband do in response?"

"Nothing. He was in shock. Baffled. He thought he'd treated this woman better than anyone else in his life. He had been deluded into believing he had rescued her from people traffickers."

"What about you? How did you react?"

"I felt calm. Lightened. As though we'd been handed a reprieve."

Daly stared closely at her. He pushed the suicide hypothesis aside for a moment and entertained the idea of jealousy, the rage of a spurned wife tipped off by the woman who had casually seduced her husband and then set about blackmailing him. But would she have been rational and calculated enough to orchestrate her husband's death to look like a suicide? He doubted it. The death scene was too contrived to have been a crime of passion, but the revelation that Lena may have tried to blackmail Fowler opened up new possibilities. He began to wonder whether their entire affair had been a trap. If so, who had set it?

Greta caught Daly's curious gaze, forced a smile, and said: "That woman did us a favor. I was getting suspicious about the hours he was keeping. The fear that he was having an affair left me sick to the stomach."

"Did you not think of kicking him out?"

"No. Not at all. I believed I could salvage our marriage. In my circumstances, women prefer security to fidelity. I hated him for his stupidity, but I wasn't prepared to run away from what we had created. Our family life together."

"What happened after you both listened to the message?"

"It was an emotional few hours. He tried to plan a course of action, got upset, and rang her number. When he got no answer, he came to me. He was like a piece of rope in a tug-of-war. When I went to bed, he was burning papers in the study. I watched the flames light up his face. He looked crumpled. Broken." "Enough to commit suicide."

"He didn't mention anything that would give me that idea. He had other things on his mind. Financial worries. But then it was always hard to tell with Jack. When I get low, everyone knows about it. But when Jack was down, he would just go quiet and say he was tired."

"I'll need to hear the message."

"Too late. I erased it."

"Why did you do that?"

"I thought it too dangerous. Especially if it was heard by the wrong person."

"Who?"

"I don't know. It was her voice. The sound of her accent. Knowing it was still on the machine was too painful for me. And embarrassing." She tried to change the subject. "Have you found her yet?"

"No."

"She's disappeared without a trace, hasn't she? Only criminals can vanish like that. Organized criminals."

"That's why I'm here. I need more information about her."

"Did she kill someone?"

"I don't know."

"That's what people are saying. I blame her for Jack's

death. She had a blank check to his heart, but that wasn't enough for her. She should be hunted by the police like any other killer. What do you think?"

Daly had learned from experience that there was little to be gained by arguing with a grieving widow. In any case, she had added some credence to his deepest concerns.

"You may be right. Perhaps she is a killer, but that's for the justice system to decide. And we are searching for her. But she's being hunted by others. People who hunt to kill. We're trying to make contact with her and encourage her to come in and talk to us. Her time for running and hiding is over."

Greta Fowler had nothing more to add. Daly produced the CD of *La Traviata*.

"This was the CD playing on the morning of your husband's death. A set of fingerprints was found on it. We haven't been able to identify them."

Greta nodded. She was staring absentmindedly out at the pool.

"The choice of CD must have some importance," said Daly.

She looked at him in surprise. "I could draw a number of conclusions from it."

"What are you thinking?"

She shrugged. "I took Jack to see a performance of *La Traviata* by the Philharmonic Society before Christmas. He wasn't a big opera buff, but he was taken by the story line. Afterward, he bought the CD and played it late at night. He said he found Violetta's plight very moving."

Daly stared at the CD. From his basic knowledge of the

opera, he recalled that Violetta was a high-class prostitute, the original whore with the heart of gold. The opera charted her relationship with her lover, which was jinxed by emotional blackmail. Perhaps it was a clue, a reference to Fowler's relationship with Lena, thought Daly.

"Thank you for your time," he said. "You've been very helpful."

"Have I? I thought we were getting nowhere. But I'm glad if what I've told you brings you closer to tracking down that bitch."

She had a black-and-white view of Lena Novak, one that Daly envied.

Before he left, she held out her hand. When he shook it, her fingers seemed to fumble in his as though she were about to lose her balance. He released them quickly.

Afterward, he sat in his car and played through the conversation in his head. Her revelations were not going to dramatically alter the investigation. In fact, they confirmed his instinct all along. Fowler's mysterious death was connected to Lena's disappearance and the border brothel in which they must have met.

26

Daly drove home, his thoughts focused on the similarities that were emerging between *La Traviata*'s plotlines and Fowler's doomed relationship with Lena Novak. It struck him how difficult it would be for a woman like Lena to build up a trusting relationship with a man, especially one whom she had met as a prostitute. Relationships change and evolve, and many romances are triggered by an act of betrayal, but how many love affairs begin with exploited sex? Not very many, he thought. Blackmail and revenge were more likely to be kindled by such a relationship, rather than new love, so he tried not to judge Lena too harshly.

He pulled up at the cottage, switched off the engine, and broke away from his thoughts. He stared through the windshield and kept his grip on the steering wheel. He groaned. The policing partnership meeting. He had completely forgotten about it. He tried ringing Boyd on his mobile, but the commander had switched off his phone. He reversed and hurried to the venue, hoping that the meeting had started late.

"Good evening, Inspector, we've been waiting for you," murmured Commander Boyd, without bothering to look up from his notes. Across the table sat the rest of the policing partnership, made up of local community leaders, four from the Catholic community, four from the Protestant. Susie Brooke, the antiracism officer, was there too. She looked up at Daly with a benign flicker of her long eyelashes. The man sitting next to her waved a finger at Daly. It was Michael Mooney. The antiracism officer and the former IRA prisoner. Now that was a pairing Daly hadn't expected. He sat down beside the chief, realizing he was going to have to take this meeting more seriously than he had intended.

"Any more late-arriving stragglers?" said the chairman, Owen Higgins, the new Sinn Fein deputy leader, staring at Daly as though he were a scab on a difficult-to-heal wound. For some of the partnership members the monthly meetings were simply a chance to refresh their contempt for the new Police Service of Northern Ireland.

Boyd began with an overview of the latest crime figures. He emphasized the police's success in tackling property theft, which had escalated alarmingly since the downturn in the economy. The figures sounded good. A 38 percent increase in the number of detections in the past year. Boyd rattled through the numbers.

"We haven't come here to be bombarded by statistics," interrupted Mooney. "At least the statistics you've successfully manipulated for public consumption."

"What do you mean?"

"What about missing person cases? From what I can gather, your detection rate there is as bad as South America's in the seventies."

There were chortles from the other Republican politicians.

"All missing person cases are taken very seriously," said Boyd.

"What if the missing person is a foreign national?"

"I presume you're talking about Lena Novak," he replied. "Cases like hers are statistically very unusual. However, the coverage given to them by the media make them very important ones in the public's perception. Inspector Daly has been assigned this particular investigation, along with his Special Branch colleague, Detective Derek Irwin."

Daly spoke up. "I can assure you we have been delving deep into this case, and that we are extremely anxious for this woman's safety."

However, Mooney had a point to make. "According to reports, another three Croatian women were reported missing this week from an illegal alcohol-bottling plant near the border, but I've yet to see a police appeal about their whereabouts. Is it the case that police officers are indifferent to foreign nationals who go missing?"

"No," said Boyd. "Not at all."

Owen Higgins leaned back in his seat. "Disappearances are a notorious border crime. During the Troubles we had many instances of men and women going missing. Usually they were branded as informers. In those days, proper searches were seldom conducted. It doesn't surprise me to see a similar nonchalance at work in the police today."

"Exactly," said Mooney. "People just don't vanish off the face of the earth because it's South Armagh. When and where was the last sighting of Lena Novak?"

"Why are you so interested in this woman?" asked Daly. Neither Mooney nor Higgins answered.

"What is it you're trying to find out here?" continued Daly. "The whereabouts of your missing peace funds?"

Boyd butted in. "Mr. Mooney, you should know that we can't reveal the details of an ongoing investigation."

"I'm just concerned that people traffickers and pimps are operating freely under the cover of police indifference."

One of the more moderate politicians, a representative of the Social Democratic and Labour Party, submitted a question. "Only a few years ago, South Armagh was a constant center of bloodshed and murder," she said. "Now we learn from the media that it's the focus for international criminal gangs. What exactly are the police doing to tackle the problem of people trafficking and is it true that these gangs have teamed up with former IRA men?"

Mooney shifted uncomfortably in his seat. He hunched his shoulders, drummed his fingers on the tabletop, and leaned over and whispered to Brooke. Daly caught his gaze and saw a pair of worried eyes flash back at him. Or was that just his imagination? The former terrorist and close friend of Jack Fowler looked anxious to get back to his heavily mortgaged, stinking concrete cell. Was it because, a decade ago, Mooney would have been one of the dark shadows from the terrorist underworld they were discussing? Daly watched him with curiosity.

"That's a good question," answered Commander Boyd. "And one we have been asking ourselves a lot in recent months."

"Is it not your job to provide answers?" asked Higgins.

"That's correct," replied Boyd stiffly.

"Well, you seem to be doing the opposite right now."

Daly watched the commander falter, anger flaring his nostrils. In a way, he felt sorry for Boyd, doing his paperwork every day, issuing new directives from headquarters, trying to keep in touch with what Special Branch officers were up to, and even interfere in what some of his detectives were doing. Telling himself that after ten years or so of shuffling papers he might be promoted back to the city, with perhaps an MBE as a glittering prize in sight. Getting heckled by Republican politicians was not part of his career plan.

Daly cleared his throat. "Police forces have their strategies and budgets. We have to reach targets for vehicle crime, street crime, and burglary, and that is where the resources go, but I think we need to realize that human trafficking is a problem that is sneaking up on us."

"How many people traffickers have your arrested in the past year?" asked Mooney.

Daly shrugged and tried to be honest. "None. Yet. You have to remember we're groping in the dark through a maze of cross-border roads and hideouts. Dissident Republicans, people traffickers, drug smugglers, fuel smugglers, cigarette smugglers, there's a hundred different types of criminal out there running in different directions. But we struggle on, doing the best we can."

Susie Brooke nodded. "This is a very new environment for the police: tackling international crime while dealing appropriately with foreign nationals; tackling racism in all its forms, especially the more covert forms such as institutional racism." She glanced at Daly. "I think as police officers we need a new kind of training and a new set of experiences to make us more effective."

The meeting progressed for another half an hour, discussing strategies to help the police reach out to the new arrivals from Eastern Europe. They decided to start with a mail drop to every house in the district with information about police services printed in different languages.

When it was over, Brooke came over and sat down beside Daly.

"I know why Lena Novak ran away from you."

He twisted in his chair. "Why?"

"She doesn't trust you. Isn't it obvious?"

"Why shouldn't she trust me? I saved her from a man who was about to kidnap her."

"There's no simple answer to that, but it's a question you can't ignore."

"Why don't you try giving me an answer then?"

She stared at him. "One aspect of her distrust is based on the fact that you're a man."

"And how do I resolve that?"

"You have to understand her world. All she sees are enemies, dangerous men who might do her harm. Try to imagine what it's like being in her shoes."

Daly was tired. He had a slight headache. If he was

honest, he had let Lena slip out of his grasp in the clumsiest way possible, not once, but twice. Deep down, he blamed himself for not arresting her on the night they first met in the abandoned farmhouse. If anything, he had been too tentative, too interested in understanding her world. He looked at Brooke.

She smiled and tipped her head slightly to one side. "Perhaps we should talk about this later."

"I agree."

"What about Hegarty's tonight? I'm heading there for a drink and a dance with some girlfriends."

He was taken aback by the sudden invitation. "Sure."

When she got up and left, Daly found himself staring across the table at Higgins and Mooney. The two Republicans exchanged meaningful glances.

"How do you get a date with a woman like that?" asked Higgins.

"Now you're asking a good question." Mooney nodded his head. "We'd all like to hear the answer to that one."

Daly felt the back of his neck turn red as they laughed.

27

Daly had decided to decline Brooke's invitation and head for home when he bumped into Irwin in the car park. The younger detective looked uncharacteristically deflated, like the captain of a football team that had lost a dozen games on the trot.

"I need a drink. Want to join me?" he asked bluntly.

Daly thought for a moment. It struck him as unusual that the Special Branch detective was leaving the police station at this late hour of the day.

"I've something to get off my chest," added Irwin, a note of desperation creeping into his voice.

On closer inspection, the Special Branch detective looked a mess. His dark hair was disheveled and his shirt rumpled. Several days' worth of stubble and a pair of sleepless-looking eyes had done dark things to his face. It occurred to Daly he might kill two birds with one stone and take Brooke up on her invite after all.

"Fancy Hegarty's then?"

Irwin shrugged his shoulders. "As good a place as any."

"Should I bring the hankies?"

"I don't need any fuckin' hankies." Irwin's tone was defensive.

Outside the pub, a row of bouncers stood guard over the closed doors. They had just turned away a group of Eastern European youths dressed in T-shirts and jeans. The young men huddled together in the shadows with the look of those condemned always to wait on the wrong side of closed doors. One of them glanced up as the two detectives passed. Daly watched the yellow streetlights glinting in his eyes before the darkness hooded his face.

Grinning and nodding, the bouncers stepped aside and ushered the detectives through.

Once they had settled into a snug, Daly asked Irwin if it was part of Hegarty's door policy to bar Eastern Europeans.

"Why not?" replied Irwin. "Isn't that the whole point of a door policy—to discriminate?" He got up to order the first round.

"We should be doing something about it," said Daly when Irwin returned with two pints of Guinness, their creamy heads spilling enticingly over the top.

"Like what?"

"I don't know. Tell our antiracism officer about it, for a start."

Irwin snorted. "And what will she do? Send in an undercover team of Lithuanian policemen to entrap the bouncers?"

"Fair enough. Forget it."

"Targeting those bouncers and their racist door policy

isn't going to solve anything. Anyway, it's not just Eastern Europeans they bar. If a group of Eskimos came up to the door, they'd probably turn them away, as well."

"I just don't like seeing it happen before my eyes."

"Whether you like it or not, people will always want to drink and party with their own. It's a fact the world over. Russians, Chinese, Africans, we're all the same."

"I don't see the bouncers turning away Eastern European girls."

Irwin's eyes glinted. "Even bouncers can forget their principles."

They were halfway through their third round of Guinness when Irwin came round to mentioning what was troubling him.

"I thought about quitting today," he confided in Daly, his voice raw. "I'm going to talk to the chief. It's the hours and the security threat. I don't mind, but it plays havoc with your personal life."

As far as Daly knew, Irwin had a healthy and colorful personal life, a pulsating soap opera of romantic conquests, furtive betrayals, fights, and makeups, involving his girlfriend, Poppy, and a cast of about half a dozen other women, most of them colleagues.

"It's Poppy." Irwin shook his head. His eyes grew watery. "She's kicked me out. I think it's for good this time."

"What makes you think that?"

"I asked her how serious this was on a scale of one to ten. She said eleven. I've hardly eaten since."

Daly nodded.

"It's not what you think. We were in love. I was going to get her an engagement ring."

"What about the other girls?"

"Poppy was different. I thought we were going to be together forever."

That was what I thought about Anna, even a year ago, mused Daly.

Irwin stared at his pint and swirled it sorrowfully, as though he were working out how the drink and he were going to manage in the big bad world without his girlfriend. He hugged the pint to his chest before placing it dejectedly on the table.

A waitress came to collect the empty drinks, but Irwin waved her away. He finished the dregs, wiping his lips as if too much had spilled from there already.

"She wasn't like the others," he said eventually. He barely glanced in Daly's direction. "That's the truth." Then he went back to the bar.

He returned with two fresh pints and several bags of crisps.

"It's not worth it, this job," he declared. "When it drives a wedge between you and your loved ones."

Daly decided to play devil's advocate.

"How do you think giving up your job will change things with Poppy?"

Irwin gulped down a mouthful and shrugged. "You're probably right. It's too late for that."

Daly remained silent. He felt a disabling echo of his own loss. He tasted once again the familiar pangs of separation, the desire to have his married life with Anna restored, the life they had enjoyed before the accident. He glanced at the younger detective and felt a twinge of empathy. It was an odd feeling. As though the circuitry of his emotions had gone awry, the polar forces reversed. He never imagined he might feel anything in common with Irwin, let alone sympathize with his predicament.

"We're all under pressure in the force these days," Daly said, sighing. "And everyone fears deep down that they're about to be blown up by terrorists."

"Bloody Republican dissidents. It's like the transfer window in the football league out there. They're bringing in a whole team of new signings from the IRA and the INLA."

They raised their pints of Guinness in mock salute to each other and drank deeply. The creamy heads slopped back to the bottom of the empty glasses.

"I don't mean to make light of your problems," said Daly after a pause. "I'm just suggesting you shouldn't lose your sense of proportion. You're letting your emotions interfere with your career."

Irwin responded to Daly's sympathy by opening up further. He recounted in detail how he had spent the last week trawling the Internet for dates. Daly listened, suspecting the real purpose behind the younger detective's frenzied search for romance was to prevent even a moment of silent reflection creeping into his life.

"It's impossible to judge how a woman looks from a photo on the Internet," complained Irwin, his face registering the memory of his disappointment. "This new woman I met online, she posted two pictures of herself. One was terrible. The other not so bad. I arranged to meet her for a date. I thought if she was somewhere in between…" His voice trailed off. The dance floor was beginning to fill with bodies. He stared longingly at the moving crowd, as though it were a train he had just missed, a train that would whisk him away from loneliness.

He picked up the thread of the story again, glancing back at Daly with a look of reproach. "Turned out, even the terrible photo of her was flattering."

"What did you do then?"

"I escaped to the nearest pub after half an hour, but then she texted to say how much she had enjoyed the date. I texted back likewise, but shame about the chemistry. Then she said she thought the chemistry had been great. So I switched off the phone and hit the bar."

Daly nodded. He wanted to say a few words, but could not think of anything that would extract the sting of disappointment from Irwin's face. On the dance floor a mixed barrage of drunken businessmen and muscled builders were launching themselves onto the circulating groups of women.

"Thanks for humoring me."

"Humoring you? I meant to do the opposite."

Irwin grinned suddenly.

"At least you can still see the funny side," said Daly.

Irwin stared at his glass. "At least I'm drunk."

A group of women, who had been sitting at a nearby table, moved closer. Irwin went to the toilet, returned, and said nothing. After his brief outpouring of emotion, he drew a gloomy mantle of suffering around himself. He sipped the froth of his pint and smacked his lips deliberately, trying to keep his deck of troubles a little closer to his chest. The woman at the nearby table laughed at a private joke, and Irwin glanced uncertainly at them. He raked his hand through his curly hair, looked at them again, and gulped down his drink. He edged a little closer to the women, as though he were keen to share the joke.

Daly was about to advise Irwin to go home and tell his girlfriend he still loved her and that she was too good for him. However, a change had overcome Irwin. The oldest of the women flashed a smile in his direction. Love was in the air, or at least lust, as Irwin blinked and grinned. He was like a thief, thought Daly, newly released from prison, who comes across a wallet on the pavement. Just as in crime, sex was always more about opportunity than motivation. Irwin went up to the bar and nerved himself with a double whiskey.

Daly surveyed the women. The oldest had bleached blond hair and heavy makeup, designed more to cover the signs of age rather than enhance the freshness of youth. All three women were ogling Irwin now, islanded in a sea of knowing sexual energy, urging him to draw closer as he returned unsteadily from the bar. Something about the directness of their invitation convinced Daly they were foreign. Local women would have feigned disinterest for longer, playing out a charade of boredom until their target had drunk himself into an inebriated stupor.

Irwin gulped down the remainder of his pint, leaned over to the women, and introduced himself. His face glistened with sweat. He beckoned Daly over, and soon the older detective found himself exchanging meaningless pleasantries with the women, who were all from Poland. They claimed to be sisters, but Daly had the suspicion that at least two, if not three, generations were represented in their company.

The disco started, and the pub began to shake with the reverberations of the music. Irwin rose to the floor with the eldest of the women and began dancing as proudly as a strutting cock. After a few songs, he sat down beside Daly again.

"She tells me she's forty," he said. "I think she's having me on. What do you think?"

"Give or take a few years—what's the difference?" It was the most comforting thing Daly could think of saying. Truthfully, he suspected she might be the youngest woman's grandmother.

Irwin rubbed his face. "At least I've moved off the Internet and into the real world." His eyes blazed with a sudden lack of caution, his mind already inhabiting the reduced reality and raised hopes of the intoxicated. His tactics had changed but the scope for deception was still as great, thought Daly, as he rose to his feet. It was the easiest parting from company he had made in a long time.

28

Daly avoided the swell of people pushing onto the dance floor and forced his way to the bar. From what he could see, it was less a disco than an exploration of how far drunken men could be teased. He scanned the crowd, looking for Susie Brooke, but there was no sign of his colleague.

One of the younger Polish women appeared out of the sweating throng and sidled up to him.

"Your friend, he's funny," she said, smiling. "A typical Irishman."

"Don't call him that," said Daly.

"What do you mean?"

"He thinks he's British."

"What about you? Are you Irish?"

"Yes."

She leaned her face close to his and, widening her eyes with mock aggression, hissed in his ear. "Tonight my country will take its revenge on you."

"What?"

She paused for a moment, drinking in Daly's uncertainty. "I'm talking about football." She grinned and pointed to the television screen. The pumping music had drowned the commentary, but Daly was able to make out that Poland was playing Northern Ireland. An international friendly match, but there was nothing friendly about the atmosphere on the terraces. Poland had scored a goal and a flurry of missiles rained down on the pitch.

Behind the Polish girl, Daly saw a familiar face enter the pub, shun the bar, and disappear into the crowd. He blinked. It was a woman with short spiky hair, pale olive skin, and a gleam of disdain in her eyes. He felt an intimate heat rise in his chest. He caught another glimpse of her shoulder, her narrow black dress, the curve of her back and waist, as she weaved through the crowd heaving on the dance floor.

Daly made off after her. He pushed past the absorbed faces of young men and women bobbing together. The black lace of the woman's dress hem slipped out of view. He forced his way down a long passageway leading to the toilets and outside smoking area. He was sure the woman had not seen him. He waited against an emergency exit and stared at the groups of smokers silhouetted against the brink of a starry night.

When she did not reappear, he pushed past the smokers. The increased tempo of their voices drowned out the beats of the disco. A young couple brushed against him and sneered, as though he were just another middle-aged man in pursuit of a woman, which, in a way, he was. What had brought him to this place, he wondered. Equal parts loneliness and work, he conceded. Perhaps he was just another pathetic drunk after all.

In the darkness, he heard the rapid sound of footsteps, a door opening, and then the heavy footfall of several bodies landing from a height. A voice cried out in pain, followed by muffled laughter. His eyes grew accustomed to the dim light. At the other end of the yard, he saw a figure drop from the wall. The woman he had been following was steadying a set of empty beer crates as a makeshift ladder, and a group of young Eastern European men were clambering down it into the grounds of the pub. They filed hurriedly past Daly. He recognized them as the youths barred entrance at the door.

He watched as the woman with short hair swept by him. She was sinewy, with a lean back and slender neck. Daly tapped her on the shoulder. She whipped round, her pale face expecting an interrogation. He saw that she was thinner faced than Lena, her features harshly shadowed, her eyes more hollow. Disappointment thickened in his throat.

"I'm not with them," she said. "I don't know where they came from."

"It's OK. I'm not a bouncer."

"What do you want then?" Her eyes glinted.

Suddenly, it was he who was searching for an explanation.

"Nothing. I thought you were someone else."

It was probably his age, he told himself. The faces of women were beginning to repeat themselves, that and the destructive effects of alcohol on his mental apparatus.

She leaned back against the wall and looked up at him, her dark eyes equipped with mascara, glittery eye shadow, and a smoldering expression. Her shoulders pressed against the wall, emphasizing the tight nexus of her waist. She smiled at Daly's downward glance. A smile that said *I can twist you around my little finger.*

"Lena Novak. Ever heard of her?" he asked.

"Are you seeing her?"

"No."

"Then who are you seeing?"

"I'm not seeing anyone." The words came out with a force that surprised him. "This is important. Do you know a girl called Lena Novak? She's Croatian, your height and build."

Her eyes rolled. "The more you run after a girl like Lena, the faster she'll run away."

He wanted to tell her he was a policeman, and that policemen don't get caught up in romance. It was bad enough being caught up in crime, but he did not want to frighten her into silence.

"This is purely business. I need to know where she is."

She was losing interest in him. Her eyes drifted to the side. "I haven't seen Lena in over a month. What's wrong? Is she in trouble?"

"Worse than she knows. But I'm her friend. If you see her, tell her Celcius Daly is looking for her. I have everything ready."

"What's everything?"

"A safe place. Legal help."

"I know what you are, Celcius Daly."

Daly said nothing.

"You're in love."

Daly flushed.

"See," she said, her smile widening.

She made to leave but then turned back.

"If you want to find Lena Novak, speak to Martha Havel. She's the boss of a cleaning company called Home Sweet Home. You'll find it on Rutherford Street. She's as hard as nails, but all the girls go to her if they're in trouble."

Daly made his way back to the bar. He glanced at his watch and wondered where Susie Brooke had gotten to. It was 11:00 p.m. and still there was no sign of her. With a sigh, he decided that sobriety was not an option with so many drunken people pressing around him. He ordered another pint of Guinness and a whiskey, which he downed in two gulps. For an Irishman, getting drunk in a packed bar was a physical imperative, like putting up an umbrella against the rain.

He was enjoying being one intoxicated single man among many when he saw a curtain fall back from the stage behind the dance floor. A shiny pole hung from the ceiling against a silver banner, advertising a pole-dancing competition. The dance music changed in pitch and grew deeper, as though the disco was slowing down. In reality, the pace was about to get a lot racier. A voice beside him shouted: "Showtime!"

Just as he was thinking it was too late for Brooke to appear, he caught sight of her. Onto the stage walked a tall woman with silver-studded hot pants and a glittering bikini top. Even in a crowded bar, Susie Brooke would not have been a difficult woman to spot, but as she sauntered scantily clad across the stage, her presence was like a searchlight filling the room. Daly sank back into the dark. Brooke's hair had gone a little wild since the last time he saw her, and her skin was covered in false tan. She looked possessed. She lifted her chin toward the audience and wrapped one strong thigh around the shiny pole.

Daly could feel the excitement billow through the crowd like wind in an eager sail. Drunken men pressed closer to the stage. The floor trembled. Susie seemed oblivious to the leering audience. She leaned back, her body straining as if she were about to somersault backward.

The DJ shouted over the thumping music. "Our first contestant tonight is Susie. In her day job she's Armagh's antiracism officer, but tonight, I think you'll all agree, she's political correctness gone mad!"

Daly's head began to spin. The dance floor tipped like the deck of a ship riding a high wave.

The pole trembled as Brooke slid up and down to the grinding rhythm of a Latin dance tune. After each flip and acrobatic move, the crowd cheered lustily. Her eyes remained half closed, her face a blank. Her body had taken over from her senses.

An overweight man bumped into Daly.

"You've the best seat in the pub!" he shouted. "Full view of the stage and within shouting distance of the bar."

Daly nodded uncomfortably.

The man leaned closer. "What do you think of her?"

Daly avoided the glare of his bulging eyes and moved

away. In the meantime, Brooke had finished her routine and stepped off the stage. She spotted him through the crowd and waved. When he raised his hand in awkward acknowledgment, she strode toward him, still on fire with the energy of her dance, her hair damp with exertion.

"That was a revelation," said Daly.

"I'm not much of a dancer," she replied. "I've only taken this up recently."

"You seem to have it backward. Compared to you, I'm an invalid."

She was so close he could see the soft boundary of skin above her bikini where the false tan stopped.

"This is my second adventure this year. Getting up there and dancing is just another source of adrenaline."

"What was your first?"

"Getting a job with the police."

"That's a lot of excitement for one year."

He tried to recall his last adventure. He had to think hard. Falling in love with Anna, he supposed, had been an adventure of sorts, but that had been a decade ago, and he'd jettisoned all his memories of that time and sent them spinning into the void. He gulped from his pint. He was overcome suddenly with the feeling that it was he who was spinning emptily into the void, cast off from the one great romance of his life.

The elastic figure of another dancer swung round the pole. Susie stared at him. He felt her tease around his silence, searching for a point of connection as though it were an ungraspable pole.

"What's bothering you?"

"Nothing."

"Is it the music or the dancing? Something tells me you're not impressed."

"I didn't realize you were going to invite me along to this."

"What do you mean?"

"Watching how long a half-naked colleague can hold her body upside down in front of a crowd of baying drunks."

She shrugged. "I find it empowering."

"Empowering? Now there's an overused word. You know, I've even heard it used to describe charging a mobile phone." He was drunk and could hear the contemptuous dismissal in his voice. "I thought women's lib was against using the body as a sex object."

"My body's not an object."

"Try telling that to the men who crowded the stage."

"If your aim is to humiliate me, then you won't succeed."

"I don't need to try. I thought you were a policewoman, not some sort of wannabe exotic dancer."

She looked disarmed. "I didn't realize you were sexist."

"Me? Sexist? Now you really are political correctness gone mad."

He watched as her face cooled and backed away, disappearing into the swirl of drunken strangers. He realized it was time to go home, before he said or did anything else he might regret.

29

In spite of the half-dozen pints, Daly believed he was in good enough order when he staggered onto the street. He had decided to leave Irwin to his own devices after seeing him take to the center of the dance floor and clear a space like Bambi on ice.

The cloying reek of oil and meat from the nearby fast-food outlets coated the night air. Farther up the street, a snatch of melody floated from a bar where a folk session was in full swing. Daly made his way toward the center of the town. The mood changed dramatically in the square. Chanting from a group of Poland supporters had attracted a rival group of local youths, who began shouting their own songs, peppered with swearing. Young men with grim, pale faces taunting one another. Meat factory workers with the kind of faces that do not wake up expecting sunshine. Daly had seen the inside of the places where they worked. He knew the sheer scale and awesome vacuum of the factory floors, the endless conveyor belts carrying meat carcasses imported from all over the world. He detected something mechanical and automatic in their violent shouting and the way they lined up in front of one another. A few of them had rolled back their shirtsleeves, revealing muscled biceps covered in tattoos.

Perhaps they were motivated by pride in their team, or some kind of patriotism, thought Daly, or perhaps they had gathered in the square because it was difficult to stay sober and rational in the hours of darkness. To express something through their bodies and voices, no matter how meaningless and violent, was the crucial thing.

Daly looked anxiously for a police patrol but saw none. Without warning, a bottle crashed on the pavement in front of him, showering his clothes with glass. He peered at the grim spectacle of youths spoiling for a fight. A few of them turned in his direction. He expected the thrower of the bottle to step forward, but instead another bottle came sailing through the darkness, smashing against the wall above him. This time, the fragments of glass rained down upon his head. It was too close to have been an accident, and the bottle flew too fast to have been thrown with drunken abandon. Daly was convinced it had been aimed straight at him.

He lurched down a side alleyway, blundering against a couple in a furtive embrace. The chanting of the youths turned to roars and shouts, rising into the night air with sudden violence. The sounds of a window smashing added glee and excitement to the drunken voices. He clambered over a low wall and ran along a series of dark alleys filled with bins. Only the noise of the mob gave him any sense of direction. There were further sounds of windows breaking and running footsteps. He caught a glimpse of a lit street, a car slowly moving sideways and then heaving over, and a column of young men clambering on top.

Ten minutes later, he emerged from the warren of alleyways onto a quiet street. He tried to flag down a taxi, but none of them stopped. Relief at having escaped the drunken crowd was undercut by anxiety as to how he was going to get home. He was no longer protected by his detective's ID; in fact, it made him a vulnerable target. He passed walls covered in crude graffiti and racist slogans. He felt stranded in a town dreaming of violence. He was on his own now, too drunk to know where he was going, too disheveled to attract a passing taxi. A car pulled up in front of him and a passenger door opened. It was a private car, not a taxi. Daly thought of clambering in, but hesitated. An arm waved at him urgently.

"What happened to your head, Daly? You're covered in blood," said a voice from the passenger seat. It was Irwin. The Special Branch detective had managed to cadge a lift with the three Polish women.

Daly breathed a sigh of relief and clambered into the back. He sank into the warm seat beside one of the women. Irwin was drunkenly entertaining them with stories about the police.

"What's it like being a detective?" asked the woman driving.

"Murder," replied Irwin and they all laughed

"Honestly, it is hell though," said Irwin. "Don't ever think of joining."

"Tell me something I've always wondered. Is it a crime to go missing, to disappear?" asked the driver a few minutes later.

"What do you mean?"

"I just want to know is it a crime? To leave behind everything, all your responsibilities and relationships. Can you be punished for that?"

"If it is, we haven't done anyone for it yet. How can you arrest someone who has disappeared? It would be like trying to punish a ghost."

"Poor ghosts," she said, and the others laughed again.

When they dropped Daly off at his cottage, he made his way to the bathroom and stared into the scrubby mirror. He tore small pieces of tissue paper and stuck them with blood onto the scratches on his forehead. When he was satisfied with the blood stanching, he examined his coat. The material was full of tiny glass shards. It glittered like a fish tail. He picked out the bigger pieces and shook the coat at the threshold of the front door. He felt relieved. Bar the few scratches, he had survived his drunken jaunt with Irwin. He drank a pint of water and crawled carefully into his bed as though he were slipping into a dark pool.

That night, Lena appeared in a nightmare, only this time their roles were reversed and she was pursuing him. He dreamed he was fishing the river Blackwater in a rowing boat, the currents pulling him deeper into border country, the banks growing wilder, tangled with winter thorns. There was just enough moonlight to make out the shapes of two horsemen searching the undergrowth in opposite directions. One of them, astride a white horse, was Jack Fowler, while the one on the black horse resembled the man who had tried to kidnap Lena.

His fishing line snagged and then jolted fiercely, almost capsizing the boat. He had hooked something from the depths of the river. He reeled in the line, and to his surprise the black-haired head of a woman broke through the waters. Then in a splash, her arms and torso appeared.

It was Lena Novak. She rose, loose limbed as a runner, from the churning water, wrenching herself free from his fishing line. The boat rocked violently, and he struggled to keep it afloat. When he looked back, her face had aged, her cheekbones grown sharper, her skin paler.

Suddenly it was Anna, rising out of the water, her bare feet tangled in weeds, her legs riding the swell of the river toward him. His impulse was to flee. He rowed to the bank as if his life depended on it. Then he took off into the forest, but no matter how hard he ran, he was unable to shake her off. Everywhere he turned, he saw the elongated shadows of Lena's running body followed by the galloping horses, but it was Anna's voice that he heard echoing in the forest, calling his name repeatedly.

He ran until he reached his cottage. He had just managed to shut the door tightly when it began to crack. It shook and fell apart, and in she stumbled, falling in a tumble across the stone-flag floor, her limbs entangling with upended furniture. The wet shroud of her dress was sodden and twisted, mud and river creatures spilling onto the floor.

When he lifted the strands of black hair that had wrapped themselves across her features, he fell back in surprise. The face of a skeletal old woman stared back at him.

He woke up, breathing hard. For a few moments, he was afraid he had completely lost control of his thoughts. He got up and took comfort from the unchanged position of his furniture, the table and chairs, and the solid presence of the locked door. The cottage's nooks and corners looked reassuringly familiar in the moonlight streaming through the small windows. He stood for a while in the middle of the room. A bird scrabbled on the roof. He tried to recall the precise details of his nightmare, to clutch at some clues it might offer as to what was going on inside his head. He wanted to know where the images of the dream had come from. Was it his subconscious trying to work through the mystery of Lena's flight, or a signal of something darker from within? The first dim light of dawn crept through the window. A lough wind swept against the glass pane, and the rooster began to crow.

He made himself a cup of tea and sat at the kitchen table. He was worried that six months into his divorce, after months of self-control and enforced celibacy, some pressure in his psyche was beginning to show signs of eruption. The catalyst had been Lena, he realized. This woman with whom he had snatched only a few minutes of conversation, and whose brief touch had set alarm bells ringing deep within; this woman who had been accused of orchestrating a blackmail plot, and who might even have the blood of two men on her hands.

There were certain people who slipped through the nets of society, he thought. Women like Lena. Women weighed down by disaster. No one wanted to know them. No one said good-bye to them. They were the people a detective should not sympathize too strongly with, because the danger was they could pull you down into the depths with them, and leave you with no way back to the surface.

30

In the early morning light, the ghost estate belonged to another dimension; an unfinished, shadowy version of the happily populated estate depicted on the advertising billboards.

In the ground-floor bedroom of number 62, Lena woke from a shallow sleep, thinking she had heard a cry, female and frightened, from one of the houses opposite—but it might have been just a dream. The sound of doors banging shut and keys turning in locks had haunted her mind all night.

She climbed out of bed and got dressed, picking her way round an empty wine bottle and a glass. After checking that no one was watching, she stepped out the back door and into a field overgrown with brambles. There were no hedges or fences separating the houses. From the back door, she stepped directly into a thorny wilderness. In the weak sunshine, she recognized the tiny cream flowers filling the bushes as blackberry blossoms from the thickets that bordered her village back in Croatia. The weather in this country changed so frequently it left her unsure about the time of the year, but she knew it was not yet the season for picking blackberries. When that time came, she hoped to be back with her family in the forests of Velebit. That would be her goal, she decided, to climb the slopes of the mountains, free of fear, and crush the ripe fat berries with her bare feet. She would no longer be an exile from the season of berry picking.

She caught a bus into town and spent the morning in the library. You could spend as much time as you liked there, as long as you were quiet. She scanned the local newspapers for stories of prostitution, smuggling, and fraud. She checked the court reports and police briefings to the press, but found herself wading through page after page of stories about motoring offenses committed by Eastern European drivers. She wondered if it was a policy of the papers to report every single crime and misdemeanor committed by a foreign national. She wondered how any reader would even venture out in a car. The news coverage gave the impression that the border roads were plagued with apocalyptic lawlessness.

She tried to match the names of perpetrators and victims with the names of the trafficked women from the farmhouse brothel. It proved difficult since the journalists often spelled names incorrectly or confused surnames with first names. In addition, she kept coming across the names of famous characters from Croatian literature and history. She suspected that some of her compatriots had provided the police with false information.

A male librarian took an interest in what she was doing. He helped her locate backdated issues and track court stories that had been heard in different jurisdictions. At one point, he leaned close to her and stared into her eyes. Then he let his gaze travel down the length of her body to the shiny leather of her boots. Though he was in his late thirties, his chin had only managed to sprout an unconvincing goatee of fine brown hair. The way in which he pushed his glasses back up the bridge of his nose to frame his expressionless eyes triggered an unpleasant image in Lena's memory.

"Where have I seen you before?" he whispered.

She sighed. Sometimes it was easier when people pretended she did not exist. She spoke clearly, breaking up the words with pauses, as though delivering an announcement to the entire library, which was filling up with pensioners, young mothers, and a few stray schoolchildren.

"The last time we met," she said, "I was in the prostitute business."

The librarian hurried away from her with such indecent haste he almost knocked over a shelf of hardbacks.

She flicked through the newspapers for another hour, but there was no sign of the name she wanted to find, even though she was alert to all its misspellings. It was the name of a man responsible for a hundred crimes, but none of them had been reported. The man who had abused her soul more cruelly than the men who ravaged her body. The only clue to his presence was a story about a twenty-six-year-old Croatian woman charged with prostitution and released on bail paid by a cousin. Her name was Dinah. According to the report, the cousin had agreed to keep her at an address on Altmore Drive.

Lena chose her time carefully. It was late evening when she slipped into the shadows of the bus shelter on Altmore Drive and waited for Dinah to show. It was important that she would have no advance warning of their encounter.

Shortly after 11:00 p.m., a taxi pulled up at a house. Lena watched a woman struggle out of the vehicle, laden with plastic bags that clinked as she staggered along the pavement. It was Dinah, all right, a pale, dark-eyed version of the fresh-faced girl Lena remembered. It had only been a month since she had said good-bye to her in the farmhouse brothel, but the girl looked as though she had spent the intervening period living on the doorstep of an off-license.

Lena slipped quietly into the house behind her. When Dinah saw the dark figure standing in the hall, her legs almost gave way. She bumped against furniture, unsure what to do. There was a strong whiff of alcohol from her breath. When she had gathered herself, she sat down on the sofa, slowly entwining her fingers with her scarf. The lid of her left eye was swollen, and an ugly bruise had mushroomed under her cheekbone.

"Why are you here, Lena?" she asked, her voice squeezed in her throat.

Lena didn't answer. She went into the kitchen, made two cups of tea, and placed one beside Dinah. She resisted the impulse to reach out and stroke her swollen cheek. Her face was a raw lump of flesh that Lena wanted to shape back to its former beauty.

"Why are you staring at me?" said Dinah.

"No reason."

"The night you were to escape from the farmhouse, I couldn't keep my thoughts straight. I was so worried about you."

"So worried you told Sergei about my plans?"

"It wasn't me, Lena. I swear." She was frantic in her denial, but her eyes darted about the room, as though there was an incriminating image in her head she was trying to avoid.

Lena felt herself flush with anger.

"What are you doing now?" she asked, keeping her tone even.

"I've a job in a nightclub. The pay is good."

Lena watched as a silent shadow fell across Dinah's exhausted face. Her eyes were empty.

"It's not too late for you, Lena," she said, imploring. "You can still come back. Jozef will find work for you." She seemed convinced that Lena would want to return to her old life.

"I'd rather die than go back."

"But Jozef will find you if you don't. He has people everywhere. He's stronger than you. He'll win in the end."

"What do you mean by win?"

"He'll kill you." The features of her face grew loose with fear, as she tried to hold back the tears.

"I have to go in a moment," said Lena. "Do you remember the doll I gave you? There was a piece of paper inside it with a telephone number and the names of the others. I need it now."

"I have it somewhere." Dinah got up and rummaged in a drawer. She handed Lena a crumpled sheet of paper.

Finally, Lena had the information she needed to set her plan in motion. She placed it carefully in her handbag. Help was only a telephone number away. Her head felt clear and bright, as though a dark cloud had suddenly dissolved. Staring at Dinah's anxious face, she felt a little guilty at the feeling of elation rising in her chest.

"Where's Mikolajek now?"

"I don't know."

"You're lying."

A look came over Dinah's face as though she was suffering from an attack of cramp.

"I'm sorry, I need a drink," she mumbled and went into the kitchen. Lena waited for a moment and then followed her. She found her standing over the sink with a mobile phone pressed to her ear. She was muttering in Croatian. When she saw Lena, she gave a guilty start.

"You have to run now, Lena," she said, stuffing the phone into a bag. She looked weak and forlorn, unable to return Lena's gaze.

"Who did you call?" Lena took the phone from her.

Dinah began to cry. "I had to tell Jozef. Otherwise he'd hurt me. He paid my bail. Without him, I'd be still in jail. He told me that himself."

Lena forgave her immediately. It wasn't her fault that Mikolajek still held her in the grip of terror. She looked in the girl's eyes and saw her past.

"I can save you, Dinah, if you come with me now."

"I can't. I have to work." Her voice was dull.

"You still have your life ahead of you. You have to

choose whether you want to stay like this or take a risk and find your freedom."

Before Dinah could answer, the phone in Lena's hand started to ring. She should have ignored it and made her exit. After all, she had everything to lose and nothing to gain, but she reasoned she had already set herself on the road that would take her back to Jozef Mikolajek. There was no turning now. She pressed the answer button.

"Hello?" she said.

The caller sighed. "Lena."

The hairs on the back of her neck stood on end.

"Lena? I know you're there. I hear you're looking for me. What's the matter? Need someone to help pack your suitcase?"

"I have things to do," she replied, prompted into speech by his sarcasm. "I'm not planning on leaving any time soon."

"You're not going anywhere, Lena. That's your problem."

"What do you mean?"

"I've watched women like you before. You've left the game and now you're in the first flush of excitement. You think you've escaped to some sort of paradise, but the chances are that feeling won't last. Have you thought of what you're going to do for money? Do you fancy cleaning floors or working in a meat factory?"

"I don't need to work. Jack said he was leaving me money. Enough to set me up for life."

"The IRA bastard told you that?" Violence poked through his voice like a nasty cough.

"He set up a bank account in my name. It was our contingency plan."

"Then why haven't you taken the money and run?"

"I need a passport to withdraw it. A form of ID. Jack was trying to get me one before he..."

Mikolajek cut her off. "How much money is in this account?"

"About £1 million."

He gave a low whistle and was silent. When he spoke again, his voice was tinged with sardonic respect.

"What if I give you a passport?"

"I don't want anything to do with you."

"But let's play if," he persisted. "Here you are with a fortune at your fingertips but no way to access it. Here I am, falling over with enthusiasm to help you. You know I kept your old passport as a souvenir. It's a bit dog-eared but I'm sure it will do."

"And what do you get out of this deal?" Lena knew that Mikolajek had no more intention of letting her take the money and disappear than he had of joining a flower-arranging class.

"I'm just a plain businessman at heart. Give me a share of the money. Say fifty percent. It's not as much as I took when you were working for me, but then you're in a stronger bargaining position now."

Lena said nothing.

"I'll send a car round to collect you now. Before the banks close today, you'll have your hands on your little nest egg." She could hear the impatience rise in his voice.

"You murdered Jack. Why should I trust you?"

Mikolajek sneered. "It was suicide. The police will never prove otherwise. By the way, you know what his last request was that morning? He wanted to listen to a piece of opera music. He said it reminded him of you. How pathetic was that?"

"I never believed it."

"Believed what?"

"That you were so full of evil. Otherwise, I never would have persuaded him to rescue me. I never would have risked myself. Or him."

"If you believe that, then why are you talking to me now?"

"Because I'm not afraid. I've been through everything bad a woman my age can experience."

"What about death?"

"I'm not afraid of that, either, but I have one thing left to do. And that is visit Jack's grave to tell him I've avenged his murder. To do that I have to find you. I have to wait for you to make your move. And when you do, I promise to cling to you and drag you all the way down to the gates of hell."

31

Daly sat in his car. During daylight, the street was drowned in traffic noises from the nearby bypass, but at night, the teeming sounds condensed into the hollow roar of single lorries speeding toward the ports. During the gaps in traffic, the street was claustrophobically quiet. He parked in the same place every evening after work, about fifty yards from number 29, but not once did he see the front door open.

A dog barked each time he rang the doorbell. Another disembodied sound mingling with the distant thunder of traffic. The animal gnashed his teeth as though it was about to burst through the locked door and spring for his throat. At other times, he heard furtive movements, but no one answered the door. A derelict sign hung above the letterbox. HOME SWEET HOME CLEANERS, it read, but the place was a poor advertisement for a cleaning company. The walls were peeling of paint, and torn-up cardboard filled the front windows in place of blinds. Even the doorbell looked dingy and neglected.

Daly had considered raiding the house, but what he really needed was a key to unlock the confidence of whoever dwelled within. Turning up on the fourth evening of his vigil, he saw that someone had smashed the front window. The next night, vandals had daubed "Go Home Scum" across the wall and spattered paint over the front door. The house resembled a target on a firing range for racists. When it got dark, a single streetlight came on. He wondered whether the others were broken or if the local council had stopped replacing bulbs as part of its spending cutbacks. It was cold and the darkness suited the house and the grim slogans. The street was blacked out, at war with itself. Little wonder that the door of number 29 never opened to unannounced visitors.

Daly tried to ask questions of the neighbors. Only one woman could be bothered to talk to him without showing bare contempt for the inhabitants of the house. She told Daly that the women who lived there came and went in secret. A van with HOME SWEET HOME CLEANERS painted on it collected them every morning before dawn. The driver made the women cover the windows with black bin bags. Then he packed the van with vacuum cleaners, detergents, and industrial cleaning machines.

"Are they illegal immigrants?" the neighbor asked Daly.

"I don't know."

"It's supposed to be a cleaning company, but God knows what else goes on behind the closed doors of that house. Some of those women don't come back till after midnight. I've seen them fall out of the van, exhausted to the bone.

None of them speak English. What can you do? I mention it to my husband, but he says mind my own business."

Daly rang the house's telephone number at least a dozen times. His tentative approach confirmed his suspicion that Martha Havel did not lead a normal, ordinary life in which people wake up, go to work, eat, watch TV, and then go to bed again. A different girl with a foreign accent answered each time he called. Each conversation proved as fruitless as the last.

"I want to speak to Martha Havel," he would begin.

"Martha's not here. Who's calling?"

"Celcius Daly. I'm a detective. I'm trying to find Lena Novak. When will Martha be in?"

"When she comes back."

"When's that?"

"Not sure. She comes and goes as she pleases."

"Who is this?"

"Try later."

Eventually his persistence paid off. He rang late one evening, and a woman's voice answered. She sounded older, in charge, but playful at the same time.

"Are you a gentleman friend?" she asked immediately.

"What's a gentleman friend?"

Her voice jingled with laughter. "The men who help pay the bills."

"What about Jack Fowler? Was he a gentleman friend?"

There was a wary silence. Daly heard a spark of interest but also fear in her next question.

"Who wants to know?"

"Celcius Daly."

"You're the policeman looking for Lena." Her voice was thoughtful.

"That's correct."

"This is Martha Havel."

"Look Martha, I know it's difficult to trust a stranger, but I need to talk to you about Lena. She's in danger."

"When can you come round?"

Daly had to wait several minutes before Martha Havel opened the door. She was blond haired and in her early forties. She barely glanced at him before leading him down a narrow corridor. Her combination of figure-hugging denim, black boots, and a tight top struck Daly as the classic Eastern European style. All that was missing was the black plastic handbag anchored to the shoulder.

A door lay open to the kitchen where a bottle of vodka and a butchered meat carcass sat on top of a table smeared with blood. Someone had been tenderizing a hunk of beef. The sight of the tattered flesh sitting raw and uncovered looked almost obscene to Daly's eyes.

She caught his stare. "Some of the men who visit work in the meat factories. Instead of roses or chocolates, they bring the girls steak."

She led him into a tiny sitting room. There were only two armchairs in the room. She sat down and gestured to Daly to take the other. Before he could accept her hospitality, there was the small matter of the man lounging in the offered seat. Tattoos and scars of abuse covered his muscled arms. He stared at Daly. There was no warmth or hospitality in his gaze. Daly caught a sour whiff of alcohol and sweat and felt nauseously sober.

Martha spoke to the man in Croatian, her voice edgy. His mouth automatically turned down into what was doubtless a practiced sneer. He glared at Daly and trudged up the stairs, returning to sleep or whatever it was pimps did during their free time. Meanwhile, Martha had moved to the edge of her seat, closer to the door, closer to the phone.

She lit a cigarette and regarded Daly with a look that suggested defiance, or was it fear?

"So you're the detective," she said. Her face disappeared behind a cloud of smoke. Only her bright red lips remained visible.

"That's right," replied Daly.

The smoke cleared a little. She flicked some ash into a beer bottle. Her eyelids fluttered in the haze.

"Before I tell you about Lena, you can do me a favor."

Daly leaned back in his chair. That there were goods to be bartered was a promising sign for their encounter.

"There's a man causing me bother."

"A client of yours."

"Just the once, then I barred him. That's the first thing you learn in my business. Watch out for the new ones. Especially the nervous types." She regarded Daly closely. "They can be right fuckin' trouble. A few nights ago he came by and smashed the front window."

"How long has he been harassing you?"

"A couple of weeks. He painted those signs on the wall."

"We have a new antiracism officer. I'll get her to give you a ring."

"Can't you just lock him up? Or do they have to be out-and-out psychos and serial killers before you intervene?" She kept her voice light and even, but Daly could see that her teeth were on edge.

"When the antiracism officer interviews you, tell her you have no idea why this man is abusing you in this manner. Tell her you believe it's racism, pure and simple. If he's convicted, he'll get a tough sentence."

She nodded. Daly saw a bruise, dark and purple, on the side of her neck. She clamped her hand to the spot as if aware of his attention.

"Have you seen Lena Novak?"

"I see lots of girls like Lena. They come to me when they're in trouble."

"What kind of trouble?"

"They get into a fight with their boss. Or fall in love with the wrong man."

Daly thought to himself that girls like Lena were already deep in trouble long before they came running to Martha for help.

"Usually they stay a while until they're ready to go back," she continued. "Lena was different."

"How?"

"She had a plan. Few of the girls who come here have ever begun to plan. All they have is running on their minds. They don't realize that escape is all about planning and money."

"Do you help them out?"

She laughed. "In spite of what it says outside, this place isn't home sweet home." Her head lolled slightly but her blond hair remained fixed. It struck him that she was wearing a wig.

"What about Lena? What was her plan?"

"She didn't tell me, but she had money. And knew how to get her hands on more."

"Where did she go after calling here?"

"Some other place."

"Where?"

"She had lots of places."

"What do you mean?"

"She had more door keys than a jailer. Houses, apartments, turnkey developments, all part of Fowler's property empire."

"Do you have the addresses?"

"She didn't tell me anything. She was too scared. Her boss is a man called Jozef Mikolajek. He'll catch her sooner or later. His contacts are everywhere."

"Everywhere? Including here?"

Martha chose not to answer the question. She inhaled and exhaled cigarette smoke.

"Perhaps Lena thought it was smarter not to stay with you," continued Daly. "What sort of business relationship do you have with Mikolajek?"

She shrugged. "He lets me run this place in peace. For a fat fee, of course. After that, I have nothing to do with him. Ask anyone. Anyone who knows."

"What about the women who work for you. Do they know?"

"You can try."

"Meaning they won't say anything."

"You can always get a translator."

Each of her answers was the verbal equivalent of stubbing out a cigarette with the heel of a boot.

"Why do you give a damn about Lena?" she asked. "She's a prostitute. An illegal immigrant. She wouldn't think twice about double-crossing you."

"I'm under no illusions."

Daly showed her a still from the CCTV footage taken at Lena's flat. She flicked it with her fingernail.

"When was this taken?" she asked.

"A couple of days ago."

"Maybe he's business. Lena's business."

"This man and whoever he is working for is trying to track her down. He tried to kidnap her outside a café in Aughnacloy, but fortunately, she was able to give him the slip. Staff at the café said Lena was a frequent visitor. If she keeps hanging around her old haunts, he'll find her again."

Martha's left knee began to jiggle as she spoke. Something was making her anxious.

"You're probably right, but what alternative does she have? Where else can she go?"

Daly didn't say anything, waiting for her tension to build.

"This man who's following her. Is he Croatian?"

"No. Irish. He walks with a limp."

She relaxed slightly. "Lena is more afraid of her

compatriots than any Irishman. No matter how far she runs, Mikolajek and his friends can always hurt her family back in Croatia."

"If you help me find her, I can arrest Mikolajek on the basis of her evidence. Put him behind bars. She'll never have to worry about him again."

"You're telling me the truth? You'll really arrest that pig Mikolajek?" She laughed. "He won't let go of this. I've seen what he has done to other girls. No one crosses him and gets away with it."

"Then you know that Lena is playing a very dangerous game. You must tell me where I can find her. Otherwise, I'll have this place turned over by my officers and Special Branch. After that I'll send in immigration, the tax man, and environmental health to mop up the dregs of whatever's left of your business."

Daly hunched forward and stared at her face, waiting for her mask to crack. Instead, a light switched on in her face. A light that made her ask the question that Daly had feared.

"Tell me one thing, Inspector. Are you here as part of an official police investigation?"

Daly said nothing. He rubbed the stubble on his face.

"Why haven't you brought more officers and raided this place? All these phone calls you make. Like a lonely obsessive. Hardly the normal behavior of a detective in charge of a missing person case."

Daly blinked. Perhaps the investigation *had* degenerated into an obsession.

She sat back with a smile on her face. Like a woman

being served an unexpected glass of champagne. "You've no authority to be here. You're working on your own."

Daly said nothing.

"And you're trying to tell me," she said, "that there's nothing the least personal about your interest in Lena Novak?"

He considered his answer carefully. "She helps keep my detective skills sharp." He felt like a man choosing the shortest piece of rope possible before passing it to a hangman.

"No doubt."

She leaned forward and gazed at Daly. He noticed that several buttons of her blouse were undone. She looked as though she were about to share an intimate secret.

"I like Irishmen," she said. "At least the ones who know what they want."

"I'm here as a detective, nothing else."

"But that's not the whole truth. Your motives for coming here are a little bit more complicated than those of an honest policeman."

She leaned back and took a long draw of her cigarette.

"I'm finally figuring you out. I should have seen it from the start. You're like a crossword puzzle where every line spells out the phrase midlife crisis. Are you married?"

"Yes. I mean, no." Daly hesitated. "You wouldn't understand."

"I understand that your love life is probably a mess."

"That's none of your business." Daly did not like the direction the conversation was going in.

"It's my business to make sure men don't feel ashamed or embarrassed. And I can see I've made you uncomfortable.

You're dedicated to your work. That's why you've come here looking for Lena. Every day you have to deal with lies and secrets, fear and violence. You're sick of sweeping the streets of crime. Deep down all you want is a girl who'll let you stop being yourself for a night."

Daly closed his eyes for a moment. He looked back at her. She had the strange talent of sounding caring yet scornful.

"It's one thing to go to a brothel and pay for a woman," she said. "It's another to be in love with a woman who is a fugitive. Forever out of your reach. What must that do for you? For your sense of psychological tension? To be constantly denied pleasure, does that make the attraction stronger or weaker?"

Daly felt the color in his cheeks betray him.

"I didn't come here to be interrogated," he said.

"No. I didn't think so."

Daly got up to leave. A few more questions and all his inner demons would have emerged, hunched and gloating, at her shoulder. He decided that Martha Havel was dangerous company. She knew too much about the dark world of fantasies that filled the human mind. That was why men paid to be with her and kept coming back. She helped lead them into the traps they set for themselves.

She followed him out to the door.

"Will you come back?"

"What for?"

"To talk. To tell me what you find out about Lena?"

"Let's wait and see."

She shivered slightly, framed against the light of the

kitchen. Daly's last sight of the room was of the crimson slices of meat lying strewn across the table like a woman's casually discarded garments.

Later, in his cottage, Daly put on the stove and made himself a cup of tea. He stared through the kitchen window at the twisted half mile of back lanes that led down to the edge of Lough Neagh. Waves rolled in from the north; not very menacing ones, but rough enough to chase even the pluckiest of fishermen back to their homes.

Fifteen minutes later, he had walked down to the empty shore. He felt the power of the wind as it whipped the waves higher and higher. He loitered for a while, watching the waves break on the stony shore. A dog from a nearby cottage gave out brief yelps above the wind.

He wondered if it was too late to save Lena. He felt divided from her by more than distance and the inevitable cultural barriers. There was also the dividing line between the sexes. She might as well have been on the other side of the world, or on some distant planet, he thought. He turned for home seeing a shower of rain advance from the west. Behind him, the waves jostled together in an uneasy lough.

32

It was the evening rush hour. Daylight dimmed and the lorries picked up speed. Bin bags and freshly laundered sheets drifted above the crashed Home Sweet Home van. As each lorry thundered by, the loose sheets pounced on each other with renewed energy before drifting back to earth and snagging on brambles and thorn trees. To the motorists speeding by, it looked as though the wind was conducting a frantic cleaning operation through the hedgerows.

A hundred yards along the road, a group of women huddled together in a bus stop shelter. Their clothes were torn, and some of them carried injuries. They looked up at the dazzle of lights from the approaching police cars as though their wait was finally over. Soon the traffic stopped and the roadside was alive with people, everyone active, everyone moving, paramedics, fire and police officers, and then, later, when they discovered the blood, the SOC officers, laying out their flickering lines of luminescent tape. The women remained glued to the bench. They stared at the labyrinth of police tape in confusion as though it had turned the crash scene into a complicated riddle, until they were eventually coaxed with the help of a translator along a path of concerned faces into the back of an ambulance.

Daly crossed the motorway and followed the trail of glass diamonds from the crashed van's windshield along the verge and into the ditch. The person he was searching for was not among the huddle of women in the ambulance. The firefighters congregated around the van with their cutting tools, but there were no bodies in the badly damaged vehicle. He made his way round the van slowly. He walked along the windblown hedge, staring at the cleaning rags and dustsheets that had escaped from the back of the vehicle. Rain and hawthorn blossoms blew in his face. In the damp grass he found a human oddity, a blond wig cut in a bob. Dropping it into an evidence bag, he caught the whiff of cigarette smoke. A feeling of unease gathered in his stomach.

A traffic police officer talked him through the accident.

"The van was traveling west at about sixty miles per hour," he explained. "Driving conditions were good and there were no hazards on the road. We believe another vehicle struck it on the side. Judging from the paint marks left on the van, it was colored black. The impact caused the driver to lose control of the vehicle. He swerved onto the grass verge; the vehicle flipped on its side and slid into the ditch, upending several small bushes. We found a pool of blood in the passenger seat and drag marks where someone had been pulled from the van. There's a set of tire marks farther along the grass verge. We found the passengers sheltering in the bus stop. They say the driver of a dark-colored Jeep forced them off the road. The van driver was able to walk free and made off on foot, but the other passenger is unaccounted for; her name is Martha Havel."

Daly raised a hand when he saw Irwin walking amid the emergency personnel. The Special Branch detective looked a little disoriented. Daly waited, watching for a change in his behavior after their heart-to-heart in the pub.

Irwin merely stared at the crashed van and said nothing, as though he had decided it was tactically best to give no comment. His eyes were withdrawn a little deeper into his skull, his face all lines and hollows in the fading light. What was the sharp expression hovering just below the customary one of barely suppressed boredom? Was it hurt or embarrassment? Daly wondered.

"You're not still hungover, are you?" he asked as Irwin leaned against the side of a police car. Gone was his air of having seen it all before.

"No. But my love life isn't in the best of health."

"At least you still have one."

Irwin stared at the crashed van with an evaluating frown.

"How can someone tell you that you're not in love?"

"Who said that?"

"Poppy. She told me I wasn't capable of knowing true love, but I told her it's the most I've ever felt for anyone. I can't imagine finding those feelings with anyone else."

Daly looked away. He wanted to tell Irwin that you did not find love through other people. It had to be awoken from within.

"You know what?" said Irwin. "I'm tired of women."

Daly was about to say he was tired of women, too, but he wasn't sure if either of them understood what that really meant. Did it mean they were tired of love or tired of sex, or just weary of trying to make sense of their feelings and sharing them with another person?

The wind picked up, catching one of the dustsheets snagged in the hedge, beating it like a trapped wing. Irwin stared at it intensely as though it was some sort of signal. His eyes flicked over the van and the ambulance full of frightened women.

"More foreign nationals," he said with a grunt. "What have we got? Drink-driving?"

"There are a few points of interest. The driver's done a runner, and a passenger's missing. A Croatian woman called Martha Havel."

"It's never simple, is it?"

Daly filled him in with what the traffic officer had told him.

"Do you think we'll get the driver?" asked Irwin.

"Of course we'll find him."

"He's probably fled across the border."

"We'll check the hospitals for any road casualties."

They looked at each other. "Just a crazy piece of driving?" asked Irwin. "Or something more sinister?"

"The driver will point us in the right direction when we find him."

They located the translator and got him to question the women in the ambulance. One of the women stood up and sat down again, mumbling in Croatian. There were fresh cuts on her face.

"What did she say?"

The translator shrugged. "She feels sick. She wants to vomit."

"Ask them where Martha Havel is," Daly persisted.

"They say she vanished off the roadside," replied the translator after conversing with the women.

Daly felt a shiver pass through him. "How?" he asked.

The women grew edgy and started to argue with one another. The intensity of their voices changed, the words hurrying out, as though blown on by the wind.

"It was the driver who forced them off the road. He dragged her into his Jeep. He had a limp. She was bleeding and her hair fell off."

Daly wanted to ask them more questions, but the women began to mumble fervently and raise their eyes to the ambulance roof.

The translator turned to Daly. "You won't get any more sense out of them. The shock has robbed them of their reason."

Some of the women began to weep.

Irwin intervened. "We'll decide how useful what they say is. You've been sent here to translate, not to comment or be involved in any way in the investigation."

"Of course," said the translator. "I understand this is important. What else do you want me to ask them?"

Irwin turned to Daly. "At least he learns fast."

"We need you to find out as much information as possible

232

about the driver of the Jeep," said Daly. "Take your time, if necessary."

They left the translator with the women and went back to the van.

"Another kidnap," said Daly. "First the attempted abduction of Lena Novak, then the women in the illegal bottling factory. And now Martha Havel. All of them Croatian. All of them linked to criminal activity."

"Who would want to hurt a vanload of cleaners, let alone kidnap one of them?" asked Irwin. "It doesn't add up."

"You forget these women are treated as property," replied Daly.

"You're suggesting the motive is theft."

"Possibly."

"There must be something more to it than that," said Irwin. "What if we can't work it out?"

"We have to," said Daly. "These people have been abducted with a specific aim in mind, for a specific reason."

"They were kidnapped once before. From their homelands. Perhaps they're being abducted and trafficked elsewhere."

Daly stared at the crashed van and its mud-spattered sign. *Home sweet home,* he thought. Even misery became a kind of home, for people who expected no better. The wind rifled through the vehicle's spilled contents, sending dustsheets and bin liners flapping through the branches of a thorn tree. He had the feeling he was still scurrying through the shadows of border country, chasing Lena

Novak's disappearing footsteps. The problem was he never knew exactly where he was going, blindly following a road that twisted and fell, pulled up by helping hands only for other hands to push him back down into darkness again.

33

The women in the houses next door to the Home Sweet Home Cleaning Company stepped out through their doors and stared up at the sky for a long time. The evening light was tinged with pink and blue. A look of surprise passed across their faces. A trail of smoke rising from one of the back gardens grew into a torrent of ash and sparks. Scraps of burning paper billowed over the slate roofs. Someone yelled and the women burst onto the street, jumping into the air, grabbing handfuls of smoldering ash.

Dark clouds advanced and broke, but it was not rain that fell. When Daly and Irwin arrived on the street, looking for the injured driver of the van, the sky was drizzling burned money. At the first sign of swirling police lights, the neighbors, some of whom had collected thousands of pounds' worth in scorched notes, ran back into the houses, slamming their front doors.

Only the door of Home Sweet Home remained ajar. The two detectives walked quickly through the house and out the back.

A young Croatian man was doing laps of the garden with a wheelbarrow, ferrying heaps of paper from a metal shed to a blazing bonfire. He had stripped to his waist, revealing an athletic build. A bandage, wrapped around his head like a sweatband, had slipped over a swollen, bloody eye.

Burning paper and disintegrating ash filled the air, like bats fleeing a cave at dusk. One of the pieces swirled in front of Daly's face. A glowing ember nibbled at the edge of the Queen's face. It was a fifty-pound note.

When the Croatian looked up and saw the two detectives approaching, he froze, the wheelbarrow poised to tip another load onto the fire.

"That's enough!" shouted Daly.

He did not refuse Daly's request. His broad face was suffused with weariness. He stared at Daly. A sharp racking cough took hold of him.

"You're injured. How can you run around a garden with a wheelbarrow?"

"I have to do what the boss says." His eyes clouded over as another coughing fit overtook him.

"And then what are you going to do?"

"Run." He swatted at a burning ember.

"Where?"

"Anywhere. You can't stop me." He tipped the contents of the barrow onto the fire. Another batch of notes left in a hurry, disintegrating into the spark-filled smoke.

"You need a doctor."

The man scratched the bandage, blood soaking through to his fingertips. He swayed on his feet, surrounded by smoke and a circling wind of exhaustion. Then the light in his eyes went out, and he collapsed to the ground.

It took two days for the police to finish questioning the injured driver and the women employed by the Home Sweet Home Cleaning Company. Officers compiled a draft report of their findings, which ran to more than fifty pages. The essence of the report was that the cleaning company, as well as operating as a brothel, had been used as a clearing house for counterfeit notes.

Fearing that a police investigation into the crash would reveal the sordid extent of his activities, Mikolajek had ordered the injured driver to burn whatever counterfeit money was in the house and any other evidence that might link him to Home Sweet Home. However, Daly was confident that the outline of his criminal empire would still take shape before the courts and ensure that Mikolajek would be locked away for a lengthy sentence. They just had to apprehend him first.

As well as ferrying the cleaners back and forth from their place of work, the Home Sweet Home van had operated two daily shifts as a mobile brothel, an early and a late, usually with two women on board. The van traveled everywhere, from agricultural shows to horse races and nightclub parking lots on weekends. The average number of clients per girl was six a shift. The women charged £60 for half an hour, and Mikolajek's "petrol money" cut was £40, the standard two-thirds. The average weekly turnover of the van and its various employments amounted to no less than £5,000.

Jozef Mikolajek knew how easy it was for police to shut up a brothel run from a house. From the back of a van was a different matter altogether. Police recovered several mobile phones from the vehicle. The scheme he had set up was simple to operate and easy to dodge police surveillance. The punter rang or texted one of a set of numbers that were advertised in the back of tabloid newspapers. "*Is Olga available today*" and "*hv u a J-lo on yr blk*" were two of the less obscene messages uncovered by police. The girls were then dispatched in the van with a description of the punter, to meet at a prearranged place. They were instructed to make the encounter look like a blind date and take him back to the van.

"Mikolajek must be shitting like a rabbit," said Irwin after he had read the report.

"It doesn't matter whether he flees the country or not, he's finished," said Daly.

"And Martha Havel, too, wherever she is."

"She's gone," said Daly. "Like Lena Novak. And the other trafficked women. I'm beginning to doubt if we'll ever find them."

34

Daly heard the squawking of his hens through his sleep. For the past few days they had been breaking out of their enclosure and showing up in a ragged troupe at his front doorstep, which they used as target practice, spattering it with excrement.

It took him a while to rouse himself. It was Sunday. He had spent the morning clearing weeds from the potato patch at the back of the house, and afterward, seated in an armchair, he had nodded off in front of a turf fire.

The fire had dwindled to a few gray ashes when he awoke. He felt the raw cold creep under the drafty door. His body ached. He walked over to the window, still drugged from sleep, wondering what had disturbed the hens. To his surprise, he saw the figure of Irwin remonstrating with the upset flock, waving his arms in the air with as much dignity as a drunken man could muster.

He opened the door and found the Special Branch detective covered in feathers.

"You don't need a doorbell with hens like these running about," said Irwin.

Daly did not reply, just backed away slightly, which Irwin took as an invitation to enter.

"It's a wonder I found you in the middle of all these twisting lanes and gable-ends of cottages," said Irwin.

He dipped his head at the lowness of the door and stumbled across the threshold.

"I've finally located your nest," he said, and then peering into the darkness, "or is it a cave. Where has all the bloody light gone?"

"What brought you out here?" asked Daly.

"Oh, this and that."

Daly stared at him. The Special Branch detective was being uncharacteristically evasive.

Irwin sprawled across the small sofa, like a tired dog taking up too much room. "Now I know why you're so introspective." He surveyed the dim interior of the living room. "Can't you at least switch on a few lights to kill the gloom?"

Daly switched on a low lamp.

"I had the day off," explained Irwin. "So I thought I'd check out the scenery around the lough shore. You've mentioned it. Once or twice."

"Who is she?"

"Who are you talking about?"

"Are you seeing a new woman? Someone who lives nearby?"

"No," said Irwin with sudden bitterness. "There's no one else." He looked to be on the verge of tears. "In fact, I haven't had sex for over a month."

He looked at Daly. "I know you've gone for longer without. What with your separation and all. But this is driving me crazy." An agony of embarrassment filled his long features. "I still love Poppy. More than makes sense to me."

Daly went into the kitchen and brewed a fresh pot of tea.

"The truth is I drove out here to visit you," said Irwin as Daly handed him a cup.

"All the way out here just to see me?"

"Yes."

"Why?"

"I thought you'd understand what I'm going through."

Neither spoke for a long time.

"Any cigarettes?" asked Irwin hopefully.

When Daly returned to the living room with an unopened packet, he found Irwin busy searching the sofa, fishing behind the cushions with the expertise of someone searching for contraband.

He grinned sheepishly at Daly. "Just curious as to what I might find."

"That was my father's sofa," said Daly. "The only things you'll find down there are tobacco and old religious magazines."

Irwin lit a cigarette and inhaled deeply. Then he stubbed it out in the ashtray. He removed a can of beer from his coat pocket and opened it.

"Poppy says we're finished, Daly. It really is over. And now she's taken Benjy." He guzzled from the can.

"Who's Benjy?"

"Our dog. I've spent more time with him than with any other living thing. Apart from Poppy, of course." He was silent for a while. "It's one thing to lose your girlfriend, but to have to say good-bye to your best friend as well—" He broke off to blow his nose. "She said Benjy doesn't belong to me, but that's not true. I know I've done bad things to Poppy, I know I've betrayed her—I admit it—but she can't do this to me."

He placed the can of beer on the floor. "I don't want to waste any more of your time, but I need a favor, Daly." His voice was stretched, pleading. "I've some stuff to collect from her apartment. I could do with a hand."

Daly sighed. "You're too drunk to drive. I'll give you a lift."

It was raining when they went outside. Daly's ten-year-old Renault spluttered in the downpour. Irwin sat quietly throughout the journey, biting the side of his thumbnail and nursing another can of beer. When they arrived at the apartment block, he pulled out a baseball cap from his pocket and pulled it low over his forehead. He checked his appearance in the sun visor mirror. The blood had drained from his face.

"Keep the engine running, Daly. I'll be in a hurry."

Daly waited, alert. Above the beat of the rain pounding the car he heard the sound of glass breaking, and an alarm going off. A few minutes later, Irwin appeared at the side of the car. He threw a large bag covering what looked to be a birdcage into the back and jumped in.

"Let's go!" he shouted. He was wearing a self-satisfied grin. "That was easier than I thought."

Daly glanced in the rearview mirror as he accelerated off. The bag shifted slightly. He looked again. The bag jerked, and something squawked from within.

"What the hell's in the bag?" he asked with alarm.

"Alfie."

"Who?"

"Poppy's precious pet. He's a parrot." A vindictive grin split Irwin's face. "She's taken Benjy, so I grabbed Alfie."

"A parrot? It'll smother in that plastic bag."

"Don't worry. I'm not asking you to look after it."

"You've lost it."

"Don't say that. I already know I've lost it." He gulped from the can of beer. "Tell me something different. Like how daring I am, or how great it is to pull one over on that bitch."

"Christ!"

"You're put out."

"How would I not be? You've just used me as an accessory to breaking and entry. Not to mention theft."

Irwin lifted the can to his mouth, but it was empty.

"You told me you just wanted to collect some things. Why did you lie?"

"Don't give me grief, Daly. It was the need-to-know principle."

"What do you mean?"

"The only people told my business are those who need to know. Anyway, I only went back to look for Benjy, but she'd taken him with her. You know she's threatened to have him put down?"

"Derek, this isn't a game." Daly tried to hold a note of patience in his voice. "With a criminal conviction for theft, you'll be kicked off the force."

"Really?" His voice was sarcastic. "I think you'll find, Daly, that this is technically a case of kidnapping. I've taken her parrot as ransom for my pet friend. My best friend." He glared drunkenly at Daly. "If you think I've done wrong, then arrest me. You're a policeman, remember. Or have you forgotten how to arrest lawbreakers?"

Daly shook his head. "Someone will have seen my car and taken down the registration. Our colleagues at the station are probably doing a search on it right now."

"Tell them you were driving by and saw someone behaving suspiciously, and that you were just investigating. I'll take my chances. If they track me down, I'll just say I was sleepwalking."

Daly sighed. "You've thought of everything, I see."

"I told you I had it planned to a tee."

He leaned so close Daly could feel his alcoholic breath condense on his cheek. A question formed in Irwin's mouth like sticky saliva. "What about your missing prostitute?"

Daly said nothing.

"I bet she'd make a hot date."

"How do you know? You haven't seen her, have you?"

"I'm just asking. Maybe she'd make an awful one, and then charge you £100 for the pleasure."

Irwin rolled down the window and chucked the empty beer can into a hedge. Daly decided that he was not equipped to deal with the fallout from Irwin's disintegrating love life. It was too risky and depressing a business for him to bear. He glanced at Irwin. It was difficult to decide how much self-destruction the younger detective was capable of wreaking on himself and those around him.

A thought crossed Daly's mind. He stared at the bag in the rearview mirror.

"What's the parrot going to do for food? Have you thought of that?"

"Shit." Irwin pulled a hand over his forehead and groaned.

Twenty minutes later, Daly dropped the detective off at his mother's house. Irwin's shoulders slumped a little as he dragged out the bag. He walked up to the front door, head bowed, like a man retracing his steps, searching for a way to correct the fundamental error of his adulthood that had brought him back to his parents' doorstep with a kidnapped parrot as baggage.

Daly had just stepped through the door of his cottage when his mobile rang.

"Hello." He could hear breathing on the other end, but no one answered.

"Hello. Who is this?" he demanded.

Silence.

"Is that you, Derek?" He looked at the caller display, but did not recognize the number.

He was about to hang up, when a voice spoke.

"Celcius, this is Lena."

He dropped into a chair in surprise.

35

"Lena, where are you?" asked Daly.

"I'm staying in one of Jack's properties," she replied. "A house in Foxborough Mews."

The place rang a bell with him. It was the ghost estate where Mooney lived. He wondered how the former IRA man would feel knowing he had company at last.

"You have to come down to the police station," said Daly, his voice terse. "You're a suspect in a conspiracy-to-blackmail case. No amount of running is going to change that. You're also in grave danger. There's a man with a limp who won't rest until he finds you."

Lena took a deep breath. "I've seen him, again. At least signs of him and his Jeep. He's always there, on the periphery. I think he's been watching me for some time."

"Here's what you must do." Daly spoke urgently. "Lock your doors. Stay away from the windows, and keep your mobile on you at all times. Tell me which house you're in, and I'll be there as soon as possible."

"I can't."

"Why not?"

She was silent.

"Listen, Lena. Every time I get close to finding you, along comes this man. I talked to Martha Havel a few days ago, and do you know what happened to her? Are you listening?"

Still there was silence on the other end.

"He forced her van off the road. Then he dragged her injured body into a Jeep. Right now, he's probably torturing her to extract the information I tried to get from her. That woman is suffering, and all because you won't talk to us. What secrets are you hiding? Why won't you let me help you?"

"There are dangerous men after me," she replied. "The lives of women are more worthless to them than animals, and so are our families. Why else do you think I'm trying to make myself invisible?"

"We can protect you. You can help us put Mikolajek behind bars for a very long time."

"The police haven't done much up till now."

"We're working round the clock." A note of anger crept into his voice. "All we can do is investigate the crimes we know have taken place. Jack Fowler died in mysterious circumstances, and his widow has accused you of blackmailing him."

"I never blackmailed Jack."

"You left a message on their phone demanding money. Are you saying it was some sort of misunderstanding?"

Her voice was lower, squeezed in her throat. "No. I can never have a relationship unless I repay my debts to Mikolajek. He will destroy me and anyone I come in contact with. He made me break off the relationship with Jack. He threatened to kill the two of us. I pretended to blackmail Jack to make sure he wouldn't come after me. It was easier that way."

"What about Fowler's money? You still gave his account a bloodletting."

"Staying away from Mikolajek costs money." There was a note of caution in her voice, as though she was afraid of saying too much.

"All this is evidence that can be used to bring Mikolajek to court."

"If I became a witness, you'd have to put me in a concrete bunker for the rest of my days. And my family, too. No, I have a better plan. One that will help you catch Mikolajek without my evidence."

"Which house are you in?"

She hesitated for a moment. "Number 74."

"OK, I'm heading there now."

She hung up.

In his mind's eye, he pictured a house, empty and lifeless, surrounded by other vacant houses, and in a window, the watchful face of a woman in hiding. An estate of unsold houses was the ultimate anonymous bolt-hole, he thought, as much of a void in the aftermath of the property boom as an empty sea.

36

Daly drove along deserted streets lined with houses devoid of life, like cutouts propped up in front of each other. It was hard to imagine he was deep in the South Armagh countryside. That was the snag about every one of the unsold properties in Foxborough Mews—their views were of many other similarly designed houses. He passed Michael Mooney's house, but there were no vehicles parked outside and the place looked empty.

At the end of the street stood number 74, one of the final properties to be built. The house was doing its best to camouflage itself in a general tangle of weeds, twisted hawthorns, and mounds of rubble. If Daly had to choose any of the houses for a hideaway, he would have picked number 74, too.

He got out and skirted the property, catching reflections of himself in the dark windows. Occasionally he thought he saw another shadowy reflection slip out of sight, but each time he stopped and looked behind him there was no one there. The estate seemed to absorb all signs of life, the windows throwing back blank reflections of a silhouetted skyline. He rapped the knocker on the front door of number 74 and waited. There was no answer. Had the estate swallowed up Lena Novak, too? he wondered. He scrutinized the windows, but the interior was hidden from view. He knocked again, louder, and waited as the echoes faded into the estate.

"Hello!" he shouted. "This is Inspector Daly."

Getting no answer, he pushed on the handle and found the door unlocked. He glanced behind once more to make sure no one was watching him and entered. The deep silence within reminded him that he was a trespasser. Slowly, he moved about the rooms, which were empty of furniture or decoration. One thing was sure, he wasn't going to need a team of officers and a search warrant to give the place a thorough going-over.

"Lena!" he shouted. "Where are you?" The solid wood floors creaked beneath his feet. He stepped into an immaculately tiled kitchen where a glass and a dirty plate were the only items out of place. Upstairs he looked into the bedroom and found a bed with a carefully folded sleeping bag. This time there were no signs that she had left in a hurry or that the house had been disturbed in any way.

"Where are you, Lena?" His voice grew urgent. She had summoned him to this lair only to perform another disappearing act. He must be patient, he told himself, and wait for her to make contact, but he feared that he was missing out on something, and that if Lena and he carried on as they were, they would be condemned to repeat the same experience, forever: she running away, but never fast enough to escape; he chasing, but never hard enough to catch her.

In the kitchen, he pulled out a chair and sat down. He checked his mobile phone and sighed. Her elusiveness was torturing him. Not only had her disappearances caused the investigation to stall, they had distracted him during the empty evenings in his cottage. Jack Fowler's relationship with Lena must have been a roller coaster of highs and dark lows, he thought. Exciting at the start, but terrifying and dizzying toward the end.

After a while, he got up and walked through all the rooms again. It was the scene of another almost crime. She had been a trespasser here, a squatter, but now she was gone. There had to be a clue somewhere, he thought. Something to explain why she had called him and then left.

He went through the rooms methodically. He was going to have to start reading between the lines. On a towel in the bathroom, he found a muddy footprint, too large to be a woman's. He wondered who had left it behind. In a drawer in the kitchen he found a sales brochure for Foxborough Mews and a set of keys. One of the houses was marked with an X, number 68. In another drawer, he found a plastic bag with money. A total of eight fifty-euro notes, crisp and clean. He placed the money back in the drawer and walked outside.

Blackberry brambles and gorse ran wild across the common ground. He followed a narrow forking path that he assumed had been made by rabbits or smaller rodents and almost tripped over an unearthed sewer pipe. He found where it ended in a bubbling mess of sewage and maggots, the reek of decay filling his nostrils.

In the soft soil at the back of the houses he noticed a series of footprints. Although they merged in places, he managed to follow a clear trail to the back door of number 68, the house that had been marked with an X in the brochure. He felt as though he was searching sideways and backward around the void left by Lena's disappearance.

A shadow twisted at an upstairs window. Then the face of a woman appeared briefly, a thinner, elfin version of Lena. He heard a shrill, protesting voice, and then the anxious face disappeared. Was it fear of him or fear of someone else in the house that was etched on her features? The image stayed fresh in his mind. It was the face of a victim rather than a criminal. Where had he seen her before? He banged at the locked door, but there was no answer from within. He stood back and saw another movement at the window. This time the face of a different woman appeared, her eyes wide and tired looking. Her face registered shock at the sight of him. He shouted, but she didn't respond.

He was surprised to find the front door unlocked. The usual dividing lines of ownership and property did not exist in places like Foxborough Mews. He felt a chill of cold air on his face as he stepped into a hallway of gleaming marble. He moved slowly along a corridor, glancing into the empty rooms on either side. The air smelled of that odd mixture of sealed-in dust and fresh paint possessed by all new houses. Upstairs, he checked each room, opening closed door after closed door. He took a deep breath and entered the room in which he had seen the women. It had square white walls and a clean cement floor and nothing else. No place to accommodate even a shadow. He looked through the window and kept a steady watch on the street, his ears straining all the time for a noise in the house. Who were the women? Squatters or lost souls? How had they disappeared?

He walked several times around the house, trying to light on a detail that would explain their disappearance or link them to Lena Novak. The only thing unusual was a picnic basket in the kitchen. Daly opened it and found a selection of cold meats and cheeses, and a bottle of champagne. In a side compartment were a pair of handcuffs, a blindfold, and a sharp knife. *Hardly the gear for a traditional picnic in the park,* he thought.

Apart from the presence of the basket, there were no signs that anyone had recently been in the house. Whoever the women were, they barely qualified as tenants. Like Lena, they were visitors that came and went without a trace, ghosts for a ghost estate.

He stepped outside and walked along the street. The setting sun briefly parted the dark clouds and was reflected in a hundred dazzling windows. A door rattled behind him, and the windows quivered. He spun round. The noise could have come from any one of a dozen houses. He tried several properties before he found one that was not locked. The front door of number 72 hung slightly ajar. He stepped inside. Vandals and thieves had ransacked the place, punching holes in the walls, ripping out copper piping and electrical wiring. He checked the rooms but found once again found no signs of life.

He was about to return to his car when something made him halt in his tracks. Something about number 72 had struck him as odd. He went back in and walked around. He memorized the layout. Then he went back to number 68. He secured the front door from the inside and retraced his steps through the sparsely furnished rooms. The houses in the estate followed a similar room plan. A kitchen, utility room, bathroom, and two reception rooms downstairs, with three bedrooms and a further two bathrooms upstairs. However, in number 68, there was a bedroom less upstairs.

Using his feet, he roughly measured the upstairs layout. He paced along the white walls of each room. Between one of the bedrooms and the bathroom, there was a space measuring about twelve feet by ten feet. He tapped the wall. It was hollow. He shifted a wardrobe and found a concealed door. He tried the handle, but it was locked. His discovery of a secret room was an unexpected development and piqued his curiosity. He had a dawning sense of danger and deception. He shouted and banged the door, but there was no answer.

The developers of the houses may have had grand ambitions, but they were unlikely to extend to the creation of concealed rooms. Someone with a secret to hide had constructed it recently. He walked over to a window and surveyed the estate. It was getting dark, but no streetlights came on. He pressed his hand lightly against the glass and felt it vibrate. He stepped back. The window quivered like a living thing.

37

A throbbing sound filled the empty rooms of number 68. Daly looked outside and watched as a familiar black Jeep reversed up to the front door. He stood, motionless. The Jeep door banged shut, and a man with a shaved head jumped out.

Daly stepped onto the landing. He heard the man try the front door, rattling it in frustration, and then pause. Then he tried again. Daly listened carefully, trying to work out the caller's next step. A lengthier silence followed as the man went through his pockets, fishing for keys. Then he knocked on the door and impatiently rapped the side window with his knuckles. Whatever he was looking for, it wasn't the rent.

Daly slipped down the stairs and out the back door. He crept round to the front of the house. The caller had gone, but the Jeep was still there, the keys sitting in the ignition. He fumbled in the dashboard compartment and retrieved an Irish passport in the name of Frank O'Neill, and a folder stuffed with bank statements and letters belonging to Jack Fowler. At last, the nameless stalker that roamed the border country had a name. Daly had made the first step in relegating the man with the limp to the status of an ordinary criminal.

He was about to return to his car and radio for help when he heard a frantic knocking from the boot. He glanced up at number 68. Still no signs of life and the driver was nowhere to be seen. Daly reckoned he might have enough time to check what was making the noise. At the sound of his footsteps, the Jeep swung slightly from side to side. Something in the boot was struggling desperately to get his attention.

He popped open the lid and found himself staring into the dark, troubled eyes of Lena Novak. Her body had been bound with ropes. There was no noise from her gagged mouth. Only her ragged breathing, rising and falling. Her eyes fixed on his. They were frosted with fear. He untied her squirming body and helped her out of the boot. Her body was still in shock, shaking slightly under his touch. She felt cold, as though he had lifted her from a freezing river.

"You're bleeding."

"He held a knife to my throat. He threatened to cut me if I struggled." She resisted his attention, but seemed reluctant to disengage from the safety of his gaze. "It's only a small cut."

Hearing a noise from the house, he grabbed her arm forcefully. Her eyes twisted up at him, anxious and surprised. "Get into the Jeep," he whispered urgently. "We don't have time to get back to my car." They jumped into the front, and Daly reversed quickly onto the street. A minute later, they were on the main road back to Lough Neagh.

"What happened?" he asked.

She rubbed her neck; her cheeks were still flushed from the struggle in the boot. "After I spoke to you on the phone, the doorbell rang," she said. "I thought it was you." She shivered. "But it wasn't. You were right. He was there all along. He wrapped his hands around my throat to make me stop screaming. Then he gagged me and tied me up. I blacked out. When I came round, I found myself locked in the boot. I shouted until my throat was raw. Thank God you came." Daly detected a thread of affection in her voice.

Driving through Armagh, he rang the station on his mobile phone. He asked for a patrol car to check out number 68, Foxborough Mews. He relayed his suspicions that a group of women were being held in the house against their will. He also told the duty sergeant his car had broken down. A recovery vehicle was sent out to tow it back to the station. He put the phone down and glanced at the cut on her neck.

"I should take you to the hospital. Get you checked over."

"No. I can't take the risk. He might be waiting for me there."

"There were some documents in his Jeep. In the name of Frank O'Neill. Does that ring a bell with you?"

"I've never heard of the name. Who is he?"

"I don't know, but I can tell you he's a professional. A trained professional who's been given orders to kidnap you."

"I got away from him," she said defiantly. "Twice." Her dark eyes glittered at him. "No man will ever take me prisoner again."

"What were you doing in Foxborough Mews?"

"Hiding."

"A ghost estate is a strange place to hide."

"Everywhere's strange to me. That's what happens when you're on the run in a country with no identity or past. I thought it would be the last place people would think of looking."

"What about the other women?"

"What women?"

He explained how a group of women had been kidnapped from an illegal alcohol-bottling plant.

"Have you seen them?" The tone of her voice changed.

"I think so."

"Where?"

"They were in number 68. I saw them look down from a window, but when I searched inside, they had disappeared."

She said nothing. He wanted to ask her more questions, but her mood had changed. He was afraid that if he started to cross-examine her, she would run away at the first opportunity. She nodded off in the warmth of the car and then jerked awake, fighting sleep. She kept her eyes open and vacant, slipping into a trance that was neither sleeping nor waking.

He tried to catalog her emotional state, the lengthy silences in their conversation. He was on guard for ominous signs in her demeanor. The detective in him compelled him to do so, but the changes he should have been watching for were those taking place within him. Her close presence shed a different light on the investigation, like the subtle light of the moon, changing the shape and direction of his detective work. Some things were beginning to make sense to him, but many more remained in the dark. Who were the women hiding in number 68? Was it a coincidence that he had found them in the same estate as Lena and Michael Mooney? Where was Martha Havel? And what sort of a picnic required the instruments of kidnap?

It was dark when Daly pulled the Jeep up at the cottage. He nosed the vehicle deep into a small orchard at the back. The headlights lit up the first of the season's apple blossoms. He helped Lena out of the Jeep and led her through deep grass overgrown with brambles. A necklace of bruises had started to discolor her neck. The sweet smell of her perfume filled his nostrils.

38

It struck him that Lena was his first female houseguest since he had moved into the cottage a year ago. Although the place was run-down and messy, it had been a sanctuary from women and work, the stricken victims and the burdened colleagues. He unlocked the door and tentatively invited her in.

The fusty dark barely revealed the cottage's antiques, the Welsh dresser with its set of ancient crockery, a shelf of books, and the cast-iron stove. For the first time, he noticed the cobwebs that had gathered in the corners of the small windows.

She walked around the cramped room, inquisitive, brushing against the furniture, like a kitten with an arched back. She opened the door into the kitchen, took a peek, and then tried the bedroom door.

"Is there a toilet?" she asked, eventually. "I need a pee."

When she returned, her face looked fresher; gone was the tiredness around her eyes.

"Why did you ring me?" asked Daly.

"I had a dream about you."

"What sort of a dream?"

"You were standing on a shore, calling out to me. Then I woke up and heard the sound of a vehicle cruising through the estate. It was a black Jeep. I panicked and phoned you, even though I wasn't planning to do so."

"I'm glad you did."

She sat down on a chair, her back still arched slightly.

"You should be worried," she told him.

"Why?"

"Whenever men try to save me, they get hurt." She crossed her arms in front of her and raised her chin slightly. He stared at the fine bones of her wrists. "When Jack visited the brothel, he was looking for some fun between the sheets, but then he met me. He thought he had netted something special, a woman that would excite him and make his life happier. He should have let me sink back to the bottom of the river."

"How did Mikolajek find out about Jack and you?"

"Jack's business empire was falling apart. He planned to do a runner to Spain or the United States, but we needed false passports. He was anxious not to alert any of his old associates, so we avoided the usual channels. He got in touch with a bunch of Romanians who specialized in false documents. They were meant to be useful and discreet. We met a man called Hedler. He was a pimp; I could tell right away. I think his instinct alerted him to something in me, as well. He took our photos, wrote down our details, and Jack paid him the money, about £4,000. Hedler winked at me while Jack's back was turned and then he made an obscene gesture at him. The anger rose within me, and I spat at him. That was the closest I came to forgetting to play my part. He provoked me on purpose. We were meant to meet Hedler the following week and collect the passports, but instead he tipped off Mikolajek."

She stared at Daly. "You probably disapprove of Jack. The type of man he was."

"I disapprove of the way he died. Unless you can convince me you played no part in his death, I have to arrest you. Is that clear?"

She shrugged. "I can't speak for the mental pressures he was under, but I'm no killer, nor a blackmailer."

"But Fowler's wife says you blackmailed him."

"If that was true, you'd be my next victim. Besides, I already explained to you why I made that call."

Her eyes bore into his, searching for any signs of doubt. It struck Daly that this was a skillful way to avoid the accusation. She sighed wearily. "If you used your imagination, you would realize that I didn't need to blackmail or kill Jack Fowler to get money from him. What else did I have to gain? A return to the life of a prostitute?"

"I have to know more," he said.

She raised her face toward him and gave him a steady look. Daly got the impression that a hidden part of her was maneuvering out of the dark.

"If you are ready for it, I shall give you something very special," she said. "Something made from sweat and tears, something that I have given to no one else. My story. It is my gift to you."

"I'm listening."

She proceeded to recount her life in Croatia, and how she had been kidnapped by Mikolajek. She talked for an hour. From time to time, he interrupted her, guiding her into areas where she showed uneasiness. Sometimes he noticed she would grow voluble, especially when talking about the other trafficked women and their homes, and then she would suddenly stop as if overcome by nostalgia or something sadder.

She told him how Jack Fowler had helped her escape from the farmhouse brothel. He had set up an accident on the road to divert the attention of the pimp Sergei Kriich. The plan, however, had backfired when Kriich crashed his car.

"Mikolajek left something for me that night."

"What?"

"A message. A warning."

"How?"

"In the form of Sergei's body, or whatever was left of him."

Daly fell silent.

"It was Mikolajek's way of showing how ruthless he was. He wanted to show he wasn't prepared to forgive even a mistake like the one Sergei had made in letting me escape. How would he then respond to my betrayal?"

Afterward, she sat at the table opposite Daly and looked at him, as though expecting him to ask more questions or set out rules. Darkness thickened in the windows. Shadows from the dying turf fire stretched across the flagstone floor.

He went outside to the shed to gather more turf. When he returned, he found her in the hall, going through the contents of his jacket pockets. He assumed that this came from her instinctive distrust of men, but he still felt a sense of unease. What other parts of his life was she going to rifle through?

"I wanted to know how much cash you had," she explained.

"Are you planning to rob me?" A note of anger crept into his voice.

It was then that she explained her plan to him.

"I think it's crazy and dangerous," he said after listening carefully.

"If you think that, then arrest me, now, before I take your money and run."

He felt a rush of resentment as he stared at her. She was calling the shots. He no longer had any way of influencing events, but, then, had that not been the case all along? The investigation had always been dependent on her accidental appearances, the only breakthroughs at her bidding. She stared back at him. The tension within him weakened. He looked at the ground and then up at her watchful face. It struck him there were worse ways of spending an evening than simmering in uncertainty under the attentive eyes of Lena Novak.

He walked over to the fire and dropped some turf onto the dying embers. He sat down and thought. He grasped for a different solution to the one she was proposing. He was reluctant to formally arrest her or report her as an illegal immigrant. That might create a trail for her pursuers to follow. There was also a serious risk that if she got bail, she would abscond and disappear forever. Besides, he had already compromised himself. There were enough irregularities in his pursuit of Lena to prompt a disciplinary investigation. No. His only way out was to trust her and go after the bad guys. And then, afterward, hope that she would quietly disappear and return to her homeland.

"I don't want you to lose your job," she said. "It would be better if I did this alone, rather than put you in danger. I will call you when I'm ready."

"I have to think more about this," he said, getting up to leave.

When he returned, she had taken off her boots and was sitting by the fire. She looked up. "You're worried," she said. "I don't blame you. You're risking a lot." He nodded, perching himself on the edge of the sofa.

"We could find ourselves in a lot of danger."

"Yes."

He said nothing of what was worrying him the most, this wayward impulse of his to follow her along the dark passage of her life, to yoke her destiny with his.

"My head is telling me we should drop the plan," he said.

"But does your heart want to?"

"No."

He had already made his decision. It was based less on self-preservation than the simple desire to not let her out of his sight for more than a minute. That seemed more important than any dull strategy to save his career.

He made up a bed for her in the bedroom. Before he closed the door, she thanked him.

"For what?"

"I had forgotten what it was like to be alone with a man and not have to sleep with him," she said.

That night as he lay in bed, the image of her body curled up by the fire gouged a hole in his sleep. After an hour had passed, he got up to go to the toilet. He stood outside her door, which was slightly opened. He listened to the sound of the rain outside intermingling with her breathing. The burden of his thoughts weighed heavily upon his shoulders as he walked back to bed. It was almost dawn before he slipped into a dreamless sleep.

39

Daly awoke on Monday morning to find the wet imprint of her bare feet fading on the floor of his bedroom. He got up with a start and dressed hurriedly. He wondered if she had been standing at his bedside, peering at him while he slept. He followed the footprints into the living room and out through the opened front door. She was sitting on a wooden seat overlooking the wild garden, combing her wet hair. She'd had a shower and pulled on an old jumper of his.

"You woke me earlier," she said.

Daly looked startled.

"You were grinding your teeth in your sleep." She smiled. "I thought a monster was crushing bones in your bedroom."

"My ex-wife complained that I gnashed at night like a brute."

"You know what that tells me?"

"What?"

"Something inside you is fighting to be heard. Something that won't be tamed."

"Then it's better kept at bay."

After breakfast, Daly got ready for work. He told Lena that her best strategy was to stay in the cottage, out of sight, and wait for his return. He traveled by taxi to the police station. Through the security gates, the first thing he saw was his car parked in the space reserved for impounded vehicles. He was relieved his colleagues had managed to retrieve it before vandals could take it apart.

Inside the station, he caught a glimpse of Commander Boyd coming down a flight of stairs. He slipped down a corridor to avoid him. A short while later he was about to open a glass door when he saw the commander approach. A look of intent emboldened Boyd's features when he recognized Daly. Again, he tried to make himself scarce within the station's labyrinth of corridors and interview rooms, but Boyd kept reappearing like the resolute anchor of a tug-of-war team, pulling in the competition. They bumped into each other outside the canteen.

"Your car was found in a housing estate last night with the keys in the ignition," Boyd told Daly. "We got a report of a man matching your description entering a number of unsecured properties. What the hell is going on?"

"I had a breakdown while house-hunting, sir."

Boyd shook his head in exasperation.

"I hope you're not still searching for this missing prostitute."

"She's the key to arresting Mikolajek. I intend to find her."

"She's toying with you. There's more going on in your head than a policeman pursuing a witness. Of course, I'm not a psychologist." He eyed Daly evenly.

"I'm glad you aren't." Daly's reply made him glare.

"You've been acting strangely all week, Daly. Not saying a word to colleagues. Wearing that hangdog look. Coming late to meetings and ignoring paperwork deadlines. I've yet to see your report on how the investigation is proceeding to date."

Daly said nothing. It struck him that if Boyd had any talent of note, it was his ability to take over an investigation and shuffle everyone off to meaningless paperwork.

"What's the matter with you, Inspector?" Boyd examined Daly's face closely. A look of suspicion formed on his face. "Has she left you?"

Daly flinched. "Who, sir?"

"Whoever she is. I've a teenage son who wears the same expression on his face most weekends. No woman is worth moping over."

Daly nodded. "I'll hand you the report when it's ready."

In his office, Daly rang Armagh Properties, the company advertised as the sellers of number 68, Foxborough Mews. He asked the estate agent who else had a key for the property. The answer did not surprise him. Michael Mooney was acting as an unofficial warden for it and a number of other houses in the estate.

At lunchtime, Daly drove to the bank. He had no idea how much he had in his savings account, and he had to ask the cashier for the figure. His separation from Anna had thrown his financial affairs into complete disarray.

"Five thousand and fifty-seven pounds and eighty-four pence," the teller told him.

"I want to withdraw it. Every penny."

He was asked for further documents and proof of identification. Daly watched the cashier count the money twice, then stuffed the wad into his wallet, next to the photo he still carried of Lena. The money would be enough to put the first stage of their plan into action.

Afterward, he followed the directions Lena had given him to a nondescript pub on the south side of the town. He sat in his car for a while, wondering whether he was making a mistake, launching himself on this path of criminality. However, he convinced himself that it was already too late. He had traveled too far down this path to turn back now.

Every Monday afternoon, Daniel Hedler set up camp in a corner of the pub. There were plenty of business opportunities in the sale of counterfeit documents, especially passports and driving licenses, in this part of town, and the pub was a suitably anonymous office in which to conduct his trade. He was careful and well organized in his business, and his henchmen were positioned throughout the bar if a deal needed a little more muscle to help clinch it.

As soon as Daly entered the bar, Hedler could tell he was a man in free fall. Not the slow-motion plummet of the afternoon men lounging throughout the pub, scuffing their heels, staring at the horse racing on TV, sipping their interminable pints. No, this one's descent was more precipitous. This one had not turned up for the company or the beer, Hedler was sure of that.

When Daly asked at the bar for Hedler, he was introduced to a meticulously shaved and groomed middle-aged man sitting in a corner with a newspaper. Daly sat down and told him he wanted two passports for himself and a female friend. He explained that it was an emergency and that he had the money ready. He adopted a blunt and hasty tone.

Hedler stared keenly at Daly, his pupils glistening, feeding eyes taking in its prey. He glanced down at the detective's photograph and the details of his new identity, and then back at Daly, subtracting one version of him from the other.

"What did you say your line of business was?"

"I didn't." Daly stared evenly at him. "At the moment, you could say I'm hiding from business. You know the story. Investments gone wrong, the banks chasing me, hunting down all my assets. I just want to get some breathing space for a while. For me and my girlfriend."

Hedler's facial muscles contorted with curiosity. "You don't strike me as a typical customer. The ones with criminal identities. Those people are very problematic."

He leaned back and examined Daly's details at greater ease. Then he lifted Lena's photo. He did not say anything for a long time, just scrutinized her picture, as if measuring millimeter by millimeter the dimensions of her face.

"I can't give you what you want," he said eventually. "Until I see her in the flesh."

"Why?"

"For reasons that would take too long to explain." His

voice was arrogant. It had the abruptness of someone who spent most of his time talking to people who wanted to disappear, ghosts moving from border to border. It was devoid of all human warmth. "She's a very pretty woman. How long have you known her?"

Daly made an effort to smile. All the time, he was taking mental notes of the Romanian, their surroundings, the other people in the bar.

"Not long enough."

"Here's a piece of friendly advice. Keep an eye on her. Don't let her out of your sight. A woman like that will crush you if you give her the chance."

"It's good advice. With women you never know."

Hedler pulled on his coat, lifting the collar around his neck. Daly took this to mean their conversation was over.

"Don't worry," said Hedler. "I will help you. I will give you what you want. A new name, a new start. You and this girl of yours. Four thousand pounds for two perfect fake passports. Then you'll have a means to escape yourselves. Come back tomorrow, to this bar. The both of you. OK?"

"Just have them ready."

Daly made his way through the outskirts of Armagh and into the wild border countryside. The overgrown hedgerows were full of spring flowers swaying in the breezes. The sky held the promise of a beautiful spring afternoon, but by the time he pulled up at Foxborough Mews, the sun had retreated into an eddy of dark clouds and the wind had begun to bluster.

Hawthorn blossoms swirled about his feet as he stepped out of the car. He was alone in the estate, with the echo of the wind among the thorn trees that had colonized the waste ground. *Paradise cursed*, thought Daly as he scanned the lonely-looking houses.

He called at number 68, but the doors were locked. He checked the windows, but there was no sign of anyone. A hollow silence pervaded the buildings. Daly's mind was a blank. He was surrounded by shut doors and vacant windows, a bricks-and-mortar pact of silence. How could he interpret emptiness? What clues were there to decipher when the victims had vanished?

He stumbled on a loose piece of rubble and grunted. A door banged shut in the direction of Mooney's house. He approached the former terrorist's home, hearing only the sounds of his footsteps echoing in the estate. His eyes caught a movement at one of the windows. The bowed figure of Michael Mooney stood close to the glass. He was staring out at the estate like a man at the center of a derailed train surveying the wreckage.

Daly rang the bell, but there was no answer. He pounded the door and waited.

Mooney eventually opened the door. He nodded when he saw Daly and beckoned him into a dimly lit hall. His scarred features looked even more like a mask than Daly remembered.

"I thought you were one of the gawkers," he explained.

"What gawkers?"

"We get lots of visitors pretending to be house hunters.

What they're really here for is a tour of a ghost estate." He offered Daly a seat. "You'd think the place was a crime scene, the way they drive slowly around in their cars, pointing at all the For Sale signs. It's been at least a year since I saw a genuine buyer."

"What about number sixty-eight? Anyone interested in that house?"

Mooney flinched. "We had a lot of strange people coming and going over the weekend."

"What about a group of Croatian women?"

Mooney thought about the question. "What do Croatian women look like, in your opinion? Don't they dress the same and look the same as Irish women?"

"I'm talking about women who may have been kidnapped and held prisoner there."

Mooney appeared not to have heard him. "I'm busy packing for a flight tonight, Inspector. Excuse me for being blunt, but I'm in a hurry." He got up to leave.

"The only place you'll need to pack for is a police cell if you don't tell me what's going on in that house."

Mooney's face looked stunned. He sat back down again.

"Has something happened to Lena Novak?"

"Why do you ask?"

"He told me he'd captured her."

"Who's he?"

Mooney sighed wearily. He explained to Daly how he had hired a former IRA man called John Ashe to trace the whereabouts of Lena Novak. His brief had been to question Lena and uncover the missing peace funds, and in return he'd given Ashe a new identity, a Jeep, and access to money.

"Unfortunately, I didn't realize he was going to double-cross me," Mooney said with bitterness.

"Tell me more."

"I still haven't come to terms with his betrayal. Last night Ashe rang to say he had Lena Novak but that his plans had changed. He was working for a new boss now, one who paid much better."

Mikolajek, thought Daly to himself. He said nothing while the horizons of the investigation changed in his mind.

"What about kidnapping women? Surely that wasn't part of the brief you gave him?"

"I handed him the keys to number sixty-eight and got some workmen to build a secret room for him. It was his stipulation. I thought it was a place for him to hide, if necessary. I left him to his own devices."

"Why did he take the women prisoner?"

"He was doing what he knew best—spreading terror. He wanted Lena Novak's attention, to force her into revealing herself."

Daly thought he knew what Mooney meant. People who believed their lives were in danger made predictable decisions. He wondered how predictable his and Lena's plans were to people like Mikolajek and Ashe, who were obviously well versed in manipulating the frightened and vulnerable.

"You have to help me find Ashe. And the missing women."

"It's too late, now." Mooney eyed Daly. "You were stupid not to have arrested him when you could. And I was twice as stupid to trust him with such a sensitive investigation. I should have known from the start that he wouldn't follow orders. Ashe was no longer political in any way. He had no loyalty to the past or to the Republican party."

"This man was following your orders. You facilitated these kidnaps. You provided him with a vehicle, identification, and money. If anyone is killed, you'll face serious criminal charges. Don't imagine you're going to wriggle out of this one."

A tremor of worry flashed across Mooney's frozen features as he imagined the new possibilities, the fresh horrors that might arise now that Ashe had switched allegiances.

"Is Ashe a killer?" asked Daly.

Mooney said nothing.

"It's an important question. I want you to think carefully about it."

Eventually Mooney answered. "A long time ago, yes. But now... I'm not sure."

Daly thought he saw a glimmer of Mooney's real face, one whose nerves were braced against the idea that he might have set a maniac in motion.

"Last night he told me he had locked Lena Novak in the boot of his Jeep."

"I know. I rescued her."

Mooney visibly relaxed. "That puts you in a dangerous situation, Inspector Daly. Look at what happened to the last man who tried to rescue Lena Novak. If I were you, I'd get as far away as possible from that woman."

Daly made to leave. "I'd contact a solicitor as soon as possible, Mr. Mooney. You're going to need one when we take you in for questioning."

When he got back into his car, he phoned the cottage but there was no answer. He drove home as fast as he could, fearing that Lena had disappeared once again.

40

In return for emptying his savings account, Daly received little more than a pensive stare from Lena when he returned home.

"Why didn't you answer the phone?" he asked.

"I was out." Her voice was calm and superior. "I went to get some clothes and women's things."

"In the Jeep?"

"Yes."

"You should have stayed here, like I told you."

"I'm not your prisoner." Her blue eyes were drenched in defiance.

He didn't know how to reply. He stood still and stared at her. Why couldn't she see what he saw—the dangerous men advancing, the chaos seeping around them, their time running out? Perhaps she no longer knew what fear was, he thought.

"All I'm saying is that it's not safe for you to be in public, especially in that Jeep. Next time ring me. Tell me what you're doing."

The hours dragged by in the cottage. Lena wandered through the rooms and the back garden like someone sitting out a sentence. To help pass the time, Daly began sorting through the boxes he had transported from his former home in the city. He unpacked his things—books, clothes, CDs, and old letters—but try as he might, he could not push away his rising sense of anxiety. He felt a pang of conscience that what he and Lena were doing was breaking the law, but he convinced himself that the end justified the means. How many more crimes would they prevent by capturing Mikolajek and making sure he was locked away?

He stared through the tiny attic window with its view of rutted bog land and the distant lough, water churning to the brim of the horizon. His father had spent his last winter, muffled in clothes, staring out at the same bleak landscape, the only landscape he had ever known. One day he might end up the same, thought Daly, watching over a view that never changed, with plenty of time to grieve over the past and his lack of nerve.

He knew that what he was planning had nothing to do with police work. All the same, he was committed to helping Lena. He could not abandon this woman whose path had crossed with his. He was prepared to do whatever it took to ensnare Mikolajek, because the crimes he had committed against women like Lena were so appalling, the injustice so great, that he had forfeited his right to liberty.

She was waiting for him when he came down the stairs.

"Do you think we'll get Mikolajek?" she asked.

"I've no way of predicting what will happen tomorrow," he said truthfully.

They went to their separate beds just after 10:00 p.m.

The next morning, they were both up early. Another dawn had brought fresh doubts to his mind over what they were doing. Every time he ran through the events of the past few weeks, and each of his encounters with Lena, he got the feeling that he was missing something important. When he asked her to explain her side of the events, the details remained unchanged, but a feeling of uncertainty still nagged at him.

Somehow, her readiness to keep going over her story and put his doubts at ease seemed slightly unnatural, like a woman patiently explaining away the details of an affair. He worried that she had come to him because she had detected a flaw in his makeup. Was she seeking his protection or comfort? Or was she using him for a darker purpose?

After breakfast, he asked her a question. "Why was Mikolajek so afraid of your doll?"

"You have so many questions." For the first time a note of impatience had crept into her voice.

"But this one's important." He tried to keep the suspicion out of his voice. "That night I met you in the farmhouse brothel. You said you'd come back to find the doll. Was it really just for sentimental reasons?"

She looked at him in a different way. "Why do you want to know?"

"Because I don't understand Mikolajek's fear, and that makes me suspicious."

"Suspicious of whom? The doll? Or me?"

"Suspicious of everyone. It's what happens when you devote your life to uncovering criminals." He stared at her, trying to read her thoughts, but they were hidden away in a language he could not understand.

Before leaving the cottage, he checked the gun in his jacket. He confirmed that the magazine was filled with the official number of ammunition rounds. It had been a long time since he had shot at anything other than a fixed target, and he hoped that he would not have to use the weapon today. He checked the safety and slipped it back into his jacket. When Lena walked outside and climbed into the car, he took out his mobile and thumbed in Irwin's number. Daly quickly explained to him the plan he and Lena had set into operation. There was a long pause from Irwin.

"What the hell are you playing at, Daly?"

"Look I don't have the time to explain everything now. Mikolajek is a dangerous criminal, but he's the key to everything. Once we have him, we'll find out what happened to Fowler and the Croatian. All I'm asking you to do is meet me at the Maghery roundabout and tail me from there."

"You've sidelined me from the beginning. You and this prostitute. It's a bit late to be calling in the cavalry."

Daly rubbed his jaw. He suddenly felt out of his depth, a long way out. He glanced out at the car where Lena was waiting. She was one of those women who had been pulled out too far by dangerous currents, who swam up from the fathoms to tug you under no matter how hard you fought to stay on the surface.

Irwin spoke again. "I think you should hand the entire operation over to Special Branch. Let the experts handle this one."

"It's not my choice. She won't cooperate with anyone else."

"OK." Irwin sighed. "Anything else?"

"Yes. Send a forensics team to my cottage. There's a black Jeep parked in the orchard. Get them to examine it thoroughly."

"Why are you driving so slowly?" Lena asked, twenty minutes later. "Are you thinking of pulling out?"

They were still ten minutes away from the pickup point for the passports. He had barely shifted out of fourth gear. The road lay before him, a relentless conveyor belt taking him to certain doom. Normally, he found driving an aid to thinking, but this morning, the pace of his thoughts was as sluggish as the Renault's old engine.

"I don't know," he lied. "I think the engine's losing power."

He pulled in at a lay-by and got out on the pretense of checking under the car's hood. He should have stuck to solving ordinary crime, he thought, as he pulled out his mobile phone. Hidden from Lena's view by the hood he made a surreptitious call to Irwin. At least hunting down a few burglars or drunk drivers was satisfyingly straightforward, with none of the intricacies of plotting revenge with a victim as complicated as Lena.

"Where are you, Derek?" he hissed into the phone. "I didn't see you at the roundabout."

Irwin said nothing for a moment. "Sorry. I had a flat tire." His tone was less than sincere.

"I'm not bullshitting you. This is deadly serious."

"Then why did you pick me to burden with your hare-brained scheme?"

"You owe me one, remember?"

"Listen, I can't get any sense out of you. Why don't you bring that prostitute straight to the police station? Tell her the whole plan was just a ruse to get her into the interview room."

"The only way out of this mess is to go through with the plan, but I need backup."

Lena appeared at the side of the van, cigarette in hand. She looked at Daly quizzically.

"What's wrong?"

Daly switched off the phone. "The mechanic thinks it's nothing too serious."

Concern shadowed her naturally melancholic face as she watched him check the coolant level. She blew out a cloud of cigarette smoke and stared at him. Her eyes focused on him with watery concentration.

"Don't worry, Celcius," she said. "The worst Mikolajek can do is kill me." Then she blew him a kiss and turned to walk away.

His phone chirped briefly. He checked the message. It

was from Irwin. It read: *Black Jeep gone from your cottage. House ransacked.* He shook his head. Madness, the entire plan was pure madness, he thought. The trap door of doubt groaned beneath his feet.

He was about to phone Irwin back and call in armed assistance when he heard the screech of brakes. A Jeep careening by halted abruptly and made a tight U-turn.

Daly dove for cover when a gunshot rang out. He heard the scampering of feet and several more shots followed by the pop of tires bursting. A car door slammed shut, and a woman's voice called out his name. When he looked up, the Jeep was speeding off in the opposite direction, and Lena was gone. He jumped into the car and shoved it into gear. He took off as hard as he could, but the wheels thumped uselessly against the road. He had two flat tires. He jumped out as the Jeep sped into the distance. Reaching into his jacket, he fumbled for his gun, but it was gone.

41

Jozef Mikolajek reminded himself that women were always late as he waited in the empty bar. He could feel the weight of his anger rising in his chest, but he forced himself to be patient. He needed to control his emotions; otherwise, they might spoil all his preparations and the game he had devised this afternoon for Lena Novak. He must be calm, he told himself. He must remember the patience of the shepherds and hunters in the mountains above Zagreb. They knew that missing sheep always returned, bleating for help, and that, sooner or later, the prey came looking for the hunter. Those were the laws of the wild. The laws he had believed in all his life.

He went over to the door and checked the street. He watched as a young woman pushed a pram past the pub doors. Try as he might, he could not remember Lena Novak's face very well. He had offered escape and a new life to so many girls from the east that recalling the details of one in particular was like trying to remember a glass of cheap wine he had drunk a long time ago. The kind of wine you gulp down carelessly, not thinking of the headache it might leave you with in the morning.

He sighed. The last few months had been some of the most difficult of his entire life. First, fearing a police swoop, he'd had to shut down the border brothel, then his fuel-laundering and bottling plant was raided, and, just a few days previously, the police had busted Home Sweet Home. Suddenly, his entire criminal empire looked vulnerable. Anger swelled inside him again. That girl had somehow been the trigger for his bad luck. She had humiliated him more than any other living person had ever dared. Over the past two months, he had stockpiled enough revenge and anger to start another war, never mind kill her. Ever since she had escaped, he could feel his compatriots point at him and mock. "Look at him, he can't even manage to control a simple woman from a mountain village." No wonder his businesses had suffered so badly.

However, revenge wasn't the principal reason he was waiting for Lena Novak in this dingy pub. It was money, or at least the promise of money. Enough money, he hoped, to put his criminal empire back on its feet again. For the first time in days, he smiled faintly. With so many personal set-backs, he had to learn how to appreciate the simple things in life: a fine wine rolled on the tongue, a good cigar, and this meeting with his missing prostitute, this promise of victory over a desperate woman. He was willing to spend the rest of the afternoon savoring her defeat.

A voice broke the silence.

"I didn't realize they allowed animals in here."

Mikolajek looked up toward Lena's voice. He hadn't heard her enter.

"Hedler's out of town today," he said. "He asked me to step in."

She glanced nervously about the deserted bar. "I knew you'd be here waiting for me."

He looked her up and down. A dim recollection came back to him of a winter landscape and a girl on a freezing cold bus. However, Lena Novak had changed since then. She stood before him dressed in a smart trouser suit with black leather shoes. Her short hair was swept back and her face carried just a hint of makeup. He raised an eyebrow. She looked like a cutthroat businesswoman instead of a whore on the run.

"Where's your policeman friend? The loser in the ancient Renault."

She ignored his question and sat down opposite him. She stared at him without blinking.

"Are you going to run again?" he asked.

She shook her head. "From the very beginning I knew you'd find me," she said. "I came here so that you would see me as I am. An elegant woman with her own life ahead of her. Not a piece of trash for you to keep abusing."

It was his turn to stare at her. Blinded by the mechanical business of selling sex, he had somehow overlooked the beauty that ran through her face and body. In her figure he saw the imprint of the girl he had known back in Croatia. He remembered a pretty dress she had worn once, held by delicate straps around her slender shoulders, but the memory quickly dissolved. A successful man never missed a business opportunity, he reminded himself, and a very important one had just fallen into his lap.

"You're going to have to stop looking at me in that way," she said.

"What way?"

"Like you want to hurt me."

"Don't worry I'm not going to harm you, Lena Novak," he said. "At least not right now. In fact, I'm going to give you a chance to win your freedom."

"That's why I'm here. I want to pay for my liberty. No woman should have to put up with you around her neck for the rest of her days."

"What about the money you owe me?"

From her handbag, she took out a bank statement, along with a money transfer for one million pounds, and handed them to him. "All this transfer needs is my signature and a passport to accompany it. You can fill out the details of the account you want the money paid into."

His eyes flicked over the bank details. She produced another piece of paper, one that was crumpled and covered in her handwriting. It was a list of the women who had been trafficked and forced to work in the border brothel. She pushed it toward him.

"What's this? Your Christmas card list?"

"I want you to free these women as well. The money will pay all our debts and compensate you handsomely for any losses."

He allowed a minute to pass as he considered her proposition.

"Before I grant you your freedom, I'd like you to play a little game with me."

He placed a set of dice before her.

"Fate set a trap for you, Lena," he said with a sympathetic smile. "It took you away from your family and brought you to this country. Now we will find out whether you and the others deserve to go home free women. Odd or even numbers—you choose. If you win, then you are free to go with your friends. If you lose, then I get the money. And you go back to the business you know the best."

"I already have my freedom. I'm not your slave anymore."

"I'm not treating you as my slave. We're equals at this table. Take the dice and when you throw make sure you don't blink."

He stared at her, awaiting her decision. "Come on, Lena. One thing I know about you is that you're not a coward. You're a woman of action. Winning and losing are part of life, except for cowards. And they never win."

"They also never lose," she replied.

She was tempted by the gamble. She felt enticed by his words, caught up by his promises, but it was not just the roll of the dice she was betting on; it was the belief that there was a kernel of honesty in his heart, in spite of all the evil that he had perpetrated. She lifted the dice.

"I take it this means yes."

"How do I know you'll keep your promises?"

"Why would I invent this game if I wasn't convinced by it? I have everything, and you have nothing but a bank account you can't access. If I wanted to, I could take the money off you right now. Throw the dice and we'll see what fate has in store for you."

She sat poised at one of those points in a life that can change everything. The dice felt cold and dead in her hands. She took a deep breath and threw them, trying not to think that a more deathly cold might await her.

42

"Your luck has run out," Mikolajek said with a sneer when the dice rolled to rest. He stood up and enthusiastically pocketed the dice along with the bank documents Lena had left on the table.

She sat and looked around her. The bar was empty. There had been no one there to wish her good luck or witness her defeat.

"Just so you know, the police know I'm here," she said without looking at him. "They'll be looking for me."

Mikolajek merely nodded. He did not appear concerned.

"Now that you've gambled your life away, Lena, I'm going to sell you for a good price," he said. "To a man who'll know how to control you. He does his business in the city. When he comes here, he'll want to have a good look at you."

"What makes you think I won't run away again?"

"That would be a reckless course of action." He removed a gun from his jacket. "Then you really would be screwing with your life."

"I don't belong to you or anyone else."

"Let's go. It's time." He grabbed her by her arm and dragged her to her feet.

"Why didn't you just kidnap me in the first place?"

"It's against the law in this country to take someone against their will." He smirked. "Gambling, however, is not. The Irish understand gambling. They understand why someone like you with nothing to lose would gamble away her entire life."

He took her out through the back of the pub, down a side street, and into a small garage. They walked into an office with a locked door. On the wall was an out-of-date calendar from Croatia showing the wrong month beneath a picture of snowy mountains and dark pine forests. It was like looking through a window at the past. The feeling of homesickness left her breathless.

Mikolajek took out a key and opened the door. Then he took down a length of rope from a shelf and shoved her into the room and onto a narrow bed. She fought him off as his hands reached to tear off her dress. This was the last time, she decided, as she felt his robust body press down on her with unrestrained lust and violence. She went down into the darkness where his groping hands did not reach. She drew strength from an inner reserve and came back up again for air just as he was coiling the rope around her wrists.

When she spoke, it was as if she were someone else, as if nothing she was saying had anything to do with her situation.

"Before you continue I have a confession to make."

"What's that?" He paused and stared at her pale face.

"I came here with a secret plan."

"What do you mean?"

"I didn't come here to collect a passport. I came to see you and learn something about myself. To discover whether I'm a coward or not."

He grinned at her, still uncomprehending. "You're a prostitute. Deep down you enjoy these little sex games."

"Perhaps you're right. But why don't you let me show you what I can do in bed. Let me be in charge. Just this once."

Chuckling to himself, he climbed off her, propped a pillow behind his back, and leaned against the headboard.

"Take off your clothes," she said, her voice commanding, with just a hint of wickedness in it. "Men always pay me to do what they want, not what I want." She leaned toward him with the rope in her hands.

Mikolajek's voice was dry. "I've done everything a man can dream of doing with a woman. And I'm still not satisfied. This time I want whatever you want."

"Then you must give me a gift."

"What are you talking about?"

"Something that truly belongs to you."

"What's that?"

"Your fear." She threw the length of rope at him. "I want you to tie yourself up."

Without hesitating, he bound his hands together and secured them to the bed rail with his teeth. The game totally absorbed him, his growing arousal distracting him from any sense of danger. He felt a vitality course through his veins that he had not experienced in months. She kneeled

293

in front of him and secured his feet with the rest of the rope. Then she stood before him. For a long time she said nothing.

He waited, growing uncertain. "Why are you staring at me like that?" he said aggressively.

She did not reply.

Arousal was beginning to drain from his body. He felt uncertain and vulnerable. "What type of game are you playing?"

He started untying his hands with his teeth, but before he could struggle free, she had removed a gun from her handbag. He was surprised to see her hold the gun correctly, like a professional. They sat at opposite ends of the bed. He was aware that she had only to let her little finger slip or be startled by a slight noise for the gun to go off.

"I can smell your fear," she said. "I can see the blood pumping in your throat." She had the confidence of someone who for the first time in her life was playing a leading role in her destiny. "You've been losing a lot of business recently." Her voice was mocking.

"What makes you think so?"

"That's the way it looks to me. First your brothel goes, and your illegal fuel plant, then your little money-laundering operation at Home Sweet Home."

"You think someone is trying to put me out of business?"

"Someone has put you out of business." She smiled. "It's been good to know that you've been suffering. I've had a lot of fun watching your evil little empire fall apart."

Mikolajek frowned. He did not like the vulnerable position he was in, and he liked even less her line of questioning. What was she hinting at? That she was somehow behind the trouble he had been having. His brain grasped at the meaning behind her words as he stared at his bound feet, which were as white and helpless as the feet of a corpse.

"No one likes having his life hurled into chaos," she said. "Think of what it must have felt like for a nineteen-year-old girl to have her heart deceived by a beast like you."

The door opened behind her. A man with a limp stepped into the room and waited discreetly as though attending the scene of an execution.

Lena turned and acknowledged his arrival with a brief nod. Then she ran the muzzle of the gun along Mikolajek's throbbing throat.

"I have given away too much pleasure, Jozef. Now all I have to offer is pain. I am Lady Death. If you want to sleep with me, you must sleep with death."

43

A hand grabbed Mikolajek and shook him fiercely, summoning him back to consciousness, to the nauseous smell of sweat and cigarette smoke, every hair on his body bristling as he took in his surroundings. Someone had placed a gag over his mouth, but left nothing to shield his eyes. Although there was more darkness than illumination in the room, he could make out a window with a set of metal bars and, in the wall to the right, a door with no handle. His body ached where they had tied him with ropes.

He watched a set of bluish shadows move and converse around him. Beneath the throbbing surface of pain, his thoughts revolved slowly, taking in the hushed voices. A sense of panic overwhelmed him when he realized he was trapped in a room full of lost people, the women he had taken from families and loved ones in the villages of Croatia and Albania. His body writhed on the ground, struggling against the ropes that bit into his flesh, until someone placed a damp rag over his nostrils and he slipped back into unconsciousness.

He opened his eyes to find himself looking at a creature with inquisitive gray eyes. This time his body was strapped tightly to a chair and he could not move. He wondered, was it a bird or an animal? Perhaps a fox or even a wolf? His body contorted and his eyes bulged as he tried to strike out, but they had tied his hands too tightly. The pair of eyes gaped closer, widening all the time, drawing him into the darkness of its pupils. He recoiled in terror, realizing that it was the face of a woman inspecting him hungrily. A smile appeared on her face.

"For God's sake, help me," he whispered in his own tongue, but she did not flinch. He kicked back in the chair and struck his head against a cement floor. Everything went black again.

The voices returned, striking through the haze of his consciousness. This time, they had blindfolded him.

"Are the others ready?" said an anxious voice. "Will they agree to be part of this?"

"Of course they will. Evil must be matched with evil. That's the only solution for women like us who are beyond the reach of justice."

He drifted back into darkness.

"How will we do it?" A woman's voice roused him again.

It seemed he had awoken at precisely the right moment in their conversation. A voice he recognized as Lena's spoke. "He will die like a dog. That is all he deserves."

Then the women spoke in unison, some of their voices

trembling, as they swore an oath of allegiance. He could not make out all the words, but the determination they expressed seared into his consciousness. A pair of hands removed his blindfold. He blinked, eyes burning in the bright light. A circle of hooded faces surrounded him, jolting him back to cold reality.

"We are your sisters," announced Lena. "Lost women from broken places. We have no names, no faces. We have taken you hostage so that we can wear your face and you can wear ours."

44

Daly spent the first hour after Lena's disappearance frantically trying to reach Irwin on his mobile. He was beside himself with anxiety for her safety. All he could hope for was that somehow she might be able to free herself and make contact with him again.

"They might kill her!" he shouted at Irwin when the detective feigned indifference on the phone. Daly promptly requested a raid at the pub where they had arranged to collect their passports.

Although it was one of the few things that Special Branch did well, the swoop proved fruitless. The bar was deserted, and there were no signs that Lena had even made it there in the first place. That evening, police officers mounted a series of roadblocks around Armagh, and Mikolajek's name and details were circulated to detectives in neighboring jurisdictions. The press was alerted, too, and an appeal for information on the whereabouts of Lena Novak made it onto the late news bulletin.

When Commander Boyd heard that Lena had in all likelihood stolen Daly's gun, he made him go over repeatedly what had happened, especially the role that Daly had played in the plot to ensnare Mikolajek.

"I want to hear the whole story, Daly. From the start. This woman is beginning to worry me, and that's something new."

They reconstructed the events and examined the decisions that Daly had made in the cold light of reality.

"If she uses your gun to kill someone, you could be charged with conspiracy to murder," Boyd warned him. "She could even arrange it so it looks like you were the murderer. The gun can only be traced to you."

Daly said nothing. His face was white. Boyd ordered him not to take part in the search. "The situation is too dangerous and you've already compromised yourself. There could be any number of dead bodies found at the end of today."

"Mikolajek may be a hardened criminal, but he's not a madman intent on killing anyone who crosses his path," replied Daly. "Perhaps his plan is to take Lena and the other women and set up a brothel somewhere else along the border."

Boyd rubbed his brow. "When did she steal your gun? Was it while you were driving?"

"I'm not sure. I barely took my eyes off the road."

"Is there any other detail of the journey you can remember?"

Daly ran through the drive that morning, the empty

road ahead, the frantic phone calls to Irwin, the pale blur of Lena's face as she mouthed a kiss at him, and then the black shape of the Jeep whipping past followed by the screech of brakes.

"Maybe she tried to say good-bye. I can't remember."

"We'll find her. We'll make this our top priority. We can't let people like Mikolajek find a new hiding place."

Daly did not know if the guilt he felt was because he had overstepped the boundaries between a police officer and a suspect, or because he had failed Lena and betrayed her through his incompetence.

That evening, he returned to the cottage and waited for bad news. He thought about the missing gun and the fact that Ashe had been able to track down the Jeep at his cottage. Lena's abduction had happened so suddenly, it left him perplexed. He recalled her face as she walked away from the opened hood. The kiss she had blown, flying through the air toward him, like a mystery or a riddle that only she knew how to answer. He froze, became rigid, his eyes wide open, as the darkness swept in from the lough like a rising wind. The dramatic events of the past week hit him at full force. He went to bed with the strong suspicion that he had played an unwilling part in a darker, more twisted plot.

The phone woke him just after dawn. He reached out and answered it without getting out of bed.

"The ceremony is about to begin," a familiar female voice whispered in his ear.

"Lena? Where are you?"

"In the middle of a forest by the border. We've kidnapped Mikolajek. When you find us, the ritual will be over and the fire out."

"What are you talking about?"

Silence. She had disconnected the call.

45

Cold rain fell on Jozef Mikolajek's bare skin. His flesh writhed as he returned to consciousness, his memory and sense of place wiped once again, as though a series of bad accidents had befallen him. He tried to stand up, but a more robust body pressed against his, robbing him of any movement. His eyes blinked as someone ripped off his blindfold. The first thing he glimpsed was a woman sitting astride him. Now that he had regained consciousness, she sat up and brushed aside a loose tangle of hair from her eyes. She had a lipstick pen in her right hand. He gagged with fear as she ran its moist edge along his throat.

Looking around, he saw that they had tied him to a pile of wood in a forest clearing. He breathed harshly, trying to quell his rising panic. What time of the day it was he did not know. The shadowy trees at the edge of the grass danced in the gathering wind. His naked body shivered. Before his feet lay a picnic rug and basket. A meal had been assembled, with different types of cold meats and breads, olives and condiments. Five women sat on the rug in various states of relaxation. When his eyes met theirs, their heads rocked back in laughter. Silent laughter, like that of ghosts with mouths opened wide.

One of the women was missing, he realized. Her absence played on his mind. He thought of all the things he had done to her, and then of all the things she might do to him. Although he had only been awake for a few moments, he was out of breath, not from exhaustion, but from terror.

Martha Havel rose from the rug and stood in front of him. She held a pocket mirror to his face. His eyes filled with icy tears of frustration as he took in his grotesque reflection. They had placed a blond wig on his head and covered his face in makeup. His lips were painted a purplish red, and his eyes caked in mascara. He felt as if he was no longer present, inhabiting his body in the way people normally do. They had replaced him with a garish mannequin version of himself. A sudden sob rose in his chest, but never reached his lips.

"Shouldn't we just kill him now?" asked Havel, removing a piece of tape that had stuck to her fingers.

"Not yet," replied a voice behind him.

He did not have to strain his neck and look round to work out that it was Lena Novak. She placed a finger under his chin and swiveled his head toward her. There was a serene look in her blue eyes as she circled around him. He knew that death was close and this was why her eyes appeared so calm. She was ready to wreak her vengeance.

"I learned this from you," she said. "To control someone, just make them feel more afraid."

Havel lifted a bottle of champagne and a set of crystal glasses from the basket. He heard a pop as she opened the bottle and then the cool fizz of glasses filling. The women raised a toast to one another and knocked down the champagne, their faces tipped back in triumph. Then they drank another glass, a light shining in their eyes, like those of wild animals. When they had finished, they danced around him, their long dresses fluttering across his feet, their bodies writhing in gestures of beckoning and mock supplication. A slim hard hand struck him across his face. And then another, and another. He bowed his head. He was alone with a pack of vengeful women, gagged and tied to an unlit bonfire in the middle of a dark forest. There was nothing upon which he could base an escape.

46

It was midmorning by the time the helicopter crews located a fire burning in Slaney Forest, about a mile from the border.

Daly ran through the trees. Spring had turned the forest into a fluttering, living thing, full of noises and scents. He dipped his head under branches and almost lost his balance several times. His police officer colleagues ran along paths on different levels of the slope, moving in and out of sight of each other. Behind him, the high-visibility jackets of a group of paramedics flashed through the spindly foliage.

The black shape of a helicopter flapped in the sky above, directing them by radio to the site of the fire. A splash of yellow that might have been sunshine reflecting on water made him veer toward the left. He came upon the clearing suddenly.

The fire had almost burned itself out, but smoke drifted in ghostly shapes through the damp air. He hesitated, smelling the stench of diesel. The site was exposed. He had no idea who might be there waiting for him. He tensed his body and tightened his hand on his gun.

A half-burned log fell soundlessly into the remnants of the fire. A ghostly quiet pervaded. Daly sifted through the ashes with his boot, looking for the smoldering remains of something other than wood, but found nothing. He inspected a circle of mud surrounding the fire. He made out the shapes of different sets of footprints that had been engaged in some sort of wild dance, trampling the grass and breaking the hard ground. He found a pair of bare foot-prints, larger than the others, forming a trail that veered away from the circle. A heedless flight that left a tattered path, as though a man had shadowboxed his way through the trees and undergrowth.

Daly broke off from his colleagues and followed the track of torn leaves and broken twigs. A blond wig flapped on a thorn branch. He advanced deeper into the dark-ness, expecting to see something or someone emerge at any moment from a hiding place. He could sense the person was close by. A sour stench of fear and diesel wafted in the air.

The shadows rolled back and the trees parted. Daly emerged at the bank of a fast-flowing river. A man kneeling at the water's edge turned to look up at him, his eyes bright with fear. His upper body was naked, his hands bound by thick wire behind his back, his face smeared with garish colors like a stage demon's, smudges of bright blues and purplish red mingling with mud and ash. His lower half was so caked in mud and forest debris it was difficult to tell if he was wearing trousers or not. The man sized Daly up, then hunched his body and jumped into the river.

"Stay where you are!" shouted Daly. He pulled out his gun, checked the safety, and then lowered it. The man, already shivering visibly from the cold, waded farther out. Daly realized it was a life ring he needed, not a gun.

"You're caught," Daly called to him. "You've come to a dead end."

The man ignored him. The fast-moving water lapped around his shoulders as he pushed on to the opposite bank and the promise of freedom. It hardly made sense for Daly to risk his life, but a frantic desire to finish the story made him jump into the water after him. The river was shockingly cold. It pummeled his body. He shouted out, but the sudden immersion had sucked the air from his lungs.

The man stopped in the middle of the river and turned back to check on Daly. The veins on his neck and tied arms stood out, taut as cables, as he swayed in the currents. Their pull was irresistible, dragging him toward whorls of dark water.

"Fuck it! I don't know where I'm going!" he shouted. Fear still burned in his eyes.

"I'm a policeman," said Daly. "You'll get tired before I do. Better you come out with me now."

The man laughed and then winced. He seemed disoriented. He looked back at the quiet trees and grimaced as another spasm of pain ran through his body. The black water lapped against his hair.

"Where are the women?" he asked.

"What women?"

"The women who organized that fucking picnic in the

forest. I blacked out so many times I can't remember how many were there."

"Was Lena Novak one of them?"

"Yes," he hissed between his chattering teeth. "She scared me half to death, but she didn't have the guts to kill me." His throat shook with a deep moan. It took Daly a moment to realize he was laughing.

"Why did she want to kill you?"

"Punishment. She singled me out to demonstrate her hatred of men. All men. You'd better be careful she doesn't come looking for you."

Daly fought against the cold heavy water and reached out to grab him by the arm. The man did not resist.

"I'm an asylum seeker," he said. "I'm seeking refuge in your country. I have no passport. No identity."

"Your name is Jozef Mikolajek, and I'm arresting you on suspicion of murder and people trafficking."

Daly dragged him back to the bank. He did not have to worry about his suspect putting up a struggle. Lena had done a good job with her knots.

47

"The flight to Rome is on schedule," the airport security guard told Daly as he led him into the observation room. A group of maintenance men working on the electrics behind the paneled wall stopped and regarded them with curiosity.

"Lena Novak has booked a ticket in business class," added the guard. "Her plane will leave in forty minutes from gate number twenty-eight."

Immediately after leaving the forest that morning, Daly had contacted the airports and ferry operators and asked them to check their passenger lists. They soon found evidence that Lena was planning to make the most of the newfound freedom her passport provided. As far as border country was concerned, she had reached the end of the road. He felt a slight sense of apprehension as he waited with the security officials, two of whom were younger men, eager to make an impression, while the third was middle-aged and carried the annoyed look of someone who had just been dragged from his bed.

Daly spent some empty minutes staring through the one-way windows at the sweeping curves of an escalator ferrying passengers to their boarding gates. He felt completely detached from the hubbub of the airport. The soft noises from a nearby coffee machine were all that broke the silence. It struck him that the airport was a vaulted building of labyrinthine corridors and escalators, a dizzying shrine to the twenty-first-century's insatiable desire to cross borders, and the ultimate escape route for people who wanted to disappear quickly.

The oldest security guard unfolded a newspaper and began flicking through the pages. The others checked their watches as time passed, punctuated by the rhythm of departures and arrivals.

Twenty minutes before the flight was due to take off, a ragged queue formed at the boarding gate. One by one, the passengers filed past the glass, behind which stood Daly, alert and out of sight. This time there were no shadows in which Lena could hide.

Daly raised his hand when one of the younger guards checked his gun.

"I only want to talk to this woman."

"I thought we were to arrest her."

"No. We're here to make sure she still has her liberty, not take it away from her."

A few women of about Lena's age walked by. Daly stepped toward the glass, scrutinizing them closely, but they were shadowy, dull versions of her, half ghosts already in transition to another border.

He waited awhile after the last passenger boarded and the gate closed. The stairs were wheeled away from the plane as it prepared for takeoff. Daly was a detective, and the situation did not need much explaining. He suspected that Lena had never intended to catch that evening's flight to Rome; she had booked the ticket as a means to distract his attention and that of anyone else still following her. He looked out at the runway. Time passed. The twilight sky filled with darkness and the exodus of thousands of lives, transported by planes to distant corners of the world, their jet trails hanging against the sky like the departing breath of lost souls.

He drove home slowly. The events of the day had been remarkable, but they had not answered the questions he had been asking himself constantly. Why had Lena dragged him into her personal scheme for revenge? Had she meant to pin Mikolajek's murder on him by using his stolen gun? And how had Mikolajek escaped? There were still questions he had to have answered.

He took a call on his mobile phone after arriving back at the cottage.

"Hello," he said.

He could hear breathing on the other end but no one answered.

"Who is this?"

"It's me, Celcius." Her voice sounded nervous.

"Lena? Where are you? Are you OK?"

"I'm on my way home," she said simply.

"You weren't on the flight to Rome."

"No. I booked myself onto another plane at the last minute. I thought you might still be looking for me."

"I was looking for you. For a while I thought you were going to end up in a body bag." There was a note of anger in his voice.

"I'm safe now."

Daly sighed. Then his relief sharpened into annoyance again.

"Why did you use me like that?"

"I didn't use you, Celcius. You were my knight in shining armor; you more so than anyone else."

"I don't understand. You kept me in the dark." His voice was neutral, suspending judgment. "What about Ashe? What part did he play in your plans?"

"Is this something the police need to know?" Her voice was deadpan.

"It's something I need to know." He wondered if she had rung him just to tease his ignorance.

He walked out to the porch as she explained what had happened from the beginning. He stood staring out at the waves of Lough Neagh, as if lost in another world.

She described how Fowler had given her Ashe's number to ring if she was ever in trouble. She had hidden the number in a rag doll along with the details of Mikolajek's trafficking operations. Enough evidence to have him locked up for a long stretch, if she was ever brave enough to take to the witness stand. When she retrieved the number after Fowler's death, she contacted Ashe and managed to persuade him to work for her, rather than Mooney and his Republican cronies.

"I thought your life was in danger," he told her. "I was as blind as a bat."

"I should have been more open with you from the start. But I was afraid you wouldn't understand."

"What do you mean?"

"I couldn't expect you to bear the weight of my darkest feelings, my desire for revenge."

"What about Ashe? What did you tell him?"

She hesitated. "Everything. He understood where I was coming from. We talked as if we were old friends. He told me about his travels, the horrible things he had done in the past, and his search for peace. He proposed some interesting ways to get my revenge on Mikolajek. We made out a plan to tear down his criminal empire, piece by piece. So, rather than fleeing to the city, I went back into border country. Not as a victim, but as an adventurer."

"You deceived me. There were numerous times when I thought Ashe was going to harm you."

She chose her words carefully. "Deep down, I wanted you to keep rescuing me, Celcius. Over and over again. I felt so corrupted by what had happened to me that I believed no honest man would ever want to save me. Your tenacity and endurance helped me regain my trust in men. Somehow, in all the turmoil, you never gave up. Each time you reached out to me, another piece of me was healed."

Perhaps she was right, thought Daly; he could never have understood her motivation, the secret desire for revenge she harbored.

"That's why I couldn't kill Mikolajek," she said. "It felt like I was forcing the cruelty upon you."

"Killing Mikolajek would have put me in a lot of trouble. Aiding and abetting a murderer for a start."

"You didn't deserve that, Celcius. John Ashe became my friend, but he stirred up feelings of anger and revenge. He awoke the worst in me. You were a better friend. Thanks to you, I am returning home with a clear conscience."

Daly said nothing. He wanted to feign indifference, but, in reality, her words had touched him.

"What about your bank account? What happened to the money Jack stashed away?"

"There never was any money. Jack kept a tight rein on his funds. He set up joint accounts in my name, but they were just a paper trail to confuse the auditors. I knew if I kept up the pretense that I had a big payout coming, it would be easier to lure Mikolajek, but I was penniless all along."

"All that excitement the secret bank account caused was for nothing then."

"I've got to go now, Celcius. I'm running late." He could hear the sound of an airplane in the background. He tried to visualize where she was standing, at a phone booth in some crowded airport, but the phone's illusion of proximity made him think she was much closer at hand, still hiding somewhere out there in the shadows of border country.

He had one final question to ask her. "Why did you shout my name at the roadside when Ashe's Jeep arrived? I thought it was the cry of a woman in fear for her life."

Her voice was hushed. "I was warning you to stay back.

I didn't want to see you hurt."

Daly paused. "I take it you won't be coming back to Ireland."

"I've taken all that I want from your country. My last memory will be of a phone conversation with a man who didn't want to use or possess me in any way."

She hung up before either of them could say good-bye.

On an emotional level, Daly felt vindicated. He had never been able to quell his wariness of her, but at least he had listened and tried to help her. He paced around the cottage and garden. He could feel blocks of frozen emotion melt and work their way through his system. He was relieved that she was free and, most importantly, safe, but another part of him yearned to have her back. In the past week, she had raised his life to a level of intensity, in spite of the nagging doubt and suspicions that had worked so negatively on his mind.

She might not have realized it, but he had gained from their relationship, too. He had pursued her, not as a hunter, but as a naïve and love-hungry man searching for a guide, a light to plumb the darkest depths of his feelings. He had been slow to realize what she represented to him. She had been that little bit of death he needed to enfold his failed marriage and its mistakes, and bear them away to the bottom of a deep dark river. He no longer had any expectations or illusions that he would be able to restore his failed relationship with Anna. In his mind's eye, he saw what was left of their relationship sinking underwater, drifting out of sight.

48

The days afterward felt like a weightless vacuum as Daly waited for Commander Boyd to conduct an internal investigation into his handling of the case. He had already answered all Boyd's questions honestly, but the commander had shaken his head as though they shed little light on what had really happened. Daly completed his own report and added it to the fat folder of growing paperwork the case had produced. Boyd took his time, scrutinizing the evidence closely, determined to cover all aspects of the investigation, from Sergei Kriich's murder at the start to the kidnapping of the trafficked women and the arrest of Jozef Mikolajek.

In the meantime, Mikolajek remained in custody, the evidence stacking against him. His fingerprints matched the ones left on the CD cover found at Fowler's mansion. In addition, Martha Havel and her van driver had turned up at a police station, declaring that they were prepared to testify against Mikolajek. The Croatian crime boss might have been ruthless, cunning, and ambitious, but he had been stopped by the efforts of a village girl left to her own devices in border country.

Daly spent the next few days at home. One warm spring afternoon, he opened all the doors and windows of his cottage. He took out the boxes he had moved from Anna's house and set light to what he no longer needed in a bonfire at the bottom of the garden. When the flames dwindled, he walked down the lane to the lough shore. Bees buzzed in the blossoming hedgerows. A tractor hugged the curves of a plowed field. Through the thorn trees, he watched rabbits scamper over the crests of rolling hills. He felt that all the jigsaw pieces of a settled happy life might lie within his reach, ready to be assembled.

Then, at the lough shore, the swell of restless waves broke the spell. The stony shore was full of surging sounds. He was reminded that the inner torment of the mind could never be soothed completely. Removing the picture of Lena from his wallet, he let it fall into the churning waves.

He toiled back up the lane to the cottage. Wanting to make himself invisible, he jumped into his car and headed south. He weaved in and out of the narrow roads that crisscrossed the border until he pulled up at the entrance to the ghost estate at Foxborough Mews. The rows of empty houses had proved such an effective refuge for people with unresolved lives.

Two men in safety helmets and high-visibility vests stood in front of the estate, poring over a map. One of them was

Michael Mooney. He looked pleased to see Daly. Grinning, he walked over and shook hands with the detective.

"Your investigation was very valuable to us, Inspector," he said. "Thanks to you, the regeneration association will be able to continue in spite of the harm Jack did."

"How come?"

"Jack was the unfortunate victim of a blackmail plot organized by a gang of ruthless Croatians. He compromised his position of trust and misused peace funds, but he was a desperate man forced into a corner. That's the story I'll be reporting to the auditors. Greta Fowler is an important witness."

"Sounds like an exercise in damage limitation."

"The association will escape without too much discredit, which will be very disappointing to some, I'm sure. Unionist politicians would have seized on the story like dogs jumping on a prize bone. There's a new round of peace funding in September. We have our application submitted already."

"And what will you do with the money? Build more homes to be peopled by ghosts?"

"Who knows? Young men need to be kept busy; otherwise they'll turn to guns and bombs. Don't you know that the devil makes use of idle hands?"

A thundering roar interrupted their conversation. Before them, a gray haze shimmered over the houses. Not fog but the dust of collapsed buildings. A line of bulldozers devoured the first row of unfinished houses, plowing them back into the boggy earth.

"What's happening?" asked Daly.

"These bulldozers are rescuing the housing market," said Mooney without a trace of sarcasm. "The country has thousands more houses than it could ever fill in twenty years. When homes aren't being built, the economy goes into free fall. This destruction is the price that has to be paid for prosperity and stability."

"It seems scandalous."

"These are scandalous times."

A bulldozer surged over a fresh mound of rubble. Daly took a last look at the homes, all clean and freshly painted and hopeful, but with little to offer prospective buyers other than crippling debt and a lifetime of worry. Ireland was a country where everything had grown out of proportion, even greed. The bricks and mortar of Foxborough Mews formed part of a straggling fault line that ran the length of the country, north and south, through scattered villages, moribund towns, and along new dual carriageways empty of traffic. A line of ghost estates that stretched like a yawning crack, threatening to drag the entire nation's finances under the surface.

"Please God, let us never see empty houses like these again," Mooney said with a sigh.

"These houses will always exist," replied Daly. "They'll haunt people's dreams for a hundred years."

A cloud of bluebottles rose from the ruptured sewers, buzzing a final farewell in their faces.

ACKNOWLEDGMENTS

I thank my agent, Paul Feldstein, as well as Otto Penzler and Rob Hart at MysteriousPress.com, all the folks at Open Road Integrated Media, and the Northern Ireland Arts Council for its support and funding.

A letter from the publisher

We hope you enjoyed this book. We are an independent
publisher dedicated to discovering brilliant books,
new authors and great storytelling. Please join us at
www.headofzeus.com and become part of our
community of book-lovers.

We will keep you up to date with our latest books, author
blogs, special previews, tempting offers, chances to win
signed editions and much more.

If you have any questions, feedback or just want to say hi,
please drop us a line on hello@headofzeus.com

@HoZ_Books

HeadofZeusBooks

www.headofzeus.com

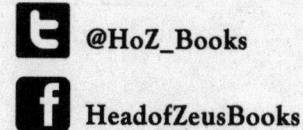

The story starts here